THE
CHILD
AT MY
DOOR

BOOKS BY SAM VICKERY

THE
CHILD
AT MY
DOOR

SAM VICKERY

bookouture

Published by Bookouture in 2024

An imprint of Storyfire Ltd.
Carmelite House
50 Victoria Embankment
London EC4Y 0DZ

www.bookouture.com

ISBN: 978-1-83790-822-6
eBook ISBN: 978-1-83790-821-9

For Jax. For your endless support and encouragement.

PROLOGUE

There was a moment, somewhere between sleep and consciousness, where I felt it. That creeping sensation that I wasn't alone. The jacket I'd thrown over myself in the absence of a sheet had slipped from my shoulders, the room still holding on to the lingering heat of the previous day, the air musty, the click of the cheap plastic clock ticking from beyond the bedroom door, but there was something else too. Not the sound of another person breathing – nothing so obvious as that. Just the cold awareness that someone was lurking there. Watching me in the darkness.

Something inside me, some sense of self-preservation – a thing I'd never been short of – forced my eyes to snap open. In the same moment, a sharp sensation seared beneath the nail of my big toe. The figure stood still at the end of the bed, a hand clamping down, securing a vice-like grip around my foot, the silvery glint of the needle protruding from the tip of a thin syringe. It took a moment for my eyes to focus on the face, too shocked to feel the fear that should have come.

'You!' I exclaimed. I followed her gaze to my foot, kicking out at her, though her grasp was surprisingly strong.

'I wouldn't do that,' she warned, pressing my ankle harder into the mattress, her fingers still gripped around the syringe forced into my flesh. The needle shifted beneath my nail and I winced as the steel collided with sensitive nerves, a jolt of pain shooting up the back of my calf.

'What the hell are you doing?'

She flashed me a smile, then – before I could stop her; before I'd had a chance to think of a way out of this predicament – pressed her thumb down on the end of the syringe. The effect was instant, her voice distorting in my ears as I felt myself sinking, the heaviness landing on my chest, robbing me of the ability to breathe.

'Good...' she said softly, her grip loosening as the needle slid slowly from my toe. 'That deals with you.'

My eyes closed against my will, the image of my four-year-old son flashing behind my retinas, a warm heat spreading over my skin as the memory of his laughter echoed in my mind. I was spinning... drowning... *dying*. The realisation was so obvious to me, and yet still there was no fear, no pain. Somewhere deep in the recesses of my mind, I knew it was a side effect of the drugs she'd flooded my bloodstream with, but I couldn't fight it. I didn't know how.

'... not the first one I've had to dispose of,' she was saying, an ethereal, alien tone tingeing her voice, making me wonder if this was even real. 'Doubt you'll be the last.'

I hadn't thought her capable of it... Had never expected this. Not from her.

There was the sound of footsteps retreating as I tried and failed to suck in a breath. And then there was only darkness.

ONE

CLARISSA

I was looking at a ghost. Either that or I was losing my mind. The boy – blonde, dressed in battered Velcro sandals, blue cotton shorts and a short-sleeved T-shirt – looked up at me with wide eyes, and I felt myself sway, the tea towel I was holding floating to the floor as I reached for the door frame. I'd been halfway through making a sponge cake for the raffle at the community centre this weekend, while listening to an interesting debate on the radio about bees. It was a perfectly ordinary Friday. So why was this child standing in my doorway with a rucksack bursting at the seams and a ragged teddy bear clutched tight in his tiny hands?

His eyes were a haunting reminder of my past – of someone I'd said goodbye to long ago. But it wasn't just the eyes. It was everything. The way his blue-and-red sandals turned inwards at the toes. The little dimple to the left of his mouth. The smattering of freckles on his upturned nose. Even the shape of his chin. He couldn't have been more than four or five.

He stared at me, unspeaking, and I glanced over his head to the taxi idling at the kerb, the driver standing next to it.

'Righto, I'm off then. Don't worry about settling up – the

little 'un's ma already paid.' The cabbie turned, making to get back in the car.

'I'm sorry, what?'

He paused, his fingers already on the door handle. 'She said to see him to your door. I've done my bit. You should be proud of the lad. Good as gold, he was.' He looked at his watch. 'Gotta dash – got a pickup at Southampton Airport in twenty minutes, and I'm pushing it at this time of day.'

'What?' I shook my head, feeling slow and stupid, trying to understand what on earth was happening.

The driver, clearly frustrated, frowned as if I was missing something that should have been obvious. He gave a shrug, then looked at the boy. 'Be good for your grandma then, fella.' He flashed him a wink, then climbed back in the cab, revved the engine and drove away.

'Grandma!' I exclaimed, staring after the car in shock as it rounded the corner, leaving me alone with the silent child. I shook my head again, helpless and confused, wondering for a brief moment if I was going senile. If I should somehow have been expecting this boy – a grandchild – to arrive. But that was impossible. I didn't have any grandchildren.

I continued to stare at the empty road, waiting to see if the taxi would reappear, the driver rushing back in a panic to tell me in an apologetic, sheepish tone that he'd got the wrong house, made a massive mistake. But the road remained silent and empty. He really had gone.

I looked down at the child to find he was staring up at me with those eyes. Those familiar blue irises that unlocked a chest full of emotions I was quite sure I wasn't prepared to face. I swallowed, then cleared my throat, taking a long, steadying breath. 'What's your name?' I asked.

He shrugged, and I saw his lip tremble. Lowering myself to my haunches, I smiled, trying to hide how flustered I was. Children needed to feel cared for; to believe they could rely on a grown-up to know what to do, in any situation.

'It's okay,' I reassured him. 'You can tell me. What's your name, darling?'

'Tommy.'

'Ah. Hello, Tommy. I'm Clarissa.'

He screwed up his face. 'Mummy said I should call you Grandma.'

'Did she?' I furrowed my brow. 'And what's your mummy's name?' I asked, holding my breath, not daring to believe he might say the word I longed to hear.

He shook his head, looking embarrassed. 'Mummy,' he whispered. 'I say Mummy. But everyone else says she's called...' He paused, looking up at me as if for permission, and I remembered my children when they were small, how they thought it was the height of cheekiness to call me by my given name.

'You can say it. It's okay,' I said with another smile.

'They call her Chloe.' He gave a shrug, looking down at his sandals.

I rocked back on my heels, the air leaving my lungs in a whoosh, my fingers gripping the door frame, nails sinking into the glossy red paint, leaving a mark that would remind me of this moment for ever. It couldn't be true. There was no way this boy was Chloe's son. He had to be mistaken. It had been fifteen years since I'd lost my children. It was impossible.

TWO

CHLOE

The hot, metallic tang of blood filled my mouth, and I turned my head to the side, letting the bitter liquid spill onto the carpet before I had a chance to think. The moment I'd done it, I regretted it. It bloomed dark and unforgiving on the worn cream surface, and the punishment was instant, the toe of his boot colliding with my shoulder blade, a gasp hissing through my teeth.

'You better clean that mess up,' Scott said, bending over me, his hand sliding through my hair, forcing me to look at the blood. 'I don't work all the fucking hours of the goddam week so you can disrespect our home like that. Show some fucking decorum.' He slammed my head back on the ground, and I tried to nod, but he was already walking away, his footsteps retreating down the hall, the door slamming hard as he left me alone.

I stayed prone and shaking on the carpet, trying to breathe through the pain, assessing the damage in a routine that had become all too familiar to me. Gingerly, I pressed my fingers to my ribs – tender flesh, new bruises covering older ones. A trail of blood and spit continued to spill from the corner of my swollen lip, and, not wanting to swallow, not daring to spit more onto the carpet, I forced myself up and over to the kitchen sink, turning on the cold tap and sticking my mouth under the stream of it, rinsing until the water ran clear.

I gripped the edge of the sink, a hollowness spreading through me now that the fear had passed. Scott wouldn't be back for hours. He never could face me afterwards. He'd slink down to the pub on the corner, blag himself pint after pint from the young, naïve barmaid who thought he was God's gift to women and then stumble back in sometime after midnight and fall asleep on the sofa. And if I could get the stain out of the carpet and erase the evidence of what had happened, he might even be in a decent mood come morning.

I opened the fridge, pulling out a packet of cheese, the only thing in there besides a half-empty pot of yoghurt, and pressing it to my swollen mouth, trying to ignore the sting, trying not to let myself think about what had just happened. My stomach churned with adrenaline, pain, anger, and I clenched my fists tight, feeling powerless and trapped.

Through the tiny window over the sink, I could see the high street below, the man who fed the pigeons daily taking up his usual spot on the bench outside the pharmacy. A group of mums were having coffee and cake, babies slung over their shoulders while the toddlers, dressed in sandals and sunhats, clambered over laps and weaved in and out of the stainless-steel tables.

I turned my head away, unable to bear the sight of them. Those mothers had no idea how lucky they were. What a gift it was to have the time, money and freedom to sit and chat over expensive slices of coconut cake, worrying about how to jump their little ones up the waiting lists for the good preschools in town. To have friends who would nod and smile and sympathise with their struggles. What I wouldn't give to trade places with them; to not be standing in this damp-ridden one-bedroom flat, where I'd never been safe... where I hadn't been able to keep *him* safe. Wasn't that the least a mother should be able to provide?

Scott hadn't even asked about his child. Hadn't seemed to notice his absence, though even through his kicks I hadn't stopped thinking about him. Worrying. *Missing* him. Putting him in that taxi, kissing his sweet little cheeks as I said goodbye, had been the most painful experience of my life, but I'd had no choice. If I could have gone with him, arrived on my mother's doorstep and asked for her help in person, I would have, but seeing her wasn't an option. I knew I'd have to face her eventually. There were questions I needed answers to – answers that only she would know. And I'd have to go back there for Tommy. I only hoped she'd forgiven me for the mistakes I'd made.

I thought of my sweet, smiling boy, the life I wanted him to have, and knew, despite how hard being apart would be, that he was in safe hands. My mother would take good care of him. Better than I could, at any rate.

I replayed the moment I'd walked back into the flat alone, feeling as if I had cut out my heart and sent it off in a box where I couldn't get it back. I'd been distraught, and if I was honest, I'd been angry too. Scott should never have forced me to make this choice. I understood that he'd been through a tough time. That his childhood wasn't the fairy tale mine had been. His mother was a hard woman, and from the little Scott had told me, it was clear she'd been cruel. I was sure his violent outbursts stemmed from his experiences with her. But he was a father now. We were supposed to be a family. It wasn't supposed to be like this.

I had hoped... I don't know what I'd hoped. That me arriving back without our son would give him the shock he needed to make him realise what he was going to lose if he didn't change. That he would wake up, see that I was taking a stand and showing him that we'd reached a crossroads. That I demanded more from him.

But it hadn't had the desired effect. He hadn't mentioned

Tommy, and perhaps, now that I thought about it, my new-found determination was what had set him off today. He'd never taken it well if he felt he was being shoved into a corner – he liked everyone to know he was the boss.

But as terrified as I was, it was too late to go back on my decision. And as much as I loved Scott, I loved my son more. I wanted a better life for him. A better role model. I wanted Scott to be the man I'd fallen in love with all those years ago when we'd met, when we'd both been teenagers running from something, and with that giddy magical hope that together we could forge a better future for ourselves. We'd been so happy back then. So sure that nothing could break us.

I still wanted that dream. I wanted to give him the chance to make it better, take back the mistakes he'd made. But he'd pushed so far, and as much as I might have put up with it if it were just me, I had a son to consider. Never again would he witness his father laying a finger on me. I'd sworn to myself I couldn't let it happen. Once was enough. Scott had crossed a line and forced my hand. I wouldn't change my mind. Either Scott changed, or I would walk away, even if it killed me to do it. There was no other choice.

But there was another reason I'd had to send Tommy away.

I crossed the room, picking up my bag from the floor beside the bedroom door, heading over to sit on the edge of the bed. The moisture evaporated from my mouth as I slid my fingers inside the compartment, touching the smooth envelope and pulling it out.

It had arrived this morning with a first-class stamp, my full name and address printed on the front. I didn't want to admit to myself just how much the slip of paper inside had contributed to my rushed decision to pile my four-year-old into the back of a taxi and send him away. It had been instinct, a panicked response, a desperate need to get him away from here, away from whatever was coming.

I unfolded the letter, rereading the words for the hundredth time since it had arrived.

I know what you did. And I will make sure that you pay for it.

I closed my eyes, wondering how it was possible that anyone could know my awful secret when I'd never told a soul.

THREE

CLARISSA

I pulled the canister of oats from the top shelf of the pantry, casting covert glances over my shoulder at the little boy sitting at my table, his backpack by his feet, his teddy clutched against his chest. Now that I looked closer, I was sure the similarities I'd thought he shared with my son had just been a figment of an overactive imagination. No doubt brought on by the shock of finding him on my doorstep in the first place. Of course my mind would go straight to something familiar, make me think of him. It meant nothing.

And then there was the other thing. The matter of his mother sharing a name with my daughter. It was unsettling. A part of me felt someone might be playing a horrible practical joke on me, but who? And why? I couldn't imagine any of the people in my circle – the friends I'd made at the Crochet and Crumpets group; the neighbours, most of whom I'd known for decades – thinking up anything so cruel. So that just left one conclusion. It was a simple mistake.

I would have to call the police. Declare his arrival, make a report. No doubt his *real* grandma was frantic with worry right now.

I poured oats into the pan, adding milk and stirring slowly, making sure to keep the heat low. 'You know,' I said, smiling over my shoulder at the frightened-looking child, 'when I had young children, if they were ever nervous of something, like going to school, for instance, or taking a test, I always made them porridge sweetened with a little dash of honey. It filled up their bellies and got rid of that nervous feeling taking up space inside them. Do you like porridge, Tommy?'

He stared at me, silent and wide-eyed, but I heard his stomach growl, and I nodded as if he'd spoken his answer, ladling the steaming mixture into a bowl. I left it on the windowsill to cool as I found a little mug, filling it with creamy milk, then drizzled honey on the porridge and walked over to where he sat, placing both down in front of him.

'Give it a try. You'll see what I mean.'

I returned to the pan, moving to rinse it in the sink, and glanced out of the window, my stomach tensing as I saw Mirium dashing past, clearly having come through the side gate. Damn, this wasn't the time for her to drop in.

'Knock-knock,' she called, letting herself in through the back door, something she always did and usually I didn't mind. 'Only me!' she announced in her sing-song voice. 'I got an extra copy of my gardening magazine through the door and thought you might like it. There're some good tips this month about rhubarb – I know you like it. Filthy stuff if you ask me.'

'Thanks,' I said, drying my hands and reaching to take the glossy magazine from her.

She turned, seeing Tommy at the table, and he looked down at his bowl, studiously ignoring her as he picked up the spoon and began to eat.

'Hello! Who's this then?' Mirium exclaimed, looking back at me with a bewildered expression on her face.

'This is Tommy.'

'Tommy?'

'That's right. Oh, how did Jeff's trip to the doctor go?' I asked, hoping she'd pick up the thread and go off on a tangent about her husband's bowel issues.

She frowned, shaking her head as if she'd missed something, her gaze lingering on Tommy's face for a moment, the crease between her eyes deepening. I cleared my throat, and she gathered herself, launching into an onslaught of complaints about the state of the NHS.

'And,' she said, finally wrapping up her train of thought, 'after waiting all that time, they only saw him for five minutes, and we're just as in the dark as we were before. The doctor told him to cut out so much from his diet he might as well not bother eating at all, so you can imagine the mood in my house right now!'

There was a clatter of metal on ceramic as Tommy dropped his spoon into his bowl. Mirium, distracted, stopped talking and stared at him again.

'Thank you, Grandma.' He gave a shy little smile. 'It *did* help. I like honey,' he added, looking at the bowl with a longing expression, as if more might appear inside it.

'You can go and watch television in the living room now, Tommy. Do you know how to turn it on?'

'I think so.'

'Well, I'll come and help you in a minute. Go on now – just through that door.'

Tommy nodded and, still clutching his bear, headed through the door with a little more confidence in his stride. I looked at Mirium.

'Did he say "Grandma"?'

I shrugged, wishing she would leave.

'But your family, your husband, your children... they, well, they're dead,' she said, mouthing the final word as if she couldn't bear to say it out loud.

I felt my stomach tense and wondered if she had any idea

how insensitive her probing was. 'Yes,' I said, the word brittle on my tongue. I took a breath. 'I *know* they are. This is just a mix-up. A simple misunderstanding.'

'I... I don't understand?'

I shook my head, thinking that in that case, she and I were in the same boat. I picked up the cloth from beside the sink and began furiously buffing the tap, needing to release the flurry of nervous energy that seemed to be building within me. How on earth was I supposed to explain the situation when I was just as confused as she was?

'Clarissa, are you all right? You seem... well, flustered. Not quite yourself. Is something going on?'

'It's a long story. And I have a lot to do today.'

'Can I help? I have nothing on.'

'No. No thank you.'

'But... the little boy... who is he? What's he doing here?' She paused, looking back towards the door as she seemed to collect her thoughts. Slowly, she raised her eyes to meet mine, and I realised she'd seen it too. 'He looks awfully like—'

'Please,' I said, holding up a hand, cutting her off. 'Don't.' I couldn't bear for her to notice the similarities. Didn't want her to be taken back to that time. I could see her thinking about it now, remembering the past. I couldn't help but think of the day I'd had to tell her Rhodri was gone, and wondered if she was thinking of that too. I didn't want to bring it all back up but she was forcing the issue, and a wave of anger like nothing I'd felt in years bubbled inside me, instinctively rejecting her questions, refusing to acknowledge those memories. I didn't want to look at the boy and see my son. It was too much. Too hard.

'I haven't seen you like this since—'

'Mirium, *please*, I'm fine,' I managed to spit out. 'The boy is lost, that's all. I'm taking care of him until... until he's collected by his mother.'

'Lost? Then why—'

'Grandma, the TV's broken,' Tommy's voice called from the front room, and I saw Mirium raise her eyebrows, her lips pressed tightly shut. I glanced at the door, hoping she would take the hint. I wasn't ever rude, but today I didn't have the patience to deal with her questions. Not when I had so many of my own. She gave a short nod and glanced behind her towards the living room, as if she wanted to ask something more, but then thought better of it.

'I'll let you get on then,' she said. 'You know where I am if you need me.'

'Thank you, Miri.'

I watched her leave with a sense of relief, the anger dissipating with every step she took. I didn't want to fall out with her, but she'd really put me on the spot.

Tommy had left his backpack on the floor. Glancing over my shoulder at the sound of *Paw Patrol* on the television, glad that he'd worked out how to use it without my help, I padded softly across the tiles, picking up the bag and sliding open the zip.

I removed the items one by one. A neatly folded pair of cotton pyjamas, bobbled and well worn. A red child-sized toothbrush. A handful of clothes, a few picture books. No photo album. No note. No indication of why he'd come here, who had sent him.

I picked up my phone, my thumb keying in the code to unlock it, and typed in 999... then paused, my thumb hovering over the call button, trepidation pooling in my gut. I deleted the number, placed the phone back on the side and repacked the little backpack. I had spent a long time avoiding the police. I wasn't about to invite them into my life now.

FOUR

CHLOE

I heard Scott leave for work and waited, pretending to be asleep as the door closed behind him. I was stiff from lying on my side all night, trying to find a position that didn't put pressure on the fresh welts and bruises that peppered my body. My neck was stiff and tense, and my eyes itched with the dryness that always came with a sleepless night. I hadn't been able to stop worrying about Tommy. Wondering if he was crying for me.

In the cold morning light, it was almost impossible not to give in to the panic that had been threatening to overwhelm me. My skin itched with anxiety as I let my thoughts run wild. What if the sudden appearance of a grandson on her doorstep had sent my mother into shock? It had been fifteen years since we'd had any contact. She didn't know if I was even alive, let alone that I'd had a child. She had no idea where I'd been, and, I realised now, I had no idea what she'd been doing since I left either. What if she had a new husband who hadn't welcomed the idea of a child under his roof? What if she'd taken on other responsibilities – a job, a dog that hated kids? I had no idea what chaos I might have caused in her routines, and it was embarrassing that I was only now considering these possibilities. I'd acted without thinking properly, my only desire being to get Tommy somewhere safe so I could mend things with Scott and find out who'd sent me that awful letter. And when it came to my notion of what it meant to feel safe, enclosed in a warm, love-filled cocoon that dulled the pain of the surrounding world, my mother was the first thing I always thought of. I wanted her to make it all better for him, and I knew, even if she had other obligations, she wouldn't let him down. It just wasn't in her nature.

The taxi driver had texted me as promised, letting me know that he'd handed Tommy over to her, so I knew he was safe. And yet the whole situation was too unsettling to bear. I felt reckless, as if I should have called to warn her of my plans. Even after everything that had passed between us, I couldn't imagine her turning her back on me when I needed her most. She had never rejected me – not even when I'd deserved it. My cowardice had been what prevented me from making contact, the shame of my past too great to overcome.

I rolled towards the edge of the mattress, easing my aching body into a sitting position with a groan I'd been containing for hours. Scott had arrived home late, stinking of beer and smoke, and had fallen into bed beside me without so much as brushing his teeth, an arm slung over my waist. He'd whispered a slurred 'Missed you, Chlo' into my ear, the earlier fire he'd vibrated with doused by alcohol, then fallen asleep, his face pressed into my spine, forcing tears into my eyes as I wished he could always be so gentle, so loving. He was capable of so much more than he was giving me, and I hated that he couldn't manage to get control of the easy anger that had broken our little family. Broken me.

I stood up, walking over to the window and pushing it open to banish the stale smell of hops and cigarettes from the flat. It was mid June, and though it was cool now, I was sure it was going to be another sweltering day.

My bag was on the floor, and I glanced at it, thinking of the letter concealed inside. I had to find out who had sent it. I'd been thinking of it all night. There had been no name, no clue as to who might have written it. I had never told anyone my secret. Never breathed a word of what I'd done to a single soul. Not even to Scott in our early days, when we'd confided everything to each other. I couldn't bear for him to see me in a different light, to watch the love evaporate from his eyes. It was something that once said out loud could never be taken back. So I'd held my tongue. Always.

So how had somebody found out? And why were they writing to me now? It could only be that what I'd always feared had happened that night. Someone had seen me.

FIVE

Then

I crossed the road, heading down the narrow alley that led to the back door of the flats that had been standing abandoned, half completed, for more than a year. Ever since I'd walked out of my family home almost ten years ago to the day, places like this had been a lifesaver for me. A roof over my head at the very least, and these ones even had fitted kitchens in some of the units, although we had to make do without running water and electricity.

I missed simple things – carpet under my feet, a fridge, heating in the winter, a duvet even – but I knew it was a thousand times better than being out in some shop doorway with a damp sleeping bag and an audience of pedestrians staring down at me as I slept. I'd done my fair share of those kind of nights when we'd been forcibly evicted from the last place, and that had given me a whole new appreciation for the simple pleasures of a solid brick wall and a locked door.

Scott and I had been squatting in this building for almost nine months, playing house, warming up noodles on a camping stove he'd pinched from an unlocked motorhome parked up at a service station. We lived day to day, still kids really, but we spent our nights dreaming of what the future would look like. I always said I wanted a farmhouse, two or three children running around, chickens, a little garden, and Scott would laugh, ask me what the hell I knew about growing vegetables. Then he'd clamber up from the bare mattress we'd dragged in off the street and, butt naked, putting on a West Country accent, he'd squat down and pretend to drive off in his imaginary tractor. 'Fancy a ride, gorgeous?' he'd say with a wink, and I'd laugh so hard I could hardly breathe. We dreamed a lot, but I always felt grateful for what we had.

But now, walking home past the piled-up litter, bags of rotting food tossed from windows – no bin collection here – fag ends and even a few needles kicked into the gutter, I saw the place in a different light. The steel door, its red paint peeling off, exposing huge patches of jagged rust, swung open, and a group of girls who'd taken up residence in a flat two floors below ours came out, hollow-eyed, wearing short skirts and halter tops. My gaze homed in on the track marks running up their arms. They didn't even bother to try to hide them. They would bring men back to their place night after night, easy money to fund their drug habit. I didn't like it, but it had never been something I spent much time thinking about. But now... now things were different.

I smiled a secret little smile to myself and wrapped my arms across my chest, hugging myself tight. I couldn't wait to see Scott's face. Tell him that we were about to take the first step towards achieving the life we'd dreamed of. Everything was going to change. It was exciting, but I was scared too. I squashed down a wave of conflicting emotions, a sudden panic that I couldn't – *shouldn't* – do this, and before I could change my mind, I ran up the stairs to the third floor and let myself into our flat.

Scott was sitting by the window, rolling a cigarette, dressed in a pair of holey boxer shorts and a faded black T-shirt. I couldn't help looking at the flat with fresh eyes too. The space was big, and if the builders had completed the job, it would have been lovely. The kitchen diner was open plan, with a big picture window looking out over the road below, flooding the room with light. The floor was just bare wooden boards – boards I frequently got huge splinters from – and a rainbow of electrical wires hung loosely from where the sockets and light switches would have been. There was a damp, stale smell to the place, and despite my best efforts, a layer of dust and grime had accumulated on the skirting boards and windows. I felt a pang of sadness, knowing that if the developers had found the funds to finish, the flat I called home would be gorgeous, though of course we would never have been able to afford to stay here if that were the case.

'All right, babe?' Scott said, looking up as I closed the door. He put the rollie between his teeth and cast around, looking for a lighter.

'I'm pregnant!'

I pressed my lips together. I hadn't meant to blurt it out like that. I'd wanted to build up to it, tell a story, get him as excited as I was, but now I'd tossed the news at him like a live grenade, and as I stood waiting for him to say something, I felt horribly exposed and vulnerable.

Scott opened his mouth, the rollie falling to the ground. He didn't seem to notice. 'You're...' A slow smile spread across his face, and he jumped up. 'Yes!' he yelled, pumping the air with a fist. 'Come to Daddy!'

He opened his arms, and I rushed into them, sure we were going to be a perfect family. Scott would be a wonderful parent. But as he pulled me in and I pressed my face to his chest, a sudden image flashed into my mind, a memory I'd never quite been able to shake.

It was funny how it had once seemed so easy, so simple to run away from home, leaving my mistakes behind me. As a fifteen-year-old, I'd been naïve enough to hope that you could escape your past if you tried hard enough. But it had never been the case. And now, with less than a year until I would become a mother, responsible for the life of a vulnerable little person, I couldn't seem to hold back the floodgates, the memories forcing themselves to the front of my mind, demanding acknowledgement.

I clung to Scott, reliving the blind terror I'd felt in the weeks before I'd run away, having realised what I had done – what I was capable of. The awful understanding that there are some things that can never be taken back, no matter how desperately you wish for a second chance. That empty single bed, the blood on the carpet...

I pressed my face closer into his chest, squeezing my eyes tightly shut as I tried to bat away the images, and realised that as much as I trusted Scott to get this right and keep our baby safe, I couldn't help but be afraid that the same might not be true for me.

SIX

'Fired? You can't fire me! I need this job.'

Mr Privett looked at me from across the desk, and I felt a surge of hatred well up inside me at the smug look on his ratty little face. I hated this job. Hated that even though he was only eight years older than me, he made me call him Mr Privett rather than Niall. Hated that ever since he'd asked me out and I'd turned him down on my first week here, he'd saved the worst jobs for me. Someone been sick in the toilets? Send Chloe to clear it up. Someone vandalised the wall outside? Chloe will stay late to scrub it clean until her hands crack and bleed.

The only reason I stuck it out, forced myself to turn up and smile and pretend not to hear his sleazy, stomach-churning innuendoes, was because I needed the money. With a three-year-old to dress and feed and a flat to keep warm, working wasn't optional, and what with my leaving school at fifteen with no GCSEs under my belt, I was hardly in a position to be choosy. And now, despite all I'd done to be nice, keep a smile on my face and not rise to his bait, he had the audacity to try to fire me? I was a good, hard worker – he had no right to let me go.

'You took a week off without notice. I had to scramble to cover your shifts. You aren't a team player.'

'Tommy had chickenpox! I told you that. They wouldn't let him go to nursery, and even if they had, he was really poorly with it. He came down with strep A and had to spend three days in bed. You *know* I didn't have a choice. And it's the first time I've taken off since—'

'Since last month when he had a stomach bug.'

I shook my head. 'I can't help it if he picks up a bug in nursery. And I worked two extra days to make up for that.'

I'd felt obligated to, though it wasn't fair that he'd asked me. I'd taken the waitressing job two weeks after discovering I was pregnant, hoping to save up enough money to buy the basics, though the pay was low and the hours long. Scott had taken it in his stride when I'd told him we couldn't stay in the squat once the baby came. I wanted so much more for our child, our family. A safe home. Parents who provided – responsible and secure.

He'd seemed only too happy to go out and find work, taking the first job he was offered – on a factory production line, assembling kitchen appliances. It was mind-numbing work, and long hours, and I knew he'd rather be sitting down the pub. To begin with, he'd been stoic about it, silently going through the motions. These days he wasn't nearly so good at hiding the resentment he felt at having to provide for us.

We were in a difficult stage of life. Everyone said the early years were the hardest, trying to get through one day at a time. But once Tommy was a bit older, things would get easier. I'd held on to that hope as tight as I could, needing it to be true. But now... now I was being fired, unjustly – illegally too, I thought. He didn't have the right to sack me for my child being ill, did he? And despite Scott's long hours, we relied on my income to get by. Our landlord had increased the rent on our tiny flat every single year, and Tommy was outgrowing his clothes faster than I could buy them. I pictured walking back in and telling

Scott we had to make do on his income until I could find another job – easier said than done with my flimsy CV – and felt my stomach drop.

'I need workers I can rely on,' continued Mr Privett. 'I already filled the position. Sarah will be taking your shifts from tomorrow.'

'Who's Sarah?'

He leaned back in his chair and grinned. 'Your replacement.'

He tapped the tip of his pen on a pile of papers on his desk, and I saw an application form, a passport-sized photo of a pretty brunette with full red lips and come-to-bed eyes paper-clipped to the top. I wondered if she had any idea of the kind of disgusting creature she'd agreed to work for; if she knew that in taking the job, she was taking away my security – the very food from my mouth.

'You can't expect money for nothing, can you?' he said, his gaze following mine to the photograph, the lecherous look in his eyes unmistakable.

I stood up, not deigning to justify myself, nor point out how much harder I worked than anyone else in this damn building. Naïve as it might be, I hadn't given up on the dreams Scott and I had shared whilst lying on that bare mattress in the abandoned flat all those years ago. The farmhouse in the country. The chickens and children and fresh air, green fields, blue sky... a little slice of heaven. I still hoped to get there, though I had no idea how. But in losing this job I was even further away from grasping hold of that reality.

'This is unfair dismissal,' I said, emotion filling my voice, making it shake.

He shrugged infuriatingly, and I felt utterly powerless, knowing that as much as I wanted to fight the decision, I had no resources for lawyers, and all my time would now be taken up searching for a new job to pay the rent at the end of the month.

'Fuck you, Niall. She won't sleep with you either.' I nodded towards the pretty girl in the photo.

'We'll see,' he replied, though his face flushed as if I'd read his mind, and he looked away.

I picked up my bag, blinking back hot, stinging tears, and before I could embarrass myself by begging him to reconsider, I strode out of his poky little office with my head held high.

The flat should have been empty at this time of day, but as I slid my key into the lock, I could hear the bass of music and smiled. Sometimes the machines at the factory jammed up, and if they needed a big fix, Scott got to come home early. I wanted to see him so badly. To tell him how Niall had treated me and have him take my side.

I slipped out of my coat and kicked my shoes off, heading in the direction of the music – the bedroom all three of us shared off the far side of the living room. The light was poor in here, a result of the condensation on the windows, the glass long since blown.

The carpet, once cream, was worn and shabby, and the few pieces of furniture we had were things we'd found for free, more often than not Scott having swiped them from a skip. It was so far from the cosy home I had grown up in, and I hated that Tommy was missing out on the comforts I'd taken for granted – not to mention the stay-at-home mum who'd baked and gardened and seemed to have an infinite amount of time to spend with me. I always felt so rushed. A part of me wished that Scott would say I could forget about looking for another job. Take Tommy out of nursery and spend these precious years with him, soak up the time before it passed too fast to snatch hold of. But we couldn't afford it. Not yet.

'Hi,' I said, pushing open the bedroom door.

Scott was lying on the bed, a cigarette hanging from the

corner of his mouth, holding a cracked CD case above his face as he read the back. He looked at me with a blank expression. 'What are you doing here? I thought you were working till four?'

I nodded, feeling drained and emotional. 'Niall sacked me.'

He raised an eyebrow, dropping the CD case on the bed and sitting up. 'What? Why?'

'Does he need a reason? He's the boss.' I shook my head. 'He accused me of not pulling my weight because I had to take time off when Tommy was poorly. But I do twice what the rest of them do when I'm there. He's been looking for an excuse for ages. I told you he doesn't like me.'

That wasn't strictly true, but I'd never let on to Scott that Niall was interested in me. He had a hell of a jealous streak at times, and as much as I would have liked to be able to confide in him, I wouldn't have put it past him to go down there and beat the living daylights out of my boss, which would mean no end of trouble for all of us.

Scott leaned forward, his head dropping to his hands.

'Hey, it's okay... I can...' I was about to tell him I would head to the job centre first thing, but his head snapped up, and instead of the worry I'd expected to see etched on his features, I saw something that made me stop in my tracks – a look of absolute rage. Was he going to beat Niall up now, after all I'd done to keep the peace? Scott getting arrested was the last thing we needed.

I opened my mouth to soothe him, reassure him, but he lurched to his feet, and before I knew what was happening, his hand was round my throat, my back slamming hard into the bedroom wall. Instinctively, I grabbed at his wrist, my fingernails digging into his skin, no thought for anything but getting a breath. When his grip tightened, I did the only thing I could. I swung my knee up hard, colliding with his groin.

The effect was instant. He released me, and I bent double,

gasping for breath, my hands going to my throat, shocked and shaken.

Scott swore, straightened and then, with blank, cold eyes fixed on mine, he slapped me so hard across the face that the back of my head ricocheted off the wall. The pain was blinding, tiny bursts of light flashing behind my retinas. What the hell was happening? Was he on something? He *had* to be. This wasn't the man I knew. He'd never even raised his voice to me before.

'Scott!' I gasped. 'Stop! Stop it!' Tears were streaming down my face, and I felt as if I was going to vomit. 'Please! What's happening? I don't understand what's happening!' I said, hearing the words leave my mouth and feeling stupid and pathetic.

He pressed the tip of his tongue to his teeth, a hard, angry expression on his face. 'I knew you were too fucking good to be true. Did you think you could just trap me into a life I didn't want? Huh? Get yourself pregnant so I'd have to work some shitty job I can't fucking stand, while you swan about on my cash, expecting to be waited on like a queen? Let me tell you something, Chloe Phillips,' he went on, stepping so close I could feel his breath hot against my cheek. 'You're no queen.' He smashed the palm of his hand against the wall, and then, with a parting look that made my insides turn to liquid, he walked out, slamming the door so hard I thought the wood would shatter.

I sank to the carpet, pulling my knees tight under my chin, unable to stop the tears from falling. I had spent our whole relationship afraid of myself. What *I* might do to *him*... To Tommy. What *I* was capable of. But now, sitting alone with nobody to call for help, nowhere to run to, I realised that maybe I was the one who was in danger.

SEVEN

CLARISSA

I paced back and forth, the phone clutched in my hand as I cast furtive glances towards the open window. I'd seen Mirium out there on the pavement an hour ago chatting to her next-door neighbour Rachel. She'd pointed towards my house, and hidden by the blinds, I'd known they were discussing me and Tommy. If only he hadn't gone and called me Grandma. His presence would have raised questions whatever he'd said, but I'd seen the look on Miri's face when he'd spoken the word, the confusion as she tried and failed to fit together all the pieces of the puzzle, only to find half of them missing.

She'd been there for me back then. Those awful days. I'd lived in this same house, in this quiet little street, for the best part of forty years, and I didn't know if it was a blessing or a curse that most of the neighbours had too. On the one hand, it meant that privacy was thin on the ground. Everyone knew everyone's business. There was a culture of gossip, and although we were all friendly, there was no such thing as a secret on this street.

I knew Bill's wife had deliberately flashed the window cleaner from her bedroom on his last three visits. I knew Susan had fast food delivered when her husband was playing golf, then told him she'd been in the gym. And old Maurice on the corner never picked up after his dog unless he saw someone watching him. If you needed someone to help you lift a heavy delivery or pop to the shops when you were ill, it was wonderful, but at other times there was no denying it could be claustrophobic. That being said, I might not have survived without these people around me in my darkest moments.

Mirium's children, along with Rachel's, Linda's, Penelope's and Fiona's, had played alongside mine when they were small, out there on tricycles and scooters riding up and down the pavements, a little tribe of noise and energy. I still saw them now, all grown up when they came home for Sunday lunches and big family Christmas celebrations. It was impossible not to look at them and wonder what my children would look like as adults. Some of them even had children of their own. Careers, husbands, houses to pay for, and it was mindboggling to me that they should have grown up when my children were locked in stasis, teenagers for all eternity in my mind.

I'd lost my husband, Reece, first, when Chloe was five and Rhodri just two. The heart attack had come out of the blue; nobody had expected it of such a vibrant man. They say the heart can be a ticking time bomb, don't they? Skinny but not fit. Arteries clogged with bacon grease and saturated fat over years and years of abuse. When it happened, the neighbours got me through. Fed me. Took the kids so I could catch my breath. I could feel their pity, but I leaned on them anyway. I had to.

But when the children were taken from me too, one after the other just a decade later, I couldn't bear those looks of horror in their eyes. I couldn't accept their help with grace. I was angry with them, with the whole world. Jealous of all they had when so much had been snatched out from beneath me. It didn't seem right, *fair*, for so much to land on my shoulders while my neighbours celebrated wedding anniversaries and dreamed of their children's futures.

I had taken to my bed, and it was months before I emerged, several stone lighter despite Mirium and the other women practically force-feeding me around the clock. We hadn't spoken of it afterwards. I never mentioned their names. I'd placed all the photographs in the loft and pretended I'd always been alone. It was the only way to keep going – keep living.

I couldn't blame Mirium for having questions about the boy. Of course she would. I did too. And I knew I had to call the police. Yet, those dimples... those eyes... I couldn't help but wonder... *hope*. Would it be so bad if he stayed a while, just until I was certain? I didn't want to get into trouble, but I wasn't ready to let him go just yet. Having him here had brought back so many memories, and I knew, even if he left now, it was too late to pretend they weren't there demanding I pay attention to them.

'Tommy,' I said, looking down at the boy playing with my knitting box on the carpet. I had no toys for him to explore, no trinkets left over from the past. 'Tell me what your mummy said to you before you came here.'

He wound a long strand of wool around his thumb, concentrating on it. 'She said she was going to see me soon. And don't forget to brush my teeth.'

'Did she say why she wasn't coming too?'

He shrugged and picked up a big blue button.

I sighed, then tried another approach. 'What does Mummy look like?' I asked, thinking of the last time I'd seen my daughter. She'd been fifteen. It was how I still pictured her – when I allowed myself to. Low-rise jeans and a white band T-shirt that showed off her tanned belly. Her hair was fine, light brown and chopped to her shoulders. She'd had her ears pierced, just once – I'd been strict about that, not wanting her to overdo it. Stick-on nails. Lipstick that was too dark for her pale freckled face.

Blue eyes that had looked at me as if I was the answer to everything. I'd never had a moment of trouble from her. She and I had been two peas in a pod, and since she'd been snatched so suddenly from my world, I had dreamed of her every single night. It's like that with daughters. Special. Inexplicable.

Tommy seemed to think for a moment, pressing the button into the carpet to watch the indent the holes made. 'She wears a nice jumper. It has a picture of a cat on the front. And she smells like...' His eyes began to well up, and he dropped the button, reaching for the bear he'd placed on the carpet beside him.

I bit my lip, seeing that I wasn't going to get anywhere with this line of questioning.

I heard a car outside and glanced at the window, half expecting to see the taxi returning for Tommy. Instead, I felt my stomach drop as I saw a police car coming to a stop outside. I shook my head, glancing at the phone in my hand, confused. When I looked back up, I saw Mirium's husband, Jeff, standing behind the police car outside their house, staring right at me through the glass, his arms folded across his chest.

I felt my teeth clamp down on the tip of my tongue, my shoulders tensing as my eyes met his. Damn him. I knew without a shadow of a doubt that he'd been the one who'd called them. He was the one neighbour I'd never got on with, always interfering, always watching in a way that made me feel uncomfortable in my own home. It wasn't the first time I'd caught him staring through my window without the slightest hint of shame. I should have guessed Mirium would share her concern with him, and he would force my hand. And now, whether I liked it or not, I would have to speak to the police about Tommy.

I gave Jeff a parting glare through the window, then turned away and went to answer the door.

EIGHT

I smiled warmly as the policewoman took a biscuit from the plate in my outstretched hand, trying to remind myself that it wasn't their fault that I'd been put in such an awkward position. No, *that* was all down to Jeff. The two WPCs looked sheepish as I made them repeat the reason for their visit, specifically so they could hear just how ridiculous it sounded.

I leaned back against the sofa cushions, meeting the eyes of the officer seated closest to me. 'As far as I'm aware,' I replied, trying to keep my tone jovial, though it felt a little strained, 'it's not a crime to have my grandson to stay with me for a few days?'

The second WPC took a biscuit, biting into it and sending a shower of crumbs over my carpet. 'Of course not,' she agreed, running her tongue over her front teeth. 'But I'm sure you understand we have to look into these types of calls. When it comes to children, you can never be too careful.'

'Oh, I completely agree. Some of the things you hear in the news nowadays don't bear thinking about. I'm only sorry I can't help. The poor parents must be mad with worry.' I paused. 'That is, I assume you've had a report of a missing child? That is why you're investigating every lead, no matter how unlikely?'

'There's been no report, no.'

'I see.' I maintained my gaze coolly. 'So why would you think...' I let my sentence trail off, expectantly.

She had the grace to blush as she answered. 'Like I said, we're just following up on the information we've been given.'

The first officer spoke again, and I forced my lips into a smile as I listened.

'Is he here now?' she asked. 'Can we see him?'

I admired her ability to be assertive in what had to be an uncomfortable situation. I certainly hadn't made it easy, I was well aware of that, but it wasn't in my best interests, nor Tommy's, to be obstructive to their investigation. And I'd been expecting this question. They wouldn't be doing their job properly if they returned to the station without having given him the once-over. I felt for her. For both of them. The police force was hardly an easy career path, and despite the reason for their visit, I couldn't help but feel a motherly sort of pride at how they'd worked through their checklists without being derailed by the awkwardness of the circumstances.

I stood wordlessly, going to the living-room door and opening it. 'Tommy, darling,' I called. 'Can you come down here for a moment?'

I turned back to the young women. 'Don't look so worried. I know you have to ask. I only wish I didn't have such nosy neighbours. It's a lovely place to live, but being in such close proximity has its downsides. You can't escape the curtain twitchers.'

I wished I could say more, but there was no need. I was certain they would have already flagged up the fact that this wasn't the first time Jeff had made a malicious complaint about me. I doubted it would be the last.

'Do you have an address for his mother? Just so we can contact her if needed?'

I shook my head. 'She's moving,' I said, hoping they wouldn't check up on my story. 'And I don't have the new address written down yet. When she calls, I'll ask her to give you a ring.' I was sure that by the time they realised she hadn't been in touch, they'd be occupied with far more pressing things. Actual crimes, even.

'Yes, Grandma?' Tommy walked into the room, his voice shy and sweet. His eyes widened as he saw the police officers sitting there.

'Hello,' they said one after the other, and I saw their assessing gazes raking him over from head to toe.

Tommy's eyes lit up. 'Hello,' he said, stepping forward, his meek demeanour erased by curiosity. 'Can I try on your hat?' he asked, more boldly than I thought him capable of.

The WPC closest to him complied, popping it on his head, and I bit my tongue, half wanting to chide him for being rude but glad that he was making a good impression. He certainly wasn't coming across as a child in fear of his kidnapper.

I walked back to the sofa and sat down as they continued to talk, picking up the last biscuit from the plate and biting into it. As far as I was concerned, Jeff could go hang. I had nothing to hide.

I flicked the switch on the kettle and pulled a pack of malt loaf from the larder, cutting a slab and eating it without bothering with a plate as the water boiled. The police had finally gone, and it had given me a smug sense of satisfaction when I'd seen Jeff still out there, watching... waiting... though for what I couldn't decide. For me to be arrested? The boy to be taken away? Whatever the case, he'd been disappointed by the lack of fanfare as I walked the two officers out to their car and waved a cheery goodbye. They'd seemed satisfied that Tommy was in no danger, apologising one last time for the interruption to my day before leaving. I'd told them I understood – they were simply doing their job.

I'd smiled sweetly at Jeff, waving at him as if it were a normal, unremarkable day, then gone back inside and vowed to have a word with Mirium about her husband. She had to be able to exert some control over his ridiculous behaviour. Calling the police on me was unacceptable; he had no right to demand details of my private business and retaliate with this kind of nonsense when I didn't give him what he wanted. He was a bully, and I felt sorry for her having to put up with him day after day.

I'd set Tommy up on the patio with a tray full of soil, a trowel and a packet of sunflower seeds, and he was happily digging through the dirt, inspecting the seeds one by one before using his chubby fingers to push them into tiny holes he'd created. His bear was lying on the step behind him, never far from his reach, and the watering can I used for my succulents stood half full by his feet. I sighed, knowing there would be a trail of mud over my floors before too long. But he was happy and quiet and had dealt remarkably well with the unexpected arrival of the police.

It had felt strange to say out loud that this boy was my grandson. That his mother was my daughter. It had been fifteen years since I'd spoken her name. Fifteen years of mourning the loss of her. But somehow, I had known there was truth behind the admission. I didn't understand what was happening – why Tommy was here – but the more I watched him, the more impossible it was to deny what I saw.

The familiarity in his features was jolting, taking me back to another lifetime, bringing forth memories I'd held at bay for so long. As much as I'd tried to resist the idea, the truth was, he was clearly a blood relative. His arrival on my doorstep wasn't a mistake, an *accident*. He'd been sent here. And if that were true, it could mean only one thing. Chloe was alive. Before too long, she would have to come for her child. And I would finally get my daughter back.

NINE

CHLOE

I stood half concealed by a postbox, my beanie pulled low over my forehead, an uneasy feeling that I was being watched making me glance at the surrounding windows. Being back on this street was like stepping into a warm bath, the longing I'd suppressed for more years than I cared to admit surfacing so fast I could hardly stop myself from bursting into tears. I looked around at the familiar houses, picturing the neighbours who might still live behind those doors. In my mind, nobody ever left this place. It was all frozen – the mums' happy chatter after the school run outside on the pavement; the grassy patch on the corner of the cul-de-sac where I used to sit and make daisy chains with a horde of other children who came out to burn off steam after school.

As a mother, the thought of letting my child go out alone to play in the street was unfathomable, but it had been different then. A peaceful, carefree existence I realised now I was lucky to have experienced.

I looked at the front upstairs window I knew to be hers. My mother's. I knew she was still here. I'd checked. *Of course* I had checked. I'd caught a glimpse of her last week coming back from the shops. I'd been in this same spot, concealed behind dark sunglasses that in hindsight had probably made me more conspicuous to prying neighbours. She'd looked older, more creased, her floral knee-length dress and pink cardigan stretched tighter at the seams, her ample bosom larger than I remembered, but other than that, she remained unchanged.

I'd wanted so much to rush across the road and reveal myself to her. Fall into her arms and hug her, the way I had done so often as a little girl. But I couldn't. I hadn't the nerve to face her – not after the way we'd left things. But I had confirmed she was there and made up my mind to send Tommy to her. He couldn't stay at the flat. Not any more.

Things between me and Scott had been growing more and more volatile. And since Niall had stripped me of my meagre source of income last year, my attempts at finding something else fruitless, I'd found myself trapped. Life was so much more complicated when you had a child to consider. I couldn't just walk out – couldn't rely on finding a squat or a shelter to tide me over. Tucking Tommy into bed with the sound of screaming druggies and fighting prostitutes all around us, never knowing if someone would break down our door while we were sleeping... it just wasn't an option.

And as much as I liked to think I might walk away from Scott if it weren't for Tommy, the truth was I'd been with him practically since I left my mother's house, and without him, the world felt like a scary place. I knew it was senseless – that right now, *he* was the one putting me and my child in harm's way – but I still couldn't forget the way he had taken me under his wing back then. I didn't know where I would be now if he hadn't looked after me. If I'd even have survived those awful years.

What I really wanted was for him to realise what he was doing. How far he'd pushed me with his behaviour. I wanted him to see that if he didn't change, go back to being the man I knew he was capable of being, he would lose us both.

The thought of not being with Tommy had been unbearable. Sickening, even. I'd deliberated, procrastinated for so long, trying to find any other solution. The idea of reconnecting with my mother made me want to run in the opposite direction and shove my head hard in the sand, but when Scott had come home in a foul mood last week and physically dragged me from our bed by the hair, waking Tommy and scaring the life out of him, something inside me had snapped. It was the first time he'd laid hands on me in front of our son. And as hard as I might have found it to send Tommy away, as scared as I was about how Scott might react when he realised what I'd done, I had known it was my only choice. It would be the last time he would ever hurt me in front of our child.

I had never felt so helpless, lying on my bedroom floor, my eyes locked with Tommy's, seeing through *his* eyes what his father was capable of as he kicked me so hard I couldn't catch my breath. Couldn't even plead with him to stop, see sense. I had been weak. A victim. Made so many excuses for the man who was supposed to love me – *us.* But he'd gone too far, and it had given me strength. I would not let Tommy live through that again. The image of his pale little face cowering beside the bed, his eyes wide as the man he trusted to protect him hurt me, flooded my vision, and I felt myself longing to hold him, hug him, smell his head. I missed him so much I could hardly stand it.

I'd had no choice other than to send him here, but I wouldn't have had the courage to come so soon if it weren't for the anonymous letter burning a hole in my pocket, reminding me of how much danger I was in.

If I'd been thinking straight, I would have insisted on going to the police back then, the night it all happened. I'd wanted to confess to what I'd done right from the start. But now, with a son to protect, knowing how much he needed me, I no longer felt that admitting the truth was an option. I *couldn't* go to prison. I had to be here for Tommy. And the only way to do that was to track down whoever had written the note and try to convince them they were mistaken. To persuade them to forget whatever it was they thought they knew about me.

As I stared at the front door of my mother's house, I made up my mind. It was time to go back. To find the answers I needed, I was going to have to face my past.

'It's really you.'

I nodded, looking into my mother's eyes, seeing the way the colour had drained from her soft, round cheeks, the tremble in her hands as she knotted her fingers tightly together beneath her chin. 'Hi, Mum.'

She gave a choked gasp and pulled me into a hug, crushingly tight. For a moment, I remained stiff, shocked by her warm reception. I hadn't known what to expect in coming home, but as the jasmine scent of her perfume filled my nostrils, I let myself sink into the familiar sense of safety I'd forgotten – buried – the moment I'd walked out of this door.

'You silly, silly girl!' she said, pulling back to hold me by the shoulders and wiping her eyes. 'You should have called.'

I nodded, swallowing a ball of shame. 'Is he okay?'

'The boy? Your son, I presume?'

'Yes.'

'He's fine. He's been in the garden almost constantly since he arrived. Very happily digging up my flower beds.'

She gave a mock frown, and I felt a surge of love for her, letting out a breath as relief flooded through me.

'Has he been asking after me?'

'We've had some tears at bedtime, but he soon settled. And he woke up thinking of nothing but his breakfast. Boys are happy as long as their plates are full and they have a project to keep them busy. I haven't forgotten,' she added.

I pressed my lips together, feeling that we were travelling dangerously close to territory best avoided. At least for now.

'Come in, then. I'm sure he'll be delighted to see you.'

She stepped back to let me in, peering out to the street as if she were looking for someone, before closing the door on the outside world.

The hallway had changed since I'd last seen it. The walls had been painted a pale green, the carpet switched to glossy laminate flooring. Following her into the living room, though, was like stepping into a time capsule. The vertical-striped pink-and-grey wallpaper. The open fire with the same cast-iron grate. The big boxy TV set that had to be twenty years old. It was all as it had been when I'd lived here. And yet there *was* one difference, I realised as I cast my eyes around the room. There wasn't a single photograph. Not of Dad. Me... Rhodri. No indication that we had ever lived here. I wondered if she kept them locked up in a box somewhere, by her bed perhaps, so she could look at them – feel close to us – when she felt lonely. Or was the reminder of the family she'd lost just too painful to bear? Had *I* done that? Caused her so much pain she'd had to erase us from her thoughts?

'I'll make some tea,' she said softly.

I nodded, following her out to the kitchen, my eyes going straight to the window. The sight of a head of white-blonde hair made my heart leap.

Seeming to sense me watching, he glanced up from the flower bed and broke into a radiant smile. He dropped the trowel, leaped up and broke into a run, and I dashed past my mother to the back door, meeting him there, scooping him into my arms, squeezing him tight against my body. In his four years of life, we had never been apart for more than a few hours. I'd never left him anywhere overnight. And I'd missed him more than I'd ever dreamed possible, a desperate yearning to be with him consuming every waking moment of my day.

He pulled back and kissed me, his muddy hands cupping my face. 'Mummy!' he cried, his tone full of excitement. His eyes were shining, happy, and there was no trace of any of the trauma I'd feared I might see having sent him to live with a stranger. But I'd known he was safe here. So much safer than he'd ever been with me.

'Come and see what I planted in the garden!' he said, taking me by the hand and leading me outside before I had a chance to answer.

As I followed him, I saw my mother watching us with an expression that made me feel both joy and crushing guilt. I hadn't let myself believe I would ever come back here, nor dared to hope that she might open the door to me if I did. She was a good mother. She always had been. But as Tommy showed me the tray filled with compost and I turned my back on her watchful gaze, I couldn't help but wonder if there was some part of her that might hate me for what I had done. That might still long for retribution after all these years.

TEN

CLARISSA

I gripped the handle of the kettle, trying to hold back my emotions as I listened to the sound of my daughter's voice carry through the hall. It was as if the last fifteen years hadn't happened. As if she'd never left. I let go of the kettle, pressing my hands to my face, taking a deep, steeling breath.

I hadn't thought I would ever see her again. There had been no warning back then that she might leave. I hadn't even considered the possibility. I could still remember emerging from my room after what felt like weeks to find her gone, her bed unmade, no note, no clues. Then the waiting... those nail-bitingly slow days, watching the clock, staring from my bedroom window in the hope I might see her walking round the corner. Keeping the curtains closed, and thus the neighbours at bay, so I didn't have to explain her absence, didn't have to admit that the last member of my family was gone too.

I had waited for so long, but there came a point eventually when the hope began to morph into something else – a slow, awful realisation that she really was gone. And with it, the fear that I might have lost her for ever – that she might have discovered the secret I'd sworn never to tell. So much had happened in the run-up to her departure, but I had never wanted any of it to come between her and me. She had been my world.

I squeezed my eyes shut, determined to keep calm, in control, to do whatever it took to welcome her back into my life, not wanting to show how desperate I was to keep her here. I squared my shoulders and made the tea, cut up an apple for Tommy and headed back to join the two of them in the living room.

Chloe was sitting on the sofa by the window, and I wished she would move to the one opposite, by the wall. I didn't want nosy neighbours peering in, seeing her here before I knew how I was going to explain her sudden appearance. A part of me didn't want to have to. I didn't have to tell them everything, after all. Didn't owe them every scrap of my life, though I knew plenty of them would disagree with that.

She looked thin, her face pale and drawn, shadows beneath her dark-blue eyes, the round flushed cheeks she'd had as a teenager long gone. She wasn't a child any more, and the fact that I had missed the transition from her girlhood into this woman sitting before me broke my heart.

She looked up at me and gave a shy smile that made me want to pull her in for a cuddle. I'd never imagined there could be a time when the two of us would be strangers, so cautious around each other, unsure how to act, what to say.

Thankfully, she broke the ice.

'Thank you for taking him,' she said, reaching down to pluck a stray thread from the back of Tommy's T-shirt, unable to quite meet my eye. 'I'm so sorry I didn't call first. It was all a bit of a rush.'

'So I gathered,' I said, handing Tommy the plate of sliced apple.

He took it without a word, concentrating on the robot toy his mum had produced from her bag. Its paint was chipped, and there was a dent in the plastic – it was clearly well loved. I sat down in my favourite armchair and offered Chloe an encouraging smile, hoping she'd keep talking and explain what on earth she'd been thinking of, sending him here without warning.

She picked up the mug of tea I'd placed in front of her, cupping it between her palms. She chewed at her lower lip, and I waited, trying to appear serene, though all I wanted was to grill her. Ask where she'd been for the last fifteen years. Who was the boy's father? Was she safe? Happy? Why had she left home without giving me the opportunity to change her mind? I took a sip of my own tea, letting the hot, sweet liquid trickle down my throat, warming me.

'I... I've lost my job,' she said. 'Well, I lost it a little while ago, actually. But things have been tight, and I haven't been able to find anything else. Tommy's nursery is so expensive, and it's difficult to find something I can fit in around his sessions.'

She looked up at me, and I could see the effort it was costing her to admit how much she'd been struggling.

'I want to be able to provide for him. Give him a good home, be the kind of mother you were to me,' she added, offering a smile that filled me with joy. 'But, well, everything's gone wrong at once, and I might need to move to a new place. I just... I really need to get back on my feet, and I wondered if—'

'You can stay with me,' I said, wanting nothing more. 'Both of you.'

She shook her head. 'I appreciate the offer. But there are things I need to fix... to figure out. And I can't do that here.'

I frowned, wondering what she meant. Was she on drugs? Did she need time to get clean? The idea made my blood fizz, anxiety filling me at the image of my little girl injecting dangerous substances into her body. Surreptitiously, I glanced at her arms for signs, but they looked smooth and free from scars or track marks. I could see there was something she wasn't telling me, but I didn't want to push the issue. Not yet.

'Okay.' I drummed my fingers on my mug, thinking fast. It

had been so long since I'd taken care of a child, but I could remember how intensive the early years had been. It would be tiring – exhausting at my age – and would cast my routines into disarray, but that didn't matter. What was important was that Chloe was back in my life, and whatever she needed, I would be only too happy to give. 'Then leave Tommy with me,' I said, making up my mind. 'You can get on with whatever you need to do and visit him here until things are sorted. He's welcome to stay as long as you need, and if you change your mind, you can come back too. This is still your home. Your room is still here.'

She looked surprised, as if she'd expected me to turn her and the boy out on the street. She opened her mouth, and I braced myself, not ready to have the conversation we'd managed to avoid so far. It wasn't the right time, and I didn't want to hear her bring up the night I'd tried for so long to forget. If I were honest, I never wanted to speak of it again.

Instead, to my relief, she closed her mouth and nodded. 'Thanks, Mum,' she said softly. 'I'm embarrassed to have to ask... I should be able to give him what he needs. I feel like I'm failing at this.'

'It's harder than it looks, isn't it?' I said, leaning across to take her hand.

'A lot harder. I had this image of what things would be like...' She gave a laugh that sounded jaded... sad. 'Nothing like this.'

I squeezed her hand. 'You'll be fine. And he's happy. Children don't want much at the end of the day. Just the simple things.'

I saw movement through the window, and my eyes locked on a figure on the path outside. My stomach clenched tight as I recognised Jeff. He was making his way to my back gate, clearly intending to barge in.

I stood up, angry and flustered. 'I'm just going to check the oven's on. You'll stay for tea, won't you?'

'Oh, okay, that would be nice.'

I hardly waited for her to finish speaking before darting out of the room and into the kitchen. I closed the door, not wanting her to hear me talking, and reached the back door at the same time as Jeff. I swung it open, blocking his way.

'Can I help you with something, Jeff?' I asked, smiling, though my tone was far from friendly. I knew it was him who had called the police this morning. I would have staked my life on it. He and my late husband had been close when we'd first moved into the cul-de-sac, but there was something about him that had always put me on edge. He was the kind of man who stared. You'd be out doing the garden or washing the car and feel the back of your neck prickle, and, sure enough, there he'd be, watching... It made me uneasy, and I'd made no secret of the fact that I didn't like him. Especially given what I'd discovered after Reece had passed away.

'Thought I'd pop in and check you're all right, seeing as we saw the old bill here earlier. Here a while, weren't they?'

'Nothing to worry about. As you can see, I'm still in one piece.'

He nodded, unsmiling. 'Left the kid with you too, I noticed. And I saw the young lass at your door. Who was that then? His mother?'

'Not that it's any of your business, but yes.'

He pursed his lips. 'Miri said the boy called you Grandma.'

I stared at him, regretting giving him anything. I should have told him to mind his own business and sent him on his way.

I glanced over my shoulder, hoping Chloe wouldn't come in now. No doubt she would recognise Jeff. He'd been a familiar figure during her childhood, always around, and he hadn't changed much in the past fifteen years. More to the point, *he* would recognise *her*. Even as much as she'd transformed into a young woman, he would know her, just as I had. I didn't want to

have to explain to her that I'd let people think she was dead –
that it was easier than admitting the truth. And why should I
have to spill my secrets to him, of all people?

I held his penetrating stare, refusing to say another word,
wondering how Mirium could cope with being married to a
man like him. He made me uneasy in my own home – a home
that had been my sanctuary for so long.

Years ago, his behaviour had become so intense, so erratic, I
had begun to feel as if I was being stalked, and I'd had to
approach Miri privately and tell her to do something about him.
She'd seemed shocked at the time, as if she couldn't see the side
of him I'd had the displeasure of witnessing, and I hadn't
wanted to overstep the mark and tell her how sometimes I was
actually frightened of him. She must have said something to
him though, because he backed off after that, but now it was as
if he had the bit between his teeth again, and I felt that familiar
sense of dread bubble to the surface once more.

He ran his tongue over his lower lip, glancing behind me to
the closed door, and I felt my hackles rise.

'I'm rather busy, Jeff. Send my best to Miri and tell her I
won't be at the community centre tomorrow as I have other
commitments.'

I closed the door before he could object, dropping the blind
as I did to block the view of his face. I waited, tense, for the
sound of his footsteps on the path, holding my breath until I
heard the creak of the gate. Then I walked across the kitchen
and turned on the oven, trying to imagine a world where Jeff
didn't exist.

ELEVEN

CHLOE

Mum served up the plates of cottage pie and peas. It was a meal I hadn't eaten in years and brought back a flood of memories, the smell making me picture those rainy winter afternoons when the sun had begun to sink low in the sky even on the walk back from school. I'd stepped into the warm hallway, shrugging off my dripping-wet coat and school bag, hanging them on the hook and breathing in that smell of comfort. She'd always met me with a hug, holding me close as she asked how my day had been, if I had homework to do later. No matter if I'd fallen on my face during PE or messed up my maths in front of the whole class, the moment I stepped through the front door, none of it had mattered. I wished it could be so simple now. That I could turn back the clock and undo the mistakes I'd made.

But then, I thought, I wouldn't have Tommy. And I wouldn't undo him for anything.

I watched him now, a fork clamped in his hand as he dug in, a serious expression on his cherubic face. There was an aware-ness that time was ticking by more quickly than I'd like. After dinner, it would be his bedtime, and I had yet to find the courage to bring up the letter. The reception had been so warm, and I didn't want to taint it with talk of things best left unsaid. My stomach knotted, and despite the delicious smells wafting from the plate, I found I couldn't bring myself to pick up my fork and dig in.

Mum looked across the table. 'I'm sorry. I know it's the last thing you want in a heatwave, but I didn't think salad would fill him up. I wanted to give him something nutritious.' She grimaced apologetically.

I shook my head. 'No, this is lovely, I remember how you used to always make such nice dinners for us.' I forced myself to take a mouthful, chew, swallow, ignoring the nausea building in my belly. 'It's delicious.'

She smiled warmly, and I could see she appreciated the compliment. We ate in silence, and despite how smoothly the afternoon had gone, I could feel the tension beginning to grow. She had refrained from asking any questions, and so far so had I, but I could sense an awareness in her now as she watched me.

Tommy finished eating, and I sent him to wash his face.

'Mum,' I began, taking the opportunity while I had it.

She picked up my plate, taking it over to the sink with hers without responding.

'I need to ask you something.'

She looked at me, her eyes narrowing. 'If it's about why you left, we don't need to talk about that.'

'I don't want to bring it all up,' I said, standing and carrying Tommy's plate over to the side. 'But, well, something's happened...'

'What do you mean?'

I pulled the note from my pocket and unfolded it, passing it to her without a word. I watched her eyebrows rise as she read it, before she handed it back to me.

I folded my arms tightly across my chest. 'I never spoke to anyone about... you know,' I said quietly. 'Did you?'

'Of course not,' she said, her voice barely more than a whisper.

'So what does this mean? Who sent it? Someone knows.' I matched her quiet tone so Tommy wouldn't hear. 'I don't understand. Why now? Why send this after all these years?'

She shook her head. 'Is this why you're here? Why you sent Tommy to stay with me? Is this why you're so scared? I can see that you're frightened, Chloe.' She reached for my hand, taking it in hers. 'Darling, it's nonsense. I expect it's a practical joke. A silly coincidence. Nobody knows what happened that night except the two of us. You don't need to worry.'

I looked at her, wishing I could believe that, but something deep inside me screamed that she was wrong.

'I need to make sure that's the case,' I replied, trying to keep my voice steady. 'Would it be okay for Tommy to stay here until I do?'

'I told you he can stay. You're both welcome here. But you're worrying over nothing, darling. Let's forget the whole thing. It doesn't help to open old wounds.' She wrapped me in a hug. 'Your secret is *my* secret. I promise.'

I nodded, allowing myself to melt into her arms. But I knew, despite her reluctance to revisit the past, I would never rest until I found out who'd sent that letter. And what they hoped to achieve with it.

TWELVE

I woke with a gasp, clawing my way free from the duvet, which had knotted around my legs, the nightmare still bright behind my closed eyelids as I grappled for the switch on the bedside lamp. My hand swung out, meeting nothing but air, my pulse thumping in my ears. I scraped my fingers along the edge of the cabinet, relieved as I caught hold of the cable and pressed hard on the little button. The room was instantly flooded with light, and I blinked, breathing hard as I surveyed the damage.

My pillows were on the floor beside the bed, Scott somehow still sleeping beside me, despite the chaos I'd caused. I looked down to the floor mattress where Tommy should have been and felt my heart seize as I wondered if he was asleep now. If he was crying for me.

He'd been happy enough when I'd told him he was going to spend a bit longer with his grandma before coming home. As young as he was, I knew he wasn't ignorant of what had been happening with his dad. He hadn't asked after him the whole time I was with him, something that was more than a little telling. I'd hugged him goodbye and promised to visit again as soon as I could.

Perhaps my anxiety over his absence had brought on the nightmare – the first I'd had for a long time.

The fact that I'd lost control like that frightened me.

After Tommy's birth, I'd been so afraid of falling asleep near him, so sure that I wouldn't be able to keep him safe, that something awful might happen if I did. Scott had been convinced I had post-partum depression, but that wasn't it. I could still remember the disbelief in his eyes when I shared the origin of my fears with him. The night terrors that plagued me, turned me into somebody else. Someone dangerous. I knew he didn't understand. Didn't really believe what I'd told him.

Still, I became obsessive about my routines. I knew that if I went to bed at the exact same time every night, got up like clockwork every morning, I would prevent the overtiredness that led to the kind of deep, out-of-control sleep that caused nightmares... night terrors.

As it turned out, since having my son, my sleep *had* been lighter, and I'd let go of some of the fears I'd carried. You're always on duty as a mother, never fully switched off, constantly ready for a little voice to speak your name and ask for help. My anxiety had been squashed, slowly and steadily, and with each month that passed, I'd relaxed a tiny bit.

But with Tommy gone, something had changed. I had lain awake far later than usual, worrying, my skin crawling with a desperate need to have him back here with me, my anger at the sleeping man beside me – the man who was supposed to protect us and yet had forced me to take such drastic action – making switching off so much harder to achieve. Eventually, I'd sunk into a deep, dreamless slumber, so much deeper than I was used to, and in doing so, had lost myself. Lost control.

I stared at Scott, watching the way his chest rose and fell steadily, wondering what *he* dreamed about. In sleep, he didn't look like the man I'd grown to cringe away from. Learned to fear. He looked so young, barely out of childhood himself.

Slowly, as the nightmare was pushed to the back of my mind, my heartbeat returned to normal, and I reached over the side of the bed, picking up one of the pillows that had fallen in the flurry of my thrashing, and leaned back against it.

Scott rolled over, his eyes half opening. ''S'going on?' he murmured.

'Nothing. Bad dream. That's all.'

'Hmm...' He reached out, taking my hand in his, squeezing it before bringing it to his warm lips.

I closed my eyes against the swell of emotion that flooded me. He wasn't the monster he had allowed himself to become. He could be better. I knew he could. But it hadn't escaped my attention that he had yet to even ask about Tommy's whereabouts. That hurt more than I wanted to admit. He raised himself onto one elbow, his eyes soft and sleepy as they met mine. He ran his finger along my wrist, up my arm, pausing at my collarbone, where a bruise, purple and tender, bloomed. So tenderly I barely felt it, he traced the outline.

'You deserve better,' he said, his voice thick with sleep. 'I'm sorry.'

I nodded but didn't have the courage to say yes.

'It hasn't been easy... since I became the sole breadwinner. It's a lot... but that doesn't excuse this.' He looked up at the ceiling, and I watched his Adam's apple bob as he swallowed. 'You know I love you.'

'I love you too.' I took a deep breath. 'And I get that it's a lot to take on. But Tommy...' I dug my fingernails into my palm, afraid to continue. I pictured my son's wide, terrified eyes when he'd seen his father towering over me, his face contorted in rage, and my resolve hardened. 'Tommy needs a safe home.'

'Where is he now?' His words were conversational, no urgency to his tone, and it irritated me that he didn't seem in the least bit concerned.

'I... I sent him to stay with a relative.'

He frowned. 'I thought you didn't have any.'

I shrugged, not wanting to get into that. 'I want him to come home. I want us to do this properly. Have the life we always talked about. I want so much for us, Scott. We can be so much more than this. Can't we?'

He didn't reply. Instead, he reached across, cupping my chin, pulling me into a kiss. I felt hope bloom inside me, sure that I had finally got through to him.

He pulled back, his hand still on my face, a familiar sultry smile playing on his lips.

'Isn't it easier when it's just us?' he said softly, his eyes sliding down, unable to meet mine. 'There's so much space to think. The pressure is gone. No noise. No constant demands to be something I don't want to be.'

I recoiled from his touch, watching his hand drop to the bed. 'What do you mean?'

He looked back to my face and smiled. 'I mean, this is better. You, me. We were good before, weren't we?' He shrugged. 'I preferred it.'

'You *preferred* it?' I repeated. 'Before Tommy, you mean?'

'I never laid a hand on you before he came along. He pushes my buttons. He wears me down. I can't be the man you want me to be when I have to give everything I have to him,' he said, his voice plaintive. 'It's too hard – I'm not cut out for it, Chlo. I never wanted a life where I had to be responsible for someone else. I want my freedom back. I want *you* back.'

He took a breath, and I felt my whole world begin to collapse around me.

'Look... wherever he is, whoever you've found to take care of him, if he's safe there, then maybe it's better for him. Maybe that's the home he's meant to have.' He kissed my fingers then lay back against the pillow, closing his eyes. 'Just consider it,' he said, stifling a wide, obnoxious yawn.

I stared at his face and felt something snap inside me. There was nothing he could do or say now to change how I'd felt hearing those words. Nothing that would ever convince me that he deserved to be a father to my son. He'd never be the man I'd hoped for, never give Tommy what he deserved. The realisation was utterly terrifying, because it meant that not only would I have to walk away from the man I'd relied on for everything since I was fifteen years old, but also that I would have to keep Tommy safe. And I wasn't sure if I could.

THIRTEEN

The first night on the streets wasn't the worst one. Maybe it was the adrenaline coursing through my veins. Or the fact that I didn't truly believe I would really be one of them – the homeless teens I'd spotted drifting around the high street, sleeping in doorways, lank hair, hollow eyes. It had felt silly, like make-believe, as if I'd thrown a toddler tantrum and run away from home. Which in essence was what I *had* done. But I never believed it was real.

Mum would wake soon to find me gone, then the search would begin. I'd be found, bedraggled, hungry, dirty, and the police would take me home to my mother, who would wrap me in her arms and tell me never to frighten her like that again. That whatever had happened, whatever I had done, she forgave me. That she didn't blame me... didn't love me any less. It was a childish notion, but I was only fifteen and I'd always been young for my age. It was funny to think of that now. How naïve I'd been. How blind to the realities of the world. A few months on the streets had erased that side of me for good. You had to grow up fast out there, or you could find yourself in a whole world of trouble.

That first night, I'd been too unsure of myself to stop, rest, speak to anyone. After getting the last bus into Southampton city centre, I'd donned my backpack, and with my head down, unwilling to make eye contact with anyone, I'd wandered up and down the high street, needing to be around people, but at the same time, not too close.

As the night crept on, two o'clock, then three, the weather turned colder, fewer people milling around. The crowds of late-night shoppers or groups eating at the nearby restaurants had long since disappeared, and in their place were what felt like a less safe variety of people. A small group of loud men discussing some drug deal, arguing over the price on offer. A man with a huge mastiff who swayed drunkenly as he passed me, mumbling something incoherent as his dog eyeballed me, its jowls dripping with drool. Once, I caught sight of a group of three girls about my age in the distance, and tentatively approached, wondering if I might join them, sure that safety in numbers had to count for something. But as I got nearer, I froze, melting into the shadows as a man in a family estate pulled up at the kerb and the girls clambered into the back, thanking him loudly, one of them calling him Dad.

I wished *I* had a dad I could call to come and get me. But then, I realised, if he were still around, I would be too ashamed to face him after what I'd done. I could never expect his forgiveness. I should be grateful he'd died of a heart attack when I was five, so he didn't have to ever look at me with the disgust and horror I knew he would feel.

It had been a long, exhausting night, and I'd hated every moment of it, but it hadn't been the worst I experienced out there. Not by a long way.

The nights it rained were the hardest. When competition for the dry sleeping spots could become fiercely aggressive. When you had to negotiate with the police, who were determined to move you on after you'd spent hours searching for somewhere to rest. Exhaustion, hunger, that awful sense of being totally out of control in your own life were all a part of daily reality.

The longer I stayed out there, the more I lost any trace of hope that I might break free from the circumstances I'd propelled myself into. And the more I began to realise I was exactly where I deserved to be. It had been stupid of me to ever think that she would want me to come home. That she could see past what I'd done and we might still be as close as ever. The very idea that we would go back to how it was before was ridiculous. That we'd bake together on Saturday afternoons. That we'd sit on loungers in the garden chatting about my schoolwork and her plans for the vegetable patch. That we could be normal. I'd ruined all of that. It was my fault. I could never expect her to take me back into her home, look at me the same way, love me still, all the while neither of us mentioning the sibling who was missing. The son I'd stolen from her. The brother I had killed.

FOURTEEN

CLARISSA

I watched through the window as the three preschoolers ran wild on my lawn, noting how reserved little Tommy was in comparison to Mirium's rambunctious grandchildren. Berty and Lola were so loud they made my nerves jangle, always on the go, never sticking to the boundaries Mirium had set. I'd specifically heard her telling them to stay on the lawn and out of the freshly dug-over flower beds, and yet there they were, stamping all over them, screaming at the top of their lungs about giants and dragons and all manner of peculiar things.

Tommy was a credit to Chloe, and to me, as he kept his voice down, stuck to the grass, watching the two of them with curious bewilderment. Every now and then he would get a burst of confidence, finding his voice to answer their questions or running along the path with them to pick up their water bottles from the patio table, the parasol up to keep it cool and shady there. I couldn't help but feel relieved that Chloe hadn't left me with children like that. How Mirium coped for a full weekend was beyond me.

I handed her the packet of chocolate biscuits, and she took one gratefully, biting down and showering herself with crumbs.

'Thanks, Clarissa,' she said, her mouth full. She swallowed and gave an exaggerated sigh. I knew her well enough to see the question on the tip of her tongue, the confusion and curiosity etched on her well-worn features. She took another biscuit before handing back the packet.

I'd been expecting her, of course. Since Jeff had arrived, firing questions my way, I had been certain it was only a matter of time before he urged his wife to come in his place, knowing I was far more likely to give her information than I ever would him. I knew the two of them didn't share everything. That was normal in a marriage. To hold some things back. Have stories you might only share with your female friends, or in some cases keep all to yourself. It had certainly been the case in my marriage, and I knew for a fact that it was the same for Mirium and Jeff. For one thing, she seemed totally oblivious to the lingering tension that remained between me and her husband all these years on. It was as if she thought the past didn't matter. His actions were just a blip, something to be brushed under the carpet and never spoken of.

She took a sip of her tea, the biscuit still pinched between her stubby fingers. The chocolate was melting, I noted, trying not to cringe at the idea of her licking them clean. I'd always had a thing about stuff like that.

'So,' she said, looking out at the children.

Tommy had borrowed the ball Lola and Berty had brought with them, and was rolling it up and down the path, chatting happily to himself. I could just make out the other two halfway up the apple tree at the end of the garden. I hoped they wouldn't fall.

'Jeff said little Tommy's mother was here yesterday.'

I nodded, bracing myself.

Miri clicked her tongue between her teeth, measuring her words carefully. 'Clarissa... I don't understand. Who is she?

Who is this boy to you? Jeff has this wild notion that it was Chloe here, but I told him that's impossible. It can't—'

'He's right,' I interrupted. 'Tommy is my grandson. And Chloe is his mother.' I met her eyes, knowing what would come next. I wanted to send her away, avoid having to admit to the lie I had told, but I knew it was too late for that. I couldn't put this conversation off for ever. 'Chloe has asked me to take care of him for a little while. She's having a difficult time and has a few things she needs to get in order before he can go home,' I said matter-of-factly.

'But... but Chloe's dead! You told me that yourself. I don't understand.' She placed the biscuit down on the coffee table and licked her fingers. I averted my eyes. When I looked back, she was wiping her hand on her jeans. 'What about Rhodri?' she asked, her words soft, quiet.

'You know he's dead,' I snapped, cross that she'd brought my son into this.

'I mean, I thought I did, but none of this is making sense to me.'

I thought back to the day I'd told her Chloe was gone, the conversation still crisp and clear in my mind. She was right. I *had* told her Chloe was dead. There had been no ambiguity in my words, and I couldn't pretend otherwise. I sighed. 'Miri... do you remember what things were like after Rhodri's accident?'

She folded her arms, her face filled with pain. 'It was so sudden,' she whispered, glancing out of the window as if she wanted to head outside and pull her grandchildren close, the memory bringing too many unresolved emotions with it. 'One day he was fine. The next – gone.' She looked down at her lap.

I nodded. 'It was hard on all of us,' I agreed. 'But Chloe more than anyone. They hadn't been all that close, but he *was* her brother. And I was having a difficult time. I wasn't myself. I didn't support her as much as I should have. She needed more, but I was dealing with my own emotions, so I guess I didn't see how much she was struggling.' I swallowed, not wanting to think about it. I hated remembering that time. 'Two weeks after Rhodri died, she left.'

'But you said—'

'I know what I said,' I snapped again. 'Sorry. God... I'm sorry, Miri. This isn't easy for me to talk about.' I chewed my lip, looking out the window. 'The Rhodri stuff was all so fresh. And with Chloe leaving me too, I was in a dark place. I wasn't able to talk about it. There were things that happened during that time that were between me and her. Things I didn't want to speak about to anyone else. I wanted to respect her privacy, but I was grieving. Desperately sad. And in a way, I felt sure she wasn't coming back. That I'd lost her for ever. So I lied. I'm sorry it caused you pain; I know it was hard to hear, but it was the only thing I could say that would get people to stop asking questions. It was final. It meant I could move forward without having to keep picking at the wound.'

Mirium sat back in her chair, eyes wide. 'I think that makes sense... I suppose. But if you'd told me, I could have helped you find her, bring her home. We could have taken over the work so you didn't have to. You know I would have done anything to help you.'

'I know.' I reached across, patting her knee, then pulled my hand back, remembering the licked fingers. 'But I knew where she was,' I went on, though it wasn't strictly true. 'And more importantly, she knew my door was always open. That she could come home any time. I just didn't think she ever would.'

'But she has now.'

I smiled. 'You have no idea how wonderful it was to see her face again, Miri. She's so beautiful. And I'm a grandmother.'

Miri smiled too, though it looked forced, and I could see she still had questions. I couldn't blame her. But I had given more than I was comfortable with already. She would have to be content with that.

FIFTEEN

CHLOE

I walked up the path to Tommy's preschool, wishing he was holding my hand, his sweet little voice chattering away as he asked questions about everything we encountered along the way. He loved to stop and watch the snails crossing the path on rainy days. He refused to touch them, still nervous of their slime getting on him, he declared, but he was concerned about them being stepped on by the other children as they rushed to get inside, and so he stood guard, made sure they reached the grass verge in safety.

There had been so many mornings I had waited, rain dripping down the neck of my cheap jacket, glancing at my watch, stressed at how this delay would make me have to literally run to make it to work in time. Mornings when I just wanted to pick up the snail and move it, though I knew Tommy would be upset, fretting about what if we put him somewhere he wasn't planning to go. But now I would have given anything to swap the sun-filled blue sky and smooth, uninterrupted journey up the path for a summer storm and a curious little boy doing his bit for the environment.

I pressed my lips together, determined not to cry. I had to

put on a front, tell the nursery the story I'd come up with – that Tommy's grandmother was in town and he would be spending some quality time with her as they'd never met before. It was close enough to the truth without my needing to share the details of what was really happening. I'd gone to extremes to ensure they never saw me with a bruise – tailoring my outfits, wearing thick make-up, whatever was needed so they never suspected domestic violence. I was terrified of social services knocking at my door, taking him from me. I was hardly going to tell them the full story now.

I pressed the buzzer, waiting for the smiley receptionist to let me in. I wanted to grab his bag of spare clothes from his peg, so that I could wash them and give them to my mum, and then let Melanie, the manager, know to hold his place. I'd be in and out in two minutes, then I could let myself have a little cry if I needed to.

I pasted on a smile, letting the receptionist know why I'd come, then headed down the corridor to the boot room, where neat rows of coats and bags hung beneath a photo and name tag for each child. There was a low bench running against the wall beneath them, below which were the wellies and spare shoes for each child.

I pulled out Tommy's little blue wellingtons, trying not to feel embarrassed at how cheap and flimsy they looked in comparison to the others. I lifted the canvas bag from his peg, glancing inside to check everything was there. There was a letter on top, and I pulled it out, opening it to read while I waited for Melanie to be free. I'd expected a notice about the lunch menu or the upcoming summer fete, but instead I felt myself freeze, my heart rate quickening as I realised what I was looking at.

You think you can get away with murder... You're wrong.

I screwed the paper into a ball, shoving it back into the bag, fearful of someone seeing it though I was alone in the boot room. The realisation that whoever was sending these notes knew where my son went to nursery was sickening. What if one of the staff had gone through his bag and found the note? Read it? It didn't bear thinking about.

I leaned against the wall, the bag clutched in my fist. It made no sense that this was happening now, not after so many years of nothing. Mum had made it quite clear that we were the only ones who could know about what I'd done, but she was obviously wrong. And to find a note here of all places – you couldn't just walk in and tamper with a child's bag. There was a buzzer system. They would have had to show ID if they weren't recognised, and sign in. So what did that mean? I pictured each of the staff members, trying to think of any uncomfortable inter-actions I might have glossed over, to figure out if any of them could be the writer, but no faces came to mind. And how could any of them know? It was impossible.

'Chloe?'

I looked up, my lips stiff as I tried to smile, stretching my face unnaturally.

'Melanie is ready for you in her office. Did you get what you came for?'

I looked down at the bag in my hands and took a deep breath. 'Yes...' I managed. 'I got it.'

SIXTEEN

I was shaking. There was no point trying to hide the fact. My fear was impossible to disguise, from my trembling lower lip to the way my left eye kept twitching against my will. I'd chosen this place *because* of how terrified I was, sure that it was the only way I could have the conversation that needed to be had between me and Scott without him knocking me unconscious before I even finished a sentence. It wouldn't have been the first time he'd done that. But even with the hiss of the coffee machine behind me, the group of men in suits picking up sandwiches on their lunch breaks – young, strong men who looked like they might step in and help me if Scott turned nasty – I couldn't help but feel sick with trepidation.

I'd chosen a seat by the window – a hard stool I had to perch on, a conscious decision over the comfy armchairs opposite. I didn't want to sink down low. I wanted to hold my head high. And, more importantly, I wanted to be ready to jump up at a moment's notice.

I watched as Scott jogged across the road, pausing to frown up at the sign above the coffee-shop door as though he thought he'd got it wrong, but then he caught my eye, and I waved for

him to come inside. He flashed a smile that would have made
my resolve melt under any other circumstances, but I was
relieved, and somewhat surprised, to realise how little effect it
had on me now.

I'd spent years trying to work out how to break free from
the hold he had over me, and now I had – and it was all his
doing. His cold, unemotional response to the thought of giving
away our son – our baby boy – to a stranger so he could spend
his days smoking, playing video games and wasting his life
had severed any attachment I might have held on to. He'd
hurt me in so many ways since Tommy had been born, and
still, despite myself, I had loved him. Let myself be reliant on
him. But with those few short words he had snuffed out the
light I'd carried in my heart, obliterating the path for the
future I'd dreamed we could share together. Now, that
crooked smile, those deep, penetrating eyes left me cold. It
wasn't even a choice. Tommy was my path now. Just the two
of us.

Scott stepped through the door, striding past the crowd to
where I sat. 'Bloody hell, Chlo. Why the fuck did we have to
meet in this place? I bet the coffee costs more than a full dinner
at Rollo's. And you can't smoke here. It's full of fucking toffs.'

'You're not supposed to smoke at Rollo's.'

He raised an eyebrow. 'That's my point. He turns a blind
eye if it suits him. They won't do that here. I hate these fucking
chain places. Makes my skin crawl to see these corporate suits
trying to scoff their overpriced sandwiches in their fifteen
minutes of freedom. Drones, the lot of 'em,' he added in a voice
loud enough to carry and make a few heads turn our way.

I ignored his rant, reaching to pick up my cup of coffee,
which hadn't been quite as expensive as I'd anticipated. 'You
getting a drink?'

'No. Let's go to the pub. I don't want to stay here.'

I shook my head. 'I have to talk to you.'

'Yeah, fine. At the pub. Once I get a cold beer in my hand, yeah?'

'No.'

He stared at me, his eyebrows raised incredulously. 'No?'

'Sit down.' I felt my heart stutter, the moisture evaporating from my mouth, but I held his gaze.

A slow smirk spread across his face, as if I were playing some kind of game, and I knew from the glint in his eye that if we were anywhere else right now, he would have already knocked me to the floor for daring to tell him what to do. I could see him silently challenging me, daring me to continue, and I had to stop myself from apologising, begging him to forgive me, going through my usual repertoire of trying to placate him and save myself from the pain I could see coming my way. Not that it ever made a difference. If anything, it only seemed to make him hit me harder to shut me up.

A broad-shouldered man at a table across from us glanced up from his paper, and I saw him give Scott the once-over as he took in the situation.

Scott flashed a cold smile his way then took a seat opposite me, speaking loudly. 'What is it you want to talk about, *darling*?' His tone was laced with fury, and I felt my shoulders roll forward, hunching over in the self-protective stance I'd learned to adopt in these moments.

'I've found a place. For me and Tommy. I already moved my stuff out while you were at work. I'm not coming back to the flat.' I let the words hang in the silence, holding Scott's glare as he absorbed what I was saying. I had no idea what to expect.

'You're *leaving* me?'

I nodded. 'I am. Tommy deserves better.' I almost added, *and so do I*, but then I wondered if that was really true.

He sat back on his stool, propping an elbow casually on the windowsill as he watched the world go by. He looked calm, and I didn't know whether to be frightened or relieved.

'So you chose the brat,' he said softly. 'I think you'll live to regret it. Kids do nothing but take. He'll bleed you dry and leave you with nothing in the end. But if that's what you want' – he shrugged – 'that's fine with me. Go. I'll be glad of the peace.'

I shook my head. 'I know you had a hard start in life, Scott. That your mum hurt you...'

I sighed, thinking of the little he'd told me about his upbringing. He'd always been reluctant to get deep about his past, but from the snippets I'd gathered, it was clear his mum had been the polar opposite of mine. He'd never fully cut ties with her though, still visiting now and then, asking for money, no shame in still mooching off her, though each time we saw her, he came away even more volatile, as if the time spent with her was triggering for him.

I watched his face, seeing the carefully blank expression he'd cultivated so well over the years. 'I know you have scars that are still healing. It's why I've always been so patient with you. Why I've put up with so much.'

'Yeah, you're a saint. Let me order a medal for you,' he said, fixing me with a sneer.

'You think you're letting it all out when you lay into me,' I said, my voice soft, measured. 'Releasing some of the hurt and anger you've collected. But it doesn't work that way, and every time you hurt me, you add more guilt and shame to the baggage you're carrying. I'm sorry things were tough for you growing up. I really am. But you're not a child now. You're a man, and nobody can break the cycle for you. That's something you're going to have to work out for yourself. But not on me. And *not* on Tommy. Find someone to talk to, someone to help you, because if you don't, *you're* going to be the one who loses out in the end. You'll have a lonely future ahead of you if you don't do something about it.'

'Yeah, right,' he scoffed. 'Don't you worry about me, babe. I'm fine. I don't need to spill my secrets to some overpriced shrink to make you feel better. You taking the kid away will do just fine.'

'Good,' I replied, jutting out my chin, trying not to let him get to me. 'But that's not all I wanted to say.'

'There's more? Well, you're full of surprises today, aren't you?' he said, a spiteful look in his eye.

'You might not be willing to raise him, but I'm not going to let him suffer. You can relinquish all contact. In fact, I want you to do just that. But you're not going to shirk your financial obligations. I can't afford to pay the deposit on the place I've found. I need money for food, bills.'

He laughed. 'Yeah? Shall I buy you a new wardrobe and a Caribbean cruise while I'm at it, Chlo? A diamond ring?'

I shuddered at the thought of that. The dream I'd once had of him proposing to me, walking down the aisle to see him waiting for me in a suit, that cheeky smile, those sparkling eyes... How stupid I had been to gloss over his faults. Thank God I had seen his true colours before it was too late.

'I'm serious,' I said.

'I'm sure you are.' He reached across the table and picked up my cup, knocking back the rest of my cappuccino before slamming it down and wiping his mouth with the back of his hand. 'Go fuck yourself, Chloe. I'm not giving you a penny.'

I'd expected this, but it didn't make it any less frightening to have to go head to head with him. 'I'll go to the police,' I said, my lip trembling. 'I have photos of every bruise you ever gave me. I kept a diary. I'll tell them everything. You'll go down.'

He shrugged infuriatingly. 'You think they'll care? You really don't have a clue how the world works, do you, love? You've got no proof that *I* did anything. The system's a mess. I'll walk.'

He stood up, and I felt panic rise in my gut. I couldn't manage without his financial contribution. It would take time to get another job, ages before I got a pay cheque. I was going to use my new-found determination to go and see my old boss, demand proper redundancy pay, compensation for the unfair dismissal, but I would have a battle on my hands. All of it meant time – time with no money to pay the bills and a hungry four-year-old to take care of. Scott was my only solution. I wouldn't ask my mother for any more help than she'd already given. I had to prove to her that I could do this. That Tommy could thrive with me, that I could give him a decent, safe home. I needed to show her I was capable of that much. It was all I wanted.

'I'll tell them you hurt Tommy!' I called to his retreating back, my voice shrill with panic, desperation.

He paused, then turned to face me, a warning glint in his eye. 'I didn't.'

I leaned forward, lowering my voice. 'I'll say that you touched him. That I caught you doing it and that's why I left.'

'Chloe! What the fuck is wrong with you? You know I never did that!'

'I don't.'

It was a lie. Awful as he had been to me, he'd never put our son in danger. And he wouldn't have dreamed of doing anything sinister to him. Even so, I saw the blood drain from his face as he realised just how determined I was to get my way. How his reputation would go up in smoke with those accusations hanging over his head. Hated and vilified everywhere he turned. It was the kind of thing that never went away. I was ashamed to be forced into the threat, but it was all I had, and I was damned if I was going to live in a hostel because he wouldn't pay his way. The time for me to be soft, pliable, *easy* was over. I was ready for a war, and I didn't care what I had to do, how low I had to sink, to get him to give me what I wanted. He'd pushed me too far.

He shook his head. 'You're sick. You're mad!'

'I'm desperate. And I'm not bluffing.' I stood up, taking a deep breath. 'I'll check my account at eight o'clock tonight. We can start with five hundred – for now. I know you have it. You get paid the first of the month, so I'll expect to see the money in my bank by the end of the second day. And that's *every* month, you understand? Every single month. And if the money isn't there, I'll go to the station. Don't test me, Scott. I mean it.'

His mouth dropped open, and I saw the moment he realised he was beaten – shock, disgust, blind rage circulating like a toxic cocktail in his blood.

He lurched forward, grabbing my collar, and for a second my vision clouded with panic as I braced myself for the pain I'd been conditioned to expect. I could feel the wrath pulsing through him, his face so close I could smell the sweat and nicotine seeping from his pores. Then, just as quickly as he'd grabbed me, I was released, a meaty hand clamping around his wrist, yanking him back. I saw the man from the opposite table squaring up to him, several other patrons rushing forward, coming to my aid, providing a sense of nurture and safety I wanted to bottle, save for another day.

'*You* need to leave.' The guy released his hold on Scott's wrist and nodded towards the door. 'Before I call the police.'

'I'm calling them now,' a woman called from the counter. She had one hand on her hip, the other gripping her phone to her ear as she fixed Scott with a stare that would have made anyone cower.

Scott looked around, saw he was surrounded, his shoulders slumping with obvious defeat. 'It's *fine*,' he said through gritted teeth. 'There's no need to call anyone, I'm fucking going.'

'You all right?' my rescuer asked in a low voice.

I saw the way Scott tensed, the resentment at being prevented from giving me the punishment he thought I deserved.

'I'm okay,' I replied, managing a shaky smile. 'Thank you for your help.'

He gave a nod and returned to his seat, his eyes still fixed on the two of us, ready to pounce.

I took a breath and met Scott's eyes. 'I'm sorry,' I whispered. 'I really am. But you forced me to do this. There's nothing I wouldn't do for my son. Nothing.'

'Bitch,' he hissed. He slammed his hand on the table, then spun and strode away.

I clasped my shaking hands in my lap as I watched him leave the café and walk out of sight. I had done the right thing by my son. I'd had no choice.

SEVENTEEN

CLARISSA

Jeff was watching us again. I could see him out there in his front garden, pruning the rosebush with his secateurs, eyes darting across the road towards my house every thirty seconds or so. He was becoming obsessive again. Too intense. It unnerved me and brought back unsettling memories of the past, reminding me of exactly why I'd never liked the man.

I hadn't forgotten the first time we'd had him over. It had been Christmas Eve, and it had been Reece's idea to throw a bit of a party, get the neighbours round for a few drinks and nibbles. I hadn't been keen. Christmas Eve was stressful enough what with trying to get Chloe to bed at a reasonable hour and preparing the food for the big day ahead. The last thing I wanted to deal with was drunk and disorderly neighbours who might spill red wine on the new rug or help themselves to food I was saving for Christmas dinner. But Reece had already invited them before speaking to me, and in the end, I'd had to suck it up and get on with it.

I hadn't known most of them well back then, having only lived there a few years. There hadn't been the same community spirit – that had come later, when the children were old enough to play outside on the street and we'd found ourselves talking on the garden path far more frequently, dropping in on each other for coffee and a natter. But I liked the other mums, despite finding some of them a bit parochial. I'd found it difficult to relate to their moderate aspirations, to get excited about a delivery of a new sofa or news that their husbands had power-washed the patio, but I'd enjoyed their company.

Reece and Jeff had hit it off over their shared interest in cars, and that night, as the party was about to start, Reece had been like an excitable puppy wanting to tell me all about his new friend, instructing me to make sure I found time to have a chat with Jeff and his wife. I'd liked Mirium right away, but Jeff had been a different story. He'd put me on edge from the off, his eyes too piercing, the way they seemed to look through me cold and analytical.

While Mirium and Reece were talking, Jeff had leaned in close to me and made a comment about how I didn't realise how lucky I was to have landed a man like Reece. I hadn't known what to say, how to take it, as he'd pulled back, lips pursed, eyes narrowed as if challenging me to disagree with him. I'd disliked him instantly. It was impossible to miss the way he looked at my husband. There was something almost predatory about it, as if he'd claimed Reece for his own, as if his short friendship with him trumped my marriage, and I couldn't help but wonder what else aside from cars the two of them had been discussing behind my back.

I tweaked the blind now, so as not to have to see him out there, then turned with a smile to my daughter, who was sitting on the sofa, my grandson on her lap.

'So,' she was saying, seemingly oblivious to my frustration with Jeff, 'I moved my things into the new flat earlier today and it's looking good. It's small, but we don't need much, and it will be nice once we get everything unpacked.'

I nodded, wanting to ask where she was moving from, how she intended to pay her rent, her bills, but since she seemed in no hurry to volunteer any information, I held my tongue. She would open up when she was ready, I was sure. She'd never been able to keep a secret as a child.

'Tommy should stay a little longer with me though,' I said. 'Just to give you time to get it all sorted. Moving is always a hassle, isn't it?' I flashed a sympathetic smile her way before sitting down heavily in my favourite armchair. 'You're sure you don't want to come here? You could stay as long as you need – I really wouldn't mind.'

She shook her head, and I saw the determination written on her features. I could tell how much she wanted me to view her as a grown-up, and I had to remind myself that she wasn't my little girl any more. She was a mother herself, as odd as it was to accept.

'Thanks, but we need our own place. It wouldn't feel right—'

'Are you sleeping?' I interrupted. I pressed my lips together, wishing I hadn't asked, yet I hadn't been able to stop myself.

Her face darkened, her gaze sliding away from mine to the floor. 'It's been a stressful time...'

'Of course. But you can't burn the candle at both ends. You need your rest, your routines.'

She looked back up, nodding slowly. 'I know that, Mum. I do.'

She took a breath, and I held my silence, wondering if we might be about to go there, finally talk about everything, but instead she squeezed Tommy tighter, then reached into her bag, pulling out a packet of jelly beans.

'I forgot to give these to you, sweetie. Got them on my way here. Your favourite.'

'Thank you, Mummy,' he said, his face lighting up. 'Can I eat them now?'

'Course.' She smiled.

'No, Tommy.' I shook my head. 'It's almost dinner – you'll spoil your appetite.' I reached to take them from him and put the packet in my pocket. 'You can have them if you eat all your dinner like a good little boy.'

His face crumpled, and he looked up at Chloe with imploring eyes. 'But you said yes,' he whispered.

She pulled him closer, hugging him, and I could see she was uncomfortable. I looked away, not wanting to be caught in the middle, but knowing I should stand firm on this. I didn't want to let her spoil him. I'd missed out on his early years and my chance to guide her in how to raise a child, and perhaps she might think I was overstepping now, but I had raised two children practically alone. I knew how important it was to get it right.

Finally, Chloe broke the awkward silence. 'Grandma's right, sweetie. I didn't realise the time. Save them for pudding.'

I felt myself relax. Tommy gave a dramatic sigh, and I worried he might be about to have a tantrum – the first since arriving on my doorstep – but then he picked up his teddy and headed out of the room. I heard the back door open and close.

'Sorry,' I apologised. 'I didn't mean to step on your toes. But boundaries are so important at his age. Otherwise you'll be in for a world of trouble down the line. I hope I didn't cause any upset.'

'No, you're right. I'm used to spoiling him. I haven't been able to give him much, so these little things make me feel like a better mum. Like I can show him I love him.'

I shook my head. 'He knows that. You don't need to do anything special. You're his mummy. That's all you need to be. And,' I added, reaching over to pour myself another cup of tea from the pot, 'if he's going to be staying with me, it's really best that he follows my rules. It will only confuse him otherwise.'

Chloe opened her mouth as if to argue, then shut it again, nodding. I was glad. I wanted him with me until I knew for sure that it was safe for him to be in her care. And by the way she was looking at me, I knew she'd considered that too.

She folded her hands in her lap. 'I got another one,' she said, her voice quiet.

'Another what, darling?'

'Another letter.' She was watching me intently, as if searching my face for clues. 'It was in Tommy's bag at nursery. I meant to bring it over, but I forgot, what with everything going on. Somebody knows, Mum.'

I shook my head. 'It's impossible.'

'Nothing's impossible. You know that. What if it's one of the staff? I don't understand how it got in his bag otherwise. I'm scared,' she said quietly. 'I can't lose my son. I won't.'

I felt my jaw stiffen as I realised that this wasn't going away. There was only one person I could think of who might have an inkling of what had gone on, and even then, I'd done everything in my power to keep them in the dark. I looked towards the window, the blinds obscuring the view, though I was certain that Jeff was still out there, still watching.

I took a long, careful breath. 'I've never spoken of it, and I won't now.' I met her eyes and stood, heading to the window, knowing that if I didn't say more, it would be an anvil hanging over us, waiting to drop.

'Come here,' I told her.

She frowned, coming to stand beside me, following my gaze to the garden across the road.

'If someone knows,' I said, taking her hand and giving it a squeeze, 'it will be him. That man has harassed me since your father died. He's always getting fixated on some idea or another. I honestly can't think how he would have tracked you down, or why now, but he gets a kick out of harassing women. I've experienced it first-hand, and this note business, it smacks of control, and that's something he feeds off.'

'Jeff? You think he knows?'

I shook my head. 'No... there's no way for him to know. But he might have heard something that night... he might suspect. Perhaps he saw you after all these years and recognised you, followed you. Made up his mind to frighten you and get you to admit to something he can't prove.' I turned to her now. 'If he had anything, he would have gone to the police. He's bluffing, Chloe. He's an odious man, and the only reason I put up with him is because Mirium needs a friend.'

Chloe raised an eyebrow, and I wondered what she was thinking. I wished we could erase the whole sordid story of the past and just focus on the future.

'I'm going to speak to him,' she said, a note of determination ringing through her voice, surprising me with her resolve.

'And say what?' I shook my head. 'If I'm wrong, if it isn't him, then why give him something to use against you? Ignore it, Chloe. It's the reaction he's after – it's what he craves. He'd love nothing more than to see you worked into a state, frightened. Don't fall into that trap. I promise, I've dealt with him for a long time. Ignore it. Be sweet, cordial, and don't ever let him think he's got one up on you.'

'But what if he goes to the police?'

'With what evidence? There's nothing to tell them.'

She shook her head, turning to look at Jeff again through the glass. 'I just want it to be over. I want Tommy to be safe.'

'I know, darling. As a mother, it's what we do. We make choices, and we're not always sure we're getting it right. I understand that. But don't rise to the bait, Chloe. Let it blow over.' I watched her, feeling the tension boil in my belly, fearful of what she might do, wondering if I'd made a mistake in throwing Jeff's name into the conversation.

Chloe had been a quiet, compliant girl growing up, but

looking at her now, I could see she'd changed into a strong, capable woman. And I wasn't at all sure what she might do in her quest to safeguard her child. I took a deep, bracing breath as I pulled her into a hug, determined not to let her make another mistake. I would protect her this time. I couldn't lose her again.

EIGHTEEN

CHLOE

Fifteen years ago

'Chloe! Chloe, wake up!'

I felt the cover ripped from my body, cold air making goose pimples spread across my bare legs. I groaned, my head still thick with sleep. It felt too early, too dark for it to be time to get up for school. I pressed my face into the pillow. 'Not yet... five more minutes.' I yawned, my eyes still glued shut, my hand reaching out to try to find the duvet, wanting nothing more than to drag it over my head and go back to sleep.

'Oh my God... Chloe, *please!*' my mum cried.

Something about the tone of her voice sent a sudden jolt of fear through me that made all thoughts of sleep vanish into thin air. I opened my eyes, sitting up on the side of the bed in one fluid motion, confused to find myself not in my room but in my brother's. My mum, fully dressed in jeans and a dark-blue fitted shirt, was pale and wide-eyed. She looked like a deer in headlights, and I blinked, trying to catch up, feeling inexplicably scared. Through the thin *Star Wars* curtains I could see the orange glow of a street lamp in the dark.

'What time is it?' I asked, rising to my feet. My legs felt leaden, and I swayed, gripping the wall as I waited for the vertigo to pass. My tongue was gluey, sticking to the roof of my mouth, and I swallowed back a wave of nausea. How long had I slept?

I pulled the curtain to one side, confirming that the sky was still an inky black, the street deserted. I turned back to my mum, blinking. 'I feel sick. I need—' I broke off, pressing my hand to my mouth, but it was too late. Bending double, I vomited onto the Death Star rug, bile burning the back of my throat, acrid and chemical.

I felt my mother reach for me, soft hands pulling my long hair over my shoulder to avoid the splash, rubbing circles into my back, soothing in her silence. Shakily, I straightened, tears streaming down my face. I always cried. It was involuntary, inevitable.

'Chloe... do you remember what happened... what you did?' Her voice was barely a whisper, but I could tell without question that there was something different about this time. I could see it in her eyes. I had done something bad.

It was a horrible feeling, waking to be told that while you slept, you had left your bed, done things you would never have dreamed of in any other circumstances. The night terrors were something I should have grown out of when I was four or five – that was what my mother had said after seeking advice from the doctor. Only I never had, and nobody could explain why. Why I would wake the whole house with screams, yelling about people in my room wielding knives and intent on revenge.

I rarely recalled anything the next day. My mum had told me that when it happened, I would thrash and fight and scream for twenty minutes or so, seeing things that weren't there, terrified of what was happening, until finally I'd collapse, burned out, and fall into a deep, dreamless sleep. And later, when I woke, other than feeling raw in my throat and the occasional bruise, I wouldn't know it had happened.

I would hardly have believed it were true if I didn't have a handful of memories for myself. Sometimes they were strong enough that nothing could erase the fear: toothless old men in grey wax coats, white stubble on weak chins, knives long enough to go right through me. The faces of the visions that came to me in the depths of sleep were burned into my soul. And so I knew it had to be true. Even so, my mother had never looked at me like she was right now.

'No,' I said. I shook my head, regretting it instantly as I was hit by another crippling wave of vertigo. I held on to her arm, breathing through the nausea. 'I don't remember anything. I don't remember how I got here.' I gestured to my brother's bed. 'Where's Rhodri? Did he go to my room? Did I scare him?'

Mum gave a choked cry, and I felt the bile churn in my belly once again, fear and foreboding chasing through my veins.

'Where is he?' I repeated. I straightened, though my head still spun, the room swaying in front of me. My fingers trailed along the wall, guiding me towards the door, but before I reached it, she grabbed me by the wrist, forcing me to stop.

'Chloe... darling... Oh, Chloe...'

'What!' I yelled, not wanting to hear but feeling terror seize my heart, making it hard to breathe. 'I didn't hurt him, did I?'

She sucked in a shaky breath. 'He... he's gone, love... He's...' She broke off, pressing her hands to her face. I watched for what felt like an eternity, frozen to the spot, trying to understand. Then slowly she dropped her hands to her sides, meeting my eyes with a look filled with sadness, regret and so much more. 'Chloe,' she said softly, carefully. 'You killed him. You killed your brother.'

I stepped back, my spine colliding with the wall, shaking my head automatically. 'No... no, I didn't! I couldn't have!' He might be younger, but at twelve years old he was almost as big as me, and certainly able to hold his own. Unless... I knew from my mum just how violent my night terrors could become – how out of control I could get. But *still*, it wasn't possible. I would have woken up. He would have fought back. 'I don't believe you. I want to see him! Where is he?' I yelled. 'Where's my brother?'

'Chloe... love.' She put her head in her hands, and I felt the world crumble around me as I saw her fear, her devastation. 'The paramedics already came... they took him. I told them...' She fixed me with a determined look. 'I said it was an accident. I lied... I lied to protect you, darling. And I think they believed me.'

'But... but he's dead?' I whispered. 'He's really gone?'

She gripped my hand, pulling me towards her, her fingers digging into my neck as she held on to me like a drowning woman. Looking over her shoulder, I saw, there on the cream carpet, a stain. A rusty-brown patch the size of the palm of my hand. *Blood.*

'I'll keep your secret... It wasn't your fault,' Mum said, her breath damp against my neck. 'It wasn't your fault.' Her hands gripped me tighter.

I stared at the blood and found I couldn't breathe.

NINETEEN

The new flat was damp. I'd overlooked that when I'd done the brief viewing, seeing only the sanctuary it could become. The little balcony where I thought Tommy and I could plant a herb garden, the unused alcove by the front door that I wanted to make into a reading nook for him. I'd let my imagination run wild with hope, possibility, but now that I was here, it was impossible to ignore all the things that were wrong with the place.

The patterned carpet that smelled of mildew. The crack in the bathtub that rendered it unusable. The abundance of mouse droppings in the kitchen cupboards, along with a decade's worth of built-up grime. I'd thought I'd been lucky to find the place and get approved so quickly, but now, without the rose-tinted glasses of a desperate woman, I could see why I'd been given the contract. Nobody who had any choice would live here, and the landlord had given the distinct impression he didn't want to be bothered. I couldn't imagine he would take my complaints well, or move fast to remedy any issues.

Even so, it was a roof over our heads, and I was grateful. I wanted to do what I could – make it cheery and homely, a place Tommy could feel safe. I'd scoured freecycle sites, then walked for miles round town picking up anything that might disguise the flat's many faults and make it look nicer. A little red rug, a carrier bag full of toys, a pair of curtains that fitted the bedroom window almost perfectly.

A kind man had said he would deliver a sofa and a mattress for a twenty-pound charge, and though it had eaten into my meagre funds, I'd agreed, and been over the moon when he'd asked if I wanted an old table and chairs he had in the back of his van too, saving him a trip to the tip. I'd packed my sheets and taken the duvet from my bed at home while Scott was at work yesterday, stuffing everything I owned into bin bags and shoving them in the back of the taxi that had brought me here. He would have been livid when he got back to find it missing, especially after our heated exchange in the café, but why should his son and I go cold while he slept soundly?

To my relief, he had paid up, saving me from having to go through with my threat of reporting him to the police. There had been no word from him, but I didn't *want* his words. Now I had money for rent and food and to pay the preschool so I could go and look for a new job, and that was all I cared about. It would be a fight to get him to keep up with his payments month after month, but I had leverage I knew I could use against him now, and I would continue to use it, despite how dirty it made me feel.

My handbag was on the bedroom floor, and I looked at it, thinking of the note squirrelled away inside. I'd been unable to throw it away, despite the stress it was bringing to my life. A big part of me wanted to set light to it, watch it turn to ash in my fingertips, but something stopped me from doing that. I thought back to my mum's suggestion that it could be Jeff. It had surprised me to hear that she had such disdain for him. I hadn't seen it before, hadn't understood the tension simmering between them; but then I had been so young when I'd seen him last. I'd had my own life. I wouldn't have given my boring neighbours more than a fleeting thought. Still, I couldn't imagine him spending his time analysing the behaviour of the family across the road. It was so long ago. Why on earth wouldn't he have spoken up at the time if he knew something?

I kicked the bag to one side, still undecided on how best to approach the situation. My mum was right about one thing: turning up at Jeff's house and making accusations would only open a can of worms, and if she was wrong about it being him, I could make things ten times worse for myself. I longed to find out who had written such a menacing note. The not knowing was making my imagination run wild.

I picked up the bag of toys from the bedroom floor, carrying it through to the tiny kitchen and emptying it onto the side. There were several brightly coloured vehicles: a digger with a working scoop, a crane with a little hook that could be wound up and down to lift things, a tractor with a trailer. A bouncy ball. A bucket full of rubbery dinosaurs. A couple of well-loved books and a little drum with beaters attached. I couldn't wait to see Tommy's face when he saw them all lined up on the shelf for him when I brought him here for the first time.

I turned on the tap, running a bowl of soapy water and tipping the dinosaurs into it, wiping each one with a cloth. I'd hoped to bring him home today. It had been the only thing that had given me the strength to pack my things, leave my flat and demand Scott's financial support. But my mother's words had shaken me. Made me doubt myself. My choice to do this alone.

Was I up to it? Was he safe with me? Scott might have been awful, but his presence had kept Tommy safe. If I'd had a night terror, tried to hurt him, Scott would have woken, would have stopped me. He had never really understood my fears when it came to sleep. The fact that sometimes I was so afraid of what I might do that I stayed awake for days on end. He would roll over to find me sitting up in bed, staring into the darkness, deathly tired but unable to give in to the rest my body so desperately craved.

Even when I tried, when I lay down and closed my eyes, waited for oblivion to take me, it wouldn't work. I would just think. Of Rhodri. That awful splat of blood. Those *Star Wars* curtains. The way my life might have been had circumstances been different.

The longer I went without sleep, the darker my thoughts would become. I'd remember little things that kept my mind busy – the sound of my dad's laughter, the smell of his aftershave and the way I had felt when I realised he was really gone. It was my earliest memory, and the feeling of absolute devastation was still as fresh now as it had been for that five-year-old child all those years ago.

There were other memories that haunted me too. The awful encounters I'd had on the street as a naïve fifteen-year-old – the group of men who had offered me a fiver each for a blow job, then followed me for nearly an hour when I'd refused. The woman who had spat in my face when I'd inadvertently taken her spot in the bus shelter. The time I'd eaten the leftovers from a box of cold chicken and chips I'd watched someone throw in a bin outside the shopping centre, because I'd been too hungry to care about standards, *germs*. I'd been disgusted with myself, but even that hadn't stopped me cramming them into my mouth. All these memories flooded my mind, making sleep impossible.

It was only after multiple nights of this unrelenting torture, of watching the sun rise and pasting on a smile to get through another day, that sleep would refuse to be rejected any longer and I would crash. When I sensed it coming, I would warn Scott to listen out for me. I would make sure we conveniently ran low on booze so he didn't drink too much, so he would be easily roused if I did anything. He would laugh. Tell me I was mad. But knowing he was there – even on the nights he'd sunk a fist into my gut – had brought me comfort, made me sure my son was safe.

Now, I would be alone with him for the first time in his life. And I was terrified.

TWENTY

CLARISSA

I listened from the bottom of the stairs, hearing nothing but silence from above. I'd put Tommy to bed half an hour ago, and he'd chatted to himself for a bit, kicking his feet up and down on the mattress, dispersing the remainder of his energy. I made a point of keeping him busy during the day, remembering how much boys his age needed to move – to be set tasks in order to exhaust both mind and body and stay out of mischief. I got the distinct impression he wasn't used to sleeping alone, but as accommodating as I'd been about taking him in, I wasn't prepared to share my bed with a wriggly four-year-old. He would soon get used to how things were done here and accept the boundaries I set – for all our benefits. Chloe would no doubt be grateful too. From the little I'd seen, she found it hard to say no to him, and I wondered if she might be overcompensating for something.

I smiled to myself, satisfied that at last I could enjoy a few hours' peace. I was tired out from the long day, unused to sharing my space. This house had been so quiet for so long, and I'd grown comfortable living that way, used to my little rituals, the routines that gave me a sense of safety and security. As much as I was glad to help, I couldn't deny I was finding the childcare tiring.

I walked through the house, checking the toys had been cleared away, the throw neatly folded over the back of the sofa. Tommy had tidied up his bricks, and the basket was neatly hidden under the coffee table. Singing a familiar melody to myself, I walked into the kitchen, and let out a gasp, my hands flying to my mouth. Jeff was standing at the back door. His eyes met mine through the glass, and before I could reach to stop him, he pressed the handle down and stepped inside. His eyes were cold and hard as they appraised me, and I felt the familiar sense of fear I always experienced when we were alone together.

'Go home, Jeff.' My words were firm, and I held his gaze, folding my arms across my chest in an attempt to hide my shaking hands.

Ignoring me, he walked further into the room, glancing around as if he were looking for something. 'Where is he?'

I frowned. 'Frankly, it's none of your business. Does Miri know you're here? *Again.*'

'She's out.' He smirked, and I felt my stomach tighten involuntarily. 'Nobody knows I'm here.'

'I have security cameras now,' I bluffed, wishing it were true.

He laughed but didn't reply, and I knew he had seen through the lie. He would have noticed if anything had changed. He never missed a thing.

'Look, you can't keep doing this. You're making me uncomfortable.'

'So call someone. Call the police.' He smiled, his face creasing, but his eyes remained hard. It was a challenge, a threat. He knew I couldn't do that. He took a step towards me, and I recoiled against the door frame. 'I want to see him.'

'What?' I asked, shocked that he would even ask. 'No! He's fast asleep in bed!'

'Is that so?' He shoved past me, and I realised he was intending to go upstairs.

'No! Don't you dare!' I cried, grabbing hold of his arm. 'You might have once been friends with my husband, but that doesn't give you the right to come barging into my home and treating it like you own the place!'

He yanked his arm free and made a beeline for the stairs, his feet heavy on the rose-coloured carpet. I chased after him, breathless, my heart pounding beneath the thick cotton of my floral-patterned dress.

The door to Chloe's old bedroom was slightly ajar, and he pushed it open, making a swishing sound against the carpet. Tommy was sound asleep, one bare leg hanging over the edge of the mattress, his mouth open as he gave little snores.

'Jeff!' I whispered urgently. 'I want you to leave! This is unacceptable. It's crazy!'

He ignored me, the mass of his body almost filling the doorway. I forced myself into the remaining space, unwilling to let him go any further. His arm was pressed against mine, and I wanted to pull away, but I wouldn't dream of stepping back to let him take control.

He was silent as he stared at the sleeping boy, his eyes raking over him, making me squirm uncomfortably. My skin prickled with fear, and I wondered what the hell I was going to do if he tried to get any closer. Could I push him out? He was a big man, tall, burly, and despite the extra weight I carried, I was perfectly aware that it was all fat, not muscle. I was no match for him. The way he was looking at Tommy brought back an unsettling recollection of how he'd once looked at *my* son. It frightened me. Perhaps I should call his bluff. Pick up the phone and call the police. Show him I wouldn't stand for this. Not again.

'I want you to leave,' I said through clenched teeth. 'Get out of my house. And stay the hell away from my grandson.'

Jeff turned to stare down at me, and it took all my courage not to cower away. 'When is his mother coming to get him?'

'That's not your concern!' I said, indignation pulsing through me.

'I want you to tell her you can't keep him. That you're going to send him to stay with Miri and me. We'll look after him until she can take him home.'

'I'll do no such thing. He stays with me! I'm his grandma!'

He gave a laugh. 'And you were Reece's wife. Rhodri's mum. We both know how much that meant to you.'

'How *dare* you,' I whispered, conscious of the sleeping child across from us. 'I don't know why you think it's reasonable to speak to me like this. If it weren't for you, they would still be here!'

'You mean you wouldn't have killed them.'

I gasped. His eyes met mine, and I could see nothing but hatred in them. 'You've got a bloody nerve. How could you even —' I broke off, pressing a hand to my lips, feeling dizzy and ill. It was too much. It had been a long time since I had dealt with anything like this, and I found I couldn't cope. I needed peace. Needed all his awful accusations to stop.

He smirked again. 'I'm not going to let history repeat itself.'

'Neither am I,' I hissed. I held his probing glare, refusing to back down. That was the crux. He blamed me for their loss. It wasn't the first time he'd said something similar. He could never admit that his unhealthy obsession with my family was a big part of why they were no longer here. He'd never been able to admit his faults, of which there were so many.

'The boy is staying put,' I said, squaring up to him, pulling the bedroom door shut to block Tommy from his sight. I met his predatory glower and felt a pulse of blinding hatred for him. If it weren't for the secrets he held over me, I'd have destroyed him, told the whole world all about him – and he knew it. We were locked in this unspoken duel, and neither of us had the courage to show our cards. I longed for the day when Mirium would divorce him and he'd move away, saving me from ever having to look at his smug, sanctimonious face again.

He folded his arms, and I felt a wave of liquid terror at the flex of muscle in his bicep, my hands shaking too hard to hide now. But then, to my relief, he suddenly turned away, striding down the stairs without a word. I heard the back door close and rushed to my bedroom window in time to see him cross back over the road and pick up his shears. A moment later, Mr Pip from round the corner ambled past and stopped to chat with him, smiling as he pointed to the tall hollyhocks lining the low fence.

I walked back to Tommy's room and pushed open the door again, staring at the sleeping child. I knew two things with absolute certainty. One: Jeff would never stop watching while Tommy was here. And two: the clock was ticking.

TWENTY-ONE

CHLOE

The flat was eerily quiet as I stepped through the front door, save for the click of the clock on the wall, the echo of the bathroom tap that never completely stopped dripping.

'Scott?' I called into the darkness. I couldn't see him, but I knew he was there. His scent – sweat interwoven with stale beer and nicotine – permeated the air. I could sense his anger, though he didn't say a word. Somehow I knew it was my fault. I rubbed my fingers into the sockets of my eyes, my heart thudding against my ribs as I walked through the pitch-black room, flicking light switches, hoping for a flash of a bulb, though of course the meter had run out again.

'Scott,' I called, hating the tremor in my tone. 'I... I brought dinner back from work. I just popped in to drop it off on my way to pick Tommy up from nursery.' I lowered the carrier bag onto the kitchen side, running my hand along the back by the kettle, trying to find the torch we kept for emergencies.

It wasn't there.

I turned around, taking small steps so as not to bump into anything as I made my way towards the bedroom.

'There was pasta left over and it was going in the bin, so—'

I heard the creak of a floorboard behind me, and then as swift as an eagle hunting its prey, his hard chest collided with my spine, and his strong, unyielding hands were around my throat, crushing my windpipe, rendering me silent against my will.

I swung my elbows back, hitting thin air, my kicks weak and ineffectual, my cheap trainers too flimsy to make an impact. His breath curdled against my cheek as panic bloomed bright in my mind. He would stop, I reminded myself. He always stopped. He had to. Even so, as I clawed against his grip, anchoring my nails deep within his flesh, all I could think of was Tommy. What would happen to him if Scott killed me now? Would he even bother to pick him up from nursery? Or would he just leave him there?

The edges of my vision distorted, white spots fizzing and crackling in the darkness, a pulse throbbing hard in my temples. I felt my arms go limp, the fight leaving me, though I fought to concentrate, to hold on. And then, with a guttural sound, Scott released me, making no attempt to cushion my fall as I collapsed at his feet.

Gasping for breath, I lay there, head spinning, fear and anger and relief all vying for precedence in my mind. His foot swung viciously, making contact with my stomach, knocking the breath from my lungs, burning bile shooting into my throat.

I rolled to the side, hating that this was what I had become.

I woke with a start, gasping for breath, my hand at my throat as I cast around the room, the terror still fresh and raw. The bedside lamp was on, giving off a soft peach-toned glow. I never turned it off. Couldn't bear to wake up and claw my way around in the darkness, wondering if I was safe. If anything had happened.

The new flat was silent, comfortingly so, unlike in the dream – the memory stolen straight from the locked chambers of my past life. How naïve I had been to think that packing my things and walking out of the home we'd shared would mean an end to the fear I'd learned to accept as a given in my world. There had been a sense of bravery in confronting Scott, in leaving, and that had propelled me to say and do things I would never have contemplated before. But now, with the adrenaline having worn off and the reality of my situation settling over me, I couldn't pretend I wasn't scared. I had seen the resentment in his expression. I knew he'd hated the threat I'd made, the ultimatum I'd served up.

If I'd cut all ties, I could imagine he would be happy. Let me go. He'd find some other girl, go back to living in a squat somewhere, resume the life he was most comfortable in. But I had a hold over him. I'd demanded action – *responsibility* – from him, and in doing so, I held him by the balls, prevented him from the freedom he craved more than anything. And now, with my hand around my throat and the memories I'd thought I'd expelled from my mind rearing their ugly head in my dreams, I realised I was afraid of what I had done. What he might feel towards me. The enemy I'd made for myself.

I picked up the little clock on my bedside table, sighing when I saw it was gone seven. Tommy would be up by now. He'd be warm and sweet-smelling, his hair tousled from his pillow.

My heart swelled painfully. I wished I could hold him, breathe him in. I hoped he was happy. That my mum had listened to him talking about his dreams as he ate his breakfast. He was lucky to have her, but still, it was no substitute for his mother, no matter how lacking I might be. I needed to bring him home – and soon.

The bus was packed with early-morning commuters, and as the doors hissed closed on the second in a row, too full to let me on,

I turned from the crowded bus stop, making up my mind to walk. It was only half an hour or so into town, and it was probably a good idea to save my cash anyway. I needed every penny I could get.

I crossed the road, unfamiliar with the streets surrounding my new place. It wasn't as far as I would have liked from the flat Scott and I had shared, but I hoped it was far enough. I didn't want to bump into him.

I stuck to the main road, afraid of getting lost as I pictured the confrontation I was heading into. The time had come to go back to my old job, confront my ex-boss. I knew he'd be surprised to see me, that he would have assumed I'd slink off with my tail between my legs and never darken his doorstep again, but just as I'd had to face up to the uncomfortable conversation with Scott, I had to do this too. I needed the money, needed to create a safe home for my son, and nothing was going to stand in my way.

Despite the early hour, the traffic fumes were already intense, exhausts blowing out toxic clouds as cars idled at the traffic lights. I found I was watching the people nearby more closely than usual. Every man who passed caught my attention; made my stomach tighten with fear. I was half expecting to see Scott's face looming over me as he emerged from the throng. I knew it was the dream. It had rattled me. Brought the very thing I was escaping right to the forefront of my mind.

It was funny. Whilst I'd been living that nightmare, I hadn't recognised the level of fear I was dealing with. I'd grown so acclimatised to the pain, the inevitable red mist that descended over him, that I'd managed to normalise it somehow. In hindsight, perhaps it had been the only thing I could do given my circumstances. I had made it okay in my mind out of a lack of any other choice. But now, having left, it was as if I were finally letting myself feel the emotions I'd suppressed for the sake of my sanity. They were vying to get free, and after shoving them down for so long, pretending everything was okay, they would no longer be silenced. I was more anxious now, living alone, away from the man who had hurt me, than I had ever been before.

Someone brushed against my arm, and I flinched, automatically stepping back to let him pass, my eyes searching his face, checking it wasn't Scott. Was this terror, this sense of unease, just a consequence of my unresolved trauma? Or was my gut trying to tell me something? That I really was in danger. That he wouldn't let me go so easily. That he'd do whatever it took to break my hold over him. I cast my gaze over my shoulder, quickening my pace, trying to force my mind to the present, convince myself I was safe. I was surrounded by people, and there was safety in numbers. He wasn't here. Wasn't lurking in the periphery of my vision, waiting to pounce.

By the time I reached the restaurant, I was sweating, my hands shaking. It wasn't yet open, but I slipped round to the side entrance, keying in the code I still remembered and pushing open the door.

It was a relief to step inside the quiet building. I could hear the low murmur of chatter from the staff as they talked in the kitchen, pots and pans banging on the work surfaces, a hoover running somewhere nearby. I wiped my hands on my jeans and checked my reflection in the mirror of my phone case to make sure I wasn't all red and flustered-looking, before walking up the stairs to Niall's office. I paused outside the closed door, taking a deep breath; then, before I could chicken out, I gave a cursory knock and pushed it open, stepping inside.

'Morning, Niall,' I said, proud of the way my voice emerged – strong and confident. I was good at faking the exterior shell needed to fit the right moment. It was why Scott had seen me as weak and apologetic, even when inside I was seething, boiling with hatred and resentment for what he'd put me through.

Niall was leaning back in his chair, his feet on the desk, his phone in his hand, a bowl of Coco Pops propped on his belly. He dropped his spoon, splattering milk on his pale-blue shirt, and swung his feet to the floor, spinning in his chair to face me, placing the bowl on his desk and dabbing ineffectually at his shirt with his fingertips. 'Chloe, what the fuck? You made me spill milk all over the place. This is going to stink!'

Ignoring his complaints, I pulled up a chair opposite him, my expression blank as I waited for him to stop flapping about his shirt.

He met my eyes. 'Who let you in here? In case you've forgotten, you don't work here any more.' He looked back down at the wet patch and shook the fabric as if it might make a difference. 'Thank God,' he muttered under his breath.

'Yeah, well, that's what I've come about, actually.'

'I'm not giving you your job back.'

I laughed. 'As if I'd want it!'

'So what *do* you want? I'm busy, and you're trespassing.'

I let my gaze roam slowly over his desk, from the YouTube video still playing on his phone to the bowl of soggy cereal. 'I think you can make time to hear me out.'

'I can't, actually. I'm about to call the suppliers.'

'That can wait.'

He raised an eyebrow, and I felt a sense of smug satisfaction at how taken aback he looked. Gone was the timid girl too afraid of losing her job to speak up. I had nothing to lose now.

'So, Niall—' I began.

'It's Mr Privett to you!'

I pressed my lips together, trying not to smile at his rapidly reddening face. '*Niall*. I've had some time to think about the way in which I was let go from my position here. I knew at the time, of course, that it was unfair dismissal, but I was in no position to fight it, as I'm sure you knew. I was too busy looking after my child to take you on. But things are different now.'

He shook his head. 'I haven't the faintest idea what you're talking about. You were sacked because you were unreliable.'

'Hmm. Interesting take on it. But no. I was sacked without warning because I had to take time off to look after my son when he was ill. I called as soon as I knew I couldn't make it, and I always tried to find cover for my shifts too, which was above the requirement in my contract. You cannot penalise me for being a mother. You have to make allowances. It's the law.' I jutted out my chin, daring him to argue with me.

He folded his arms. 'I don't bloody care if it's the law. The government aren't paying my bills, forking out for my staff's wages, are they?'

I shrugged. 'Not my problem.'

He gave a sneer. 'I don't know what you're expecting, but like I told you, I'm not giving you another job.'

'I want what I'm owed.'

'*Owed?*'

'That's right. Did I ever tell you my uncle's a lawyer? Specialising in employment law, to be specific.'

I watched his face blanch as I spoke the lie. It was so easy, came so naturally, just as my threat to Scott had. I couldn't help but reflect how the circumstances I'd been pushed into had changed me, made my previously black-and-white world far more opaque. Was it wrong to tell him a white lie if it meant getting what I wanted? What I needed for Tommy's sake?

I smiled. '*He* says I have a strong case against you. That if I took you to court, the payout could be quite large.' I picked up the little ornamental Zen sandbox from his desk, dragging the tiny wooden rake back and forth in zigzags, knowing it would wind him up. 'And of course,' I continued, 'the papers would no doubt have a field day. There's such a lot to the story. The sexual harassment. The hygiene standards here. To be honest, I'm not sure the restaurant could survive it.' I plonked the sandbox back on the desk, leaning back in my chair.

'You wouldn't.'

I shrugged.

He stared at me, then gave a slow nod, his mouth turned down in a sour expression of defeat. 'How much? For you to drop this?'

'I want a glowing reference.'

'Done.'

I gave a laugh. 'That isn't all.'

He sighed. 'Go on.'

'Five grand.'

'You're having a laugh. No.'

'Give me a counter-offer.'

'Two hundred quid. And your sodding reference.'

I stood up. 'I think I'd be better off taking my chances in court, don't you?' I strode towards the door, hoping he wouldn't call my bluff.

Just as I reached for the handle, he blurted out, 'Three grand. Call it a redundancy package. I can't do more than that. Head office would ask too many questions.'

I turned, considering, enjoying the pleading expression on his face, his wide eyes, the bloom of slowly drying milk spread across his belly.

'I accept. On the condition you write both the cheque and the reference now, so I don't have to ever come back here.'

He met my eyes, and I could see him physically squirming, trying to find a way to get out of it, hating having to concede to my demands. I held my position, unwavering, a breath trapped in my lungs as I feigned nonchalance. Then he slumped back in his chair and picked up a pen. I had won.

I headed out onto the street, the reference and cheque stored safely within my bag. The high I felt at having got what I'd come for – and far more than I had expected at that – was swiftly replaced by a gnawing anxiety at how many people were outside now, my eyes scanning all the male faces, still unable to stop myself looking out for him. I stepped close to a woman as she pressed the button at the pelican crossing, waiting for the signal. I folded my arms, making myself small, imagining Scott watching me, having followed me to the restaurant. It was pure paranoia. Nothing more. It was ridiculous, and it needed to stop.

Behind me stood a young mum with a toddler eating a pear in the confines of her buggy, and an elderly couple discussing the best place to buy free-range eggs. I tried to force myself to relax, my gaze travelling to the small group of people waiting on the other side of the road.

My heart stuttered, my throat seizing in a choke almost as tight as the one I had dreamed only hours before. Because there, dressed in a smart navy suit, his dark hair gelled close to his head, was a man I recognised. A man who was the spitting image of my father, whose photograph I spoke to day in day out. A man who could only have been one person – a person I knew to be dead.

My brother.

TWENTY-TWO

I didn't wait to consider what I was doing as the little green man began to flash, the intermittent beep indicating that the cars had stopped, and the man my eyes were locked on started to cross the road, heading in my direction. My heart was pounding frantically as I sidestepped the other pedestrians pushing forward, changing tack as I fell into step behind the stranger, following him along the pavement in the direction I'd come from. He walked fast, an expensive-looking leather briefcase grasped in his left hand, and I could smell a rich, spicy aftershave wafting in his wake. Some sane part deep within my brain told me to turn back, that I was obviously mistaken. That it wasn't possible.

For the first few years after I killed my brother, I had seen him everywhere. His brown eyes would meet mine across a supermarket aisle, or I'd recognise his walk as he rounded a corner. Hear his voice and be unable to stop myself from searching for where it had come from. But each time, I'd been embarrassed. Disappointed. And eventually I'd stopped letting my imagination run wild. Had accepted he was never coming back, awful as it was to admit to myself.

But this was different. This wasn't just one familiar trait. His face was the mirror image of our father's. His hair the exact same rich brown colour. I had so many pictures of the man who'd died when I was just five – I still longed for him in a way I knew would never dull, longed for the man who might have raised me, who would never have allowed his little girl to live with a man who beat her. There had been so many occasions when I'd wondered if things might have been different if he hadn't died. I'd been so very young. Had the trauma of losing him sparked the sleeping disorder that led to Rhodri's death? I stared at the back of my brother's head and wondered if I was going mad. How could he be here when I knew what I had done?

He led me on a walk through the park, round the back of a row of shops. I paused as he darted inside a little newsagent's, unsure whether to follow him, but he re-emerged moments later with a bottle of lemonade in his free hand, a sandwich tucked under his arm. I pretended to look at my phone, surreptitiously snapping a photo, relieved that it was set to silent, though I'd forgotten to check. I let him go a few paces ahead and then resumed my shadowing.

A couple of minutes later, he came to a stop outside an estate agent's and, without hesitation, pushed open the door and stepped inside. I walked up to the window, pretending to look at the ads for houses, watching as he strode to the back of the room, dropped his briefcase and sandwich on a desk and cracked open the bottle of lemonade. He drank deeply, wiped his mouth with the back of his hand, then put the cap back on and turned to the two other people sitting at their computers, saying something that made them both laugh.

I stared at him, wanting to go inside, to tell him my name and watch his reaction. To ask him how he could be standing there as plain as day when he'd been dead for more than a decade.

I suddenly thought of my mother. How would she react when she found out the son she thought she'd lost was still walking around, laughing and joking with his colleagues as if we hadn't mourned him all this time?

But... I shook my head, my hand pressed against the window. It didn't make sense. *She* had been the one to break the news. She had been the one who had called for an ambulance, had his death confirmed by the paramedics. She wouldn't have made a mistake like that. Was it possible I had this all wrong? That I was seeing something that wasn't there? That the lack of sleep, the stress of walking away from my relationship, of not being with Tommy, had made my imagination run out of control? Had I lost my grip on reality? I couldn't let that happen. I had responsibilities. A child to be there for.

I looked at the face that was almost as familiar as my own, and I was certain I hadn't got it wrong.

I had to speak to her. Had to ask some difficult questions before I waded in with both feet. I didn't know what was happening, but one thing was certain, and that was that this was a delicate subject. I needed to think through how to approach it.

With a shaking hand, I wrote down the name of the estate agent, relieved at least that I would know where to find him again.

TWENTY-THREE

Tommy was wearing different clothes – clothes I would never have chosen for him, and certainly never for playtime at Grandma's house. A white button-down shirt. Smart grey trousers. It looked like a school uniform, something he shouldn't be wearing for another year at least, and it made my heart hurt to see him in it, so sweet and earnest and grown-up. A swell of resentment rose inside me. *I* should have been the one to buy his first uniform. I would have wanted to be there, to do up the little buttons and see his face light up with pride as he caught his reflection in the mirror for the first time.

I'd been unable to stop myself from making a comment about it when I'd arrived, shocked to see the boy I still considered my baby looking so composed, so handsome. I knew Mum was only trying to help me out. She said he'd got grass stains on his trousers, and though she didn't mention the fact that I'd only had one pair to send, it had been impossible not to pick up on the unspoken message behind her words. I'd forgotten to bring the spares from nursery – not that they were anything like up to this standard. They were just cheap second-hand bits I'd got at the charity shop.

For a moment, I'd felt judged at my inability to provide the basics for him, and then, looking at his neatly brushed hair, the crisp white cotton shirt, the way he seemed to hold himself a little straighter, an unconscious consequence of his fancy new clothes, I felt sad. As if I'd missed too much time with him already.

Mum was singing softly as she pottered around the kitchen, a habit of hers I'd forgotten about. It took me right back to my childhood, something I'd always found comforting – her voice strong, capable of capturing a thousand emotions. I tried to force a smile for her, pretend I wasn't on the verge of tears. 'How has he been today?' I asked, sipping the mug of tea she'd made for me.

'Energetic.' She opened the fridge, pulling out carrots, parsnips, a pack of steak, placing them on the side.

I nodded. 'I know it can be a lot. He's probably missing his friends from nursery – they run around for hours, and he always comes back calmer and ready to relax. I was going to say, actually, he still has his sessions paid for there. I kept it going for when I find a new job. It would give you a break if you wanted to make use of the time? They're fantastic with him,' I added, watching as she wrinkled her nose; shook her head.

She picked up the vegetable peeler, starting on the carrots. 'It's a nice thought, but I prefer to keep them close when they're little. Not that that's a judgement on you. You can't help your circumstances, can you?' she said.

I winced, feeling sensitive and raw. *Did* she judge me for not being the stay-at-home mum she had been? Did she feel I was giving him second best?

'What's happening with your job hunt?' she continued, oblivious to my reaction. 'Any leads?'

I placed my mug down, trying to bring myself back to the present. 'Not yet,' I replied. 'I've applied for several, so hopefully I'll get a few interviews. And I have a glowing reference from my old boss, so that should help.'

'How come you decided to move on?'

The question was tossed in casually, but it made me tense. It was the first time she'd ventured to ask, the first time either one of us had mentioned life outside this house – my past. On the surface, it should have been safe territory, but I was afraid it was only the start, an opening to all the unspoken conversations we needed to have sooner or later.

'My boss didn't like the fact I had a child. And he was horrible to work for.'

'I see...' She paused her chopping, regarding me with inquisitive eyes. 'And the boy's father? You haven't mentioned him. Is he in the picture?'

I shook my head, feeling a strange sense of shame creep over me. It felt as if I'd let her down. She'd married young, and as far as I knew, my dad had been the only man in her life. I could only assume that she'd never got over the loss of him. She'd raised us alone but always made a point of stating that she was a widow, not a single parent.

'He was,' I said, not wanting to get into the story of what had happened to the man I'd thought I would be with for ever. I didn't want to have to explain that I'd made the wrong choice time and again. That I still couldn't walk down the street without feeling his eyes on my back, scared of him coming for me, going that final step further and ending my life. I didn't want her to look at Tommy and see a boy from a home like that. It would taint her view of both of us. 'Unfortunately, things didn't work out with him.'

She made a noise like a snort and I frowned.

'What?' I asked, my tone defensive.

'Just very different to how things were in my day. There was no such thing as not working out. People didn't give up so easily back then.'

'It wasn't easy, I can assure you.'

'Oh, I don't mean *you* did anything wrong. It just makes life all the more complicated when you have to raise a child alone, doesn't it? You have to be militant in your organisation, your plans. You have to be the fun parent and the disciplinarian, the breadwinner and the one who puts them to bed. It's a lot, darling. But you have me now. I can take some of the strain from you. There's no need to keep up the nursery place. I'm sure it costs a fortune. Once you go back to work, Tommy will continue to come here. It makes far more sense.'

I swallowed, unsure how to respond. Her offer was generous, and she was right that it would save me a lot of money, but I didn't want him missing out on that time with his friends. It was good preparation for when he went to school. And it was likely a lot more fun than playing alone in his grandmother's back garden, day in, day out.

'Yeah, maybe.' I nodded, deciding to tackle the issue later. She would probably be worn out by the time I got a new job anyway, and be looking forward to having her days freed up again.

Feeling suddenly braver, now that she'd been the one to broach the past, I decided to change the subject and ask the one question that had been running through my head on a loop since my trip into town that morning. I took a deep breath, and before I could back out, balled my hands in my lap and, in a shaking voice, said, 'I wanted to ask *you* something, actually. I know we've spoken about the letters. And I'm trying to ignore all of it; get on with my life.'

'Good, that's what you need to do.'

'But you and I never actually talked about what happened, did we?' I went on in a rush. 'And, well, I have some questions. About Rhodri.'

TWENTY-FOUR

CLARISSA

I froze, the knife embedded in the fat parsnip, my hand clamping in a tight fist around the handle. Chloe, her gaze travelling back and forth between Tommy and me, was unable to meet my eye, and it didn't surprise me. I had never imagined there would come a time when we would have this conversation. Everything we needed to say, we'd said back then – in the aftermath. I'd made it clear that I didn't blame her. That it wasn't her fault. That she wasn't a bad person. I'd tried to be the mother she'd needed – though admittedly, I'd been reluctant to seek therapy for her. They were all charlatans, out to rob you blind, filling your head with nonsense as far as I was concerned. It couldn't have helped her. Not by the time I'd properly considered it anyway.

I slid the knife through the parsnip, running my tongue over my teeth, feeling the tension in my cheeks, my face frozen. My whole body felt stiff, unyielding, as I stood gripping the knife, unable to relax for fear of the long-buried emotions that might break free. There was just no point. It was done. Over. I picked up another parsnip, pretending I hadn't heard her speak, hoping she would drop it.

'Mum...'

I ignored her, chopping faster now.

'Mum!'

'What!' The knife clattered onto the board. 'For heaven's sake, what is it, Chloe?' I exclaimed, frustration and trepidation mingling inside my belly.

Tommy, seeming to pick up on the tension, climbed down from his seat at the table. 'Mummy, I want to go outside.'

Chloe stood, opening the back door, caressing his cheek before he darted off to play. She watched him go, then turned to me, waiting.

Reluctantly, I raised my eyes to meet hers. 'I don't want to talk about him.'

She nodded. 'I get that. But there's something I need to ask. I know it sounds strange, but... did I have any other brothers – brothers I didn't know about? Did Rhodri have a twin? Or a cousin of around the same age even?'

I blinked, stunned by her question. It had been the last thing I'd expected to hear her ask. I shook my head. 'What? No, of course not. What are you talking about? You don't have any cousins, and I had no other children. You already know that.'

She bowed her head, not offering an explanation for her strange question.

A sudden fear hit me, and I heard the words leave my mouth. 'Why did you ask that, Chloe?'

She sighed, glancing out of the window to Tommy. 'I... I saw him. I saw Rhodri.'

I closed my eyes. 'No, darling.'

'I did. I followed him.'

'It wasn't your brother, darling. He's gone.'

'No... I saw him.'

My voice was kind but firm as I spoke. 'You didn't, Chloe.' Slowly I walked around the counter until I was face to face with her. Without a word, I pulled her into a tight hug. 'How long has this been happening?'

She shook her head against my shoulder. 'What?'

'How many times did you see him?'

'Just once.'

'And have there been others?'

'*Others?*' She pulled back. 'What others?'

'People who don't belong. People you know to be dead. People who aren't really there.'

'I... I don't understand what you mean.'

'It's my fault, I suppose,' I muttered, squeezing her arm. 'I should have taken you to a doctor. But I was so afraid they would take you away. I couldn't bear to lose you too. And I thought you'd grow out of it. That it was just a little quirk, like your sleeping. Lots of children have imaginary friends. Although I think, if I'm honest, I always knew it was more than that. Don't you remember Annie?'

She shook her head again. 'No.'

'She was a little girl who lived across the road, next door to Mirium. The two of you became good friends when you were both eight – you were in the same class at school, so you spent a lot of time together. Then her dad got a job in Norway, and they moved over half-term. It all happened so quickly, and there was no time for you to say goodbye. You were devastated.

'A few weeks later, you got back from school all smiles, and I was so relieved. You said you'd been playing with your best friend and that she'd come home with you. I was worried – you were only little, and I thought she'd come over without letting her mum know. I was in a panic, imagining how worried she would be when her child didn't turn up, but when I followed you to the front door, there was nobody there.'

I could see the expectation on her face, waiting for me to finish the story.

'You spoke like she was real,' I continued. 'Like you could

see her. And you called her Annie. I should have expected it, I suppose. The same thing had happened with your dad. There were others too, over the years. It was as if you couldn't cope with the loss, so your mind came up with a reality that was more acceptable for you.'

'I don't remember.'

'I don't suppose you would. To you, it was nothing out of the ordinary. You believed it to be real. But it frightened me. I'm sure as a mother yourself now, you can understand why.'

Chloe frowned, rubbing her eyes with her hands. 'I'm not sure what a childhood imaginary friend has to do with my having seen Rhodri. I'm not mad, Mum. Not some fanciful child letting my imagination run wild. I know what I saw. It was him. I would stake my life on it.'

'*Don't*. Don't say that, Chloe.' I looked out to the garden at Tommy, busily digging in the soil. 'You were mistaken.'

'I—' She broke off, her face creasing, and I could see she wanted to disagree.

Her level of conviction scared me. All the same, I could tell she wasn't going to argue her side now. She wanted to let my words simmer for a while. It was clear she really believed she'd seen him, though of course that wasn't possible.

She chewed her lip. 'Perhaps you're right.' She gave a heavy sigh. She didn't sound convinced, and I watched her closely, trying not to let on how unsettled I was. 'Maybe it's the stress of being apart from Tommy. I'm not used to it. I miss him. I worry.'

I nodded, understanding, yet I was afraid of what she might say next. She wasn't ready to take him back. Especially given what she'd told me today. Seeing people who weren't there, failing to question it even though logically she had to know it was impossible. 'You need rest. A few good nights' sleep. And Tommy is perfectly happy here. He's safe with me, Chloe,' I added softly, letting my unspoken words hang in the air.

A frown crossed her pretty face, and I saw the moment she bit back a retort, giving a frustrated shake of her head.

I knew I should leave it, but I couldn't seem to stop myself from asking, 'What?'

Her eyes met mine. 'You make it sound like I'm not fit to be his mother. That you don't trust me with my own son. I've done all right so far, haven't I? He's been safe with me.'

I didn't miss the bitter tone behind her accusation. A part of me wanted to placate her, tell her it was obvious to me she was a good mother, but I couldn't bring myself to say the words, too afraid of what it might mean. I didn't want to risk her deciding it was time to take him home with her. There was still so much that needed resolving before that could happen. Instead, I did the only thing I could think of. Said the one thing I knew would make her see sense, though I hated to hurt her.

'So was your brother for the first twelve years of his life. It only takes once, Chloe. One mistake for everything to change.'

Her mouth dropped open, and I tried not to show how deeply her hurt affected me. I picked the knife back up and continued to prepare dinner, slicing the beef steak into cubes. Chloe made a sound in her throat – disbelief, I imagined, at how I could have brought up something so painful.

I glanced up through the shield of my lowered lashes to see her grab her bag and walk out the back door. She crossed the lawn to Tommy, and I watched, afraid of what she might do next, the knife still gripped tight in my palm. But after hugging him, she said something that made him smile, then, with a final kiss, left through the side gate, leaving him behind.

I swiped the meat from the chopping board into the pan and heaved a sigh of relief.

TWENTY-FIVE

CHLOE

I closed the gate with as much restraint as I could summon. I was reeling – absolutely seething with anger – but I didn't want to frighten my son. *Because* I was a good mother. *Because* I had self-control. And because, no matter what *she* might think me capable of, I would do *anything* to keep him safe.

I hardly saw the road in front of me as I crossed, intending to head back to the bus stop, home to my empty little flat. How dare she insinuate that I was seeing things! That out of the blue I'd conjured up my dead brother to ease my guilt or some such nonsense.

Granted, I'd been thinking of him a lot lately, going through that night over and over, fearful of how I would manage without Scott to watch over me as I slept. But thinking about a person didn't make them magically appear from thin air. I knew what I had seen.

I was so blind with impotent rage, half tempted to go back and give her a piece of my mind, that I didn't notice the man step out onto the path ahead of me until I'd collided with him. Half winded, I stepped back, apologising breathlessly.

'Jeff!' I gasped, holding my side.

A woman I recognised from my childhood glanced up from the other side of the hedge. Her eyes widened as she stripped off her gardening gloves and walked briskly round to where we stood on the pavement. I thought she would stop next to her husband, but instead she barrelled forward, embracing me tightly. She smelled strongly of lavender, and I felt my body go rigid, my arms remaining by my sides as I waited for her to release me.

I glanced over her shoulder at Jeff, wondering if my mother was right. Had he been sending me those awful notes? Stalking me to my son's nursery? Lurking in the shadows trying to frighten me? He was staring with open curiosity, but I couldn't detect a trace of malice, and I felt more confused than ever.

Mirium pulled back, touching my cheek in a way that felt overly familiar – maternal even. I struggled to remember if we'd ever had that kind of relationship in the past. I didn't think so. In fact, my overarching memory of the couple had been a deep-seated feeling that my mother merely tolerated them out of a duty towards neighbourly manners. I'd picked up on her lack of warmth and had followed her lead, and now, with her recent revelations about Jeff harassing her, I felt even cooler towards him.

'Hi, Mirium,' I said, stepping back awkwardly.

She smiled, her eyes wide and watery. She looked so much older than she had last time I'd laid eyes on her. Unlike my mum, whose plump cheeks kept her youthful, Mirium had lost weight over the years, and it had aged her.

'Chloe,' she breathed. 'So, it really is you. I never imagined —' She broke off, looking up at Jeff, her hand going to his chest for support.

I nodded, glancing over her shoulder for an escape, then forcing my face into a smile. 'It's me. Have you been keeping well? How's...' I tried to recall their son's name. He'd been around the same age as Rhodri, but my memory couldn't summon any details about him.

Rhodri had slept over at their place quite often, and I remembered hearing him and my mum arguing, her not being happy about it and him insisting he wanted to keep going. Now that I thought about it, it had to have been close to the time he'd died. Had he been afraid of what I might do to him in the middle of the night? Had he already known the danger he was in and tried to get away from me?

Mirium was looking at me with a patient expression, as if I could take all day to finish my sentence and she wouldn't interrupt.

'How's life treating you?' I improvised, feeling suddenly drained, devoid of every last scrap of energy. All I wanted was to head home. I wasn't in the mood for making small talk, answering difficult questions about my fifteen-year absence.

She took my hand, oblivious to my attempts to create a little distance between us. 'We've been fine. We met your little boy. Such a credit to you. He's a darling. But it was quite a shock. The last thing we expected given—'

'He *is* a wonderful child, thank you,' I said, cutting her off, unwilling to hear her thoughts on how I was too young, how she would have expected me to get married first.

She shook her head, her eyes welling up again. 'To see you standing here, strong and healthy and beautiful, it's like a miracle, isn't it, Jeff?' she exclaimed, looking to the man who stood rigid and unsmiling beside her. 'We thought you were dead.'

I let out a laugh, pulling my hand away. 'Why on earth would you think such a thing? I'm fine. Alive and well.' I wondered if there was something going on with her. Dementia, perhaps. Or maybe she was confusing me with someone else.

'We can take the boy.'

I froze, frowning, as Jeff met my bewildered gaze. 'Sorry?'

'It's too much for your mother. We'll take him while you get things sorted. Your personal business, I mean.'

'I—' I broke off, wondering if Mum had been complaining behind my back about the burden of taking on her grandson. She hadn't given me any indication – in fact, she seemed not only keen but insistent that Tommy continue to stay with her. 'Uh, that's kind of you, Jeff,' I managed, wondering what his intentions were. Was this some trick? 'You too, Mirium. But I'll be taking him back with me very soon.'

From their open front door came the shrill sound of a phone ringing.

'Drat,' Mirium said, looking over her shoulder towards the house. 'I really must take that. It'll be Joseph telling me what time to expect him. I hope we'll have a chance to catch up properly soon, Chloe love.'

I nodded non-committally as she rushed inside. Jeff was still standing watching me, and as I stared back at him, I made up my mind. There were too many questions left unanswered, and now I had an opportunity, I wasn't going to shy away from asking them.

'I'm glad I bumped into you, actually,' I said, my eyes not leaving his as I searched them for clues. 'I've received some unsettling letters recently from an anonymous source.'

'Right?' He frowned, clearly confused as to where I was going.

'Letters referring to my brother.'

He looked at his feet, his shoulders hunching as he sighed. When he said nothing, I folded my arms.

'Do you remember much from that time? When Rhodri died, I mean?'

Jeff looked back up at me. 'It's not something I would forget.' He glanced over at Mum's house. 'I'll never forgive myself for not doing more... I heard screaming in the early hours of the morning. I went outside and realised it was coming from your house... from his room. The girl from next door had come out on her lawn to investigate too – I remember it well because we were debating whether to knock or call the police or something. But then the screams stopped, the light went out upstairs and a moment later, a light was switched on in the living room. Annie and I decided it must have been you having a nightmare – you used to have them a lot – so we left it. Went back inside. But the next morning, everyone was talking about the news, saying that Rhodri had died in the night.' He shook his head. 'I couldn't believe it... Just a child...' He looked away.

I shook my head. 'Annie?' I repeated, thinking of the friend my mother had told me about earlier. 'But she would have been fifteen then. The same age as me. Mum said she moved away when we were eight. You must be mistaken.'

He shrugged as if I was focusing on the wrong detail of the story. 'No, I remember it well. They moved not long after it all happened. Said the street wasn't the same after that.'

I looked at him, wondering if he was lying or just forgetting the details, wishing I could trust his version of events. It didn't make sense. Mum had made a point of telling me about how impacted I'd been by Annie leaving. Jeff had to be thinking of someone else.

I glanced at my watch. 'Okay... well, thanks.'

'Do you want to come inside? Mirium would love it.'

'Sorry,' I said, shaking my head as I stepped around him. 'I can't stop.'

I paused, casting one last look at his face, hoping to see something there, but there was nothing – no sign of any smugness at having got one up on me, no indication of what he might be thinking. But I knew only too well how easy it was for people to hide their true nature in plain sight. Scott had been the first person to lead me into a false sense of security. It was sad, I realised, how little trust I had in anyone any more. My gut was telling me the letters hadn't come from Jeff, but if not him, then who?

'Consider what I said,' he called after me. 'About us taking the boy.'

I held up a hand in a half-wave, rushing down the street towards the bus stop. I could feel his eyes burning into my back with every step.

TWENTY-SIX

The key jammed in the lock of the flat, and I had to give the door several hard kicks before it would budge. The sound echoed through the dimly lit hallway, and I glanced over my shoulder, seeing movement in the shadows, my stomach tightening involuntarily. The key clicked just as a figure rounded the corner, and I darted inside, slamming the door behind me.

Squinting through the peephole, I saw the back of a man in a baseball cap retreating up the stairs. Probably one of my new neighbours. Not my ex. The paranoia was becoming exhausting. Constantly looking over my shoulder, expecting to see Scott, to feel his fist around my ponytail, his voice in my ear as he whispered all the ways I had ruined his life.

The visit to my mother's had done little to ease my anxiety. I dropped my bag by the door and went to run a bath in the damp-smelling bathroom. I'd filled in the crack with Polyfilla and was hoping it would hold up. Right now, I was too tired to care.

Sinking into the hot water, I let my heavy eyelids close as I pictured my son, tried to imagine the sweet sound of his laughter carrying through from the living room to where I lay. I should have brought him back here, not let my mother's fears cloud my judgement. The longer he stayed with her, the more she seemed to think she had a right to tell me what to do.

My thoughts drifted to what she'd told me about the girl across the road, Annie. The friend who had once been real but who I'd refused to let go of and had turned into a figment of my imagination, though I couldn't remember doing so.

Tommy had never had an imaginary friend, but he did frequently get lost in immersive games with his toys. There had been the dinosaur obsession, during which his three chosen favourites had accompanied us everywhere we went. We'd had to stop to hunt their appropriate food along the way, which had meant we were late for everything. And then there was the month he'd insisted he was a dog rather than a boy, and I'd had to give him a treat every time he carried something in to me – with his mouth, of course. He'd refused to be called Tommy during that one, only responding to Rocco, and woofing when I asked him a question. It had been harmless fun. A simple game that he'd soon lost interest in, moving on to the next fad. That was what kids did – there was no deep-seated meaning to any of it. And yet the message I'd got from the talk with my mother today had been quite different. She'd led me to feel that it had been more than just play in my case. That I'd been unstable. *Ill* even.

And then there had been the confusion Jeff had added to the mix, changing the timeline so it no longer aligned with my mother's. I couldn't understand why they would both be so set on their version of events when one of them had so obviously got it wrong. And I couldn't imagine why I had no memory of this girl, who had clearly meant a lot to me.

I closed my eyes, leaning back against the tub, trying to picture my childhood friends, to summon this Annie to consciousness. It wasn't as simple as I might have liked. Those childhood years felt separate, as if they belonged to someone else, the years after I'd left home my true reality. I'd walked away from everything I knew and let myself forget what had been because it was easier that way.

I thought of my old classroom, trying to remember details that had long since been erased from my mind. There'd been a teacher I'd liked, in Year 3 – was it Mrs Price? Mrs Proud? She'd had red hair and would let us work outside in the summer when the classroom got too hot.

I opened my eyes as the memory hit me, a face coming to the forefront of my mind. *Annie.* She'd plaited my hair when the teacher read to us. She'd had dark, smiling eyes and a smattering of freckles on her pale nose. And she wore glasses, but only when we were watching cartoons.

It came like a tsunami, the memories of the two of us sitting on my living-room floor laughing at *Sooty & Co.* on the little TV. Daring each other to swing higher in the park. Swapping outfits for our favourite baby dolls.

I tried to recall a moment of sadness, hearing that she'd left and wasn't coming back, but all I could picture was us having fun. Was my mum right? Had I been so obsessed with this girl, so desperate to keep her as a friend, that I'd forced myself to imagine a version of her that had never left me? Surely I would recall something like that. And how had it come to an end? I hadn't seen a therapist, a doctor. Had I grown out of it, as children do?

Whatever the case, I was certain that this thing with my brother wasn't the same. Nothing about it made sense, but I knew I wasn't imagining the man I'd followed today. It *had* to have been him.

Standing so suddenly that water splashed over the side of the bath, I clambered out, pulled my towelling dressing gown around my damp skin and went in search of my phone. I perched on the edge of the sofa, bringing up the photograph I'd taken outside the newsagent's. Annoyingly, it was blurry, the man's face half turned away, and I opened a search engine instead, typing in the name of the estate agent's, tense and impatient as my slow internet connection loaded the site.

The home page showed a photograph of a group of well-dressed agents, men and women with slick hair and smart suits, and there in the centre was the man I'd seen today, the reincarnation of my father. I read the brief biography below the photo and felt a surge of intense pride as I realised that he was the owner – the boss. Except the name beneath his picture was Paul. Not Rhodri.

There were a lot of houses listed on the sales page – he was clearly getting plenty of business – and I clicked on one of them, a mansion going for just over a million pounds. Before I could lose my nerve, I pressed the button that prompted me to *call agent* and held the phone against my ear, my fingers trembling. It was gone six. Perhaps nobody would answer. And there was no way I was leaving a message – I wouldn't know how to begin. But the phone had barely rung once before somebody picked up. A man, but I couldn't be sure if it was him. *Rhodri. Paul.*

'Emerald Estate Agents, how can I help you?'

'Oh, hi, I would like to view a property, please. As soon as possible.'

'Certainly. Which of our listings was it you were interested in?' came the smooth reply.

'The five-bedroom, on Windsor Avenue.'

There was a brief pause, then he cleared his throat. 'Of course – that won't be a problem at all. It's a beautiful property. May I ask what your position is? Do you have an agreement in principle with a mortgage company? And will you be relying on selling your own home before you can proceed? Only the vendors are quite keen to have a quick sale and—'

'I'm a cash buyer. There's no chain,' I said, matching his smooth tone, determined to make the booking. I was sure the owner of the agency would be the one to conduct the viewing on a house like this. If I'd chosen any other place, it would have been too risky – I didn't want to turn up and find I'd been met by some teenage Saturday girl.

'Fantastic. I'll just take a few details from you,' he said, and I heard his fingers clicking on a computer keyboard. 'Can I have your name, please?'

I opened my mouth to reply and then stopped myself just in time. I couldn't possibly tell him my real name. If he *was* my brother, he had to have made a concerted effort not to be found. He'd left home, faked his death, changed his name. He wouldn't want to see me. 'Annie,' I said, saying the first name that came to mind. I looked around the room, seeing the fruit bowl on the side. 'Annie Plum.'

'How's tomorrow, Annie? Ten a.m.?'

'That would be perfect. I'll meet you there. I didn't catch *your* name.'

'It's Paul.'

I closed my eyes, picturing his face. 'And you'll be doing the viewing, will you?' I asked, as casually as I could manage.

'I certainly will. I'll call the vendors now and get that booked in. Looking forward to showing you the house.'

'Me too,' I managed.

I hung up, feeling trembly and excited. I didn't understand how it was possible, but he was alive. Thriving. I'd just had my first conversation with my brother in over fifteen years, and tomorrow I would get to see him in person. I placed the phone on the table, lowered my wet body onto a chair and felt a blast of blind terror as I wondered if I was going mad.

TWENTY-SEVEN

CLARISSA

I couldn't seem to stop replaying the look in Chloe's eyes when I'd asked the question that had been burning on my tongue since she'd arrived on my doorstep. The mention of Tommy's father had elicited a response she'd tried hard to hide, but even now, with all these missed years between us, I knew my daughter well enough to see when she was lying to me. There was a lot more to the story than she was letting on, and it had me worried. Plenty of things had me worried after the way she'd been today.

Since she'd left home, I'd managed to compartmentalise her absence. The first weeks had been the hardest, waking up to an empty house, walking into her room to find it just as I'd left it. No smell of Impulse body spray lingering in the air. No laundry in the basket. I had changed her sheets every week, though they were never slept in. I'd forgotten that. Forgotten the way I'd continued to buy clothes I thought she might like from our favourite shops. The drive I'd taken to the woodworking course she'd been going to. I had sat outside in the car, watching the other teenagers head in, picturing my daughter laughing and joking with them.

I don't know at what point I'd begun to shut down the emotions associated with her name, let myself live again, but now, so many memories were flooding back and with them a tidal wave of anxiety, fear for the future, for her and for Tommy. I didn't want to pretend not to see the elephant in the room any longer. I craved answers. Where exactly had she been these past fifteen years? Who was the man she had walked away from, and why now?

I cleared away the dinner things, momentarily distracted to see that for the first time since arriving here, Tommy had eaten his vegetables without complaint. He acted as if he'd never seen half the things I served him for dinner, and I couldn't help but let my mind wander to the life he might have had until now. It was going to be up to me to remedy those missing experiences for him. It wouldn't do for him to not have a healthy childhood because of money or circumstance. Even if it did mean a few uncomfortable conversations with my daughter.

I pushed the dishwasher door shut with my foot and stood in the middle of the kitchen, my lips pursed as a thousand unanswered questions raced through my mind. I didn't want to let myself think about the conversation Chloe had initiated about Rhodri. I wasn't at all ready to deal with the emotions that came up when I thought of my son. Like I'd done with Chloe, Rhodri and Reece were compartmentalised in a vault deep inside my mind, and I was happy – no, *determined* – for them to remain that way. I was dealing with more than enough as it was. It would do none of us any favours to bring it all up now off the back of some hopeful fantasy of hers. Chloe had always seen what she wanted to see.

Impulsively, I turned, walking into the hallway and pulling open the door to the cupboard under the stairs. Tommy's backpack was hanging on a hook, and I plucked it off, carrying it back into the kitchen. I'd already been through the meagre contents Chloe had sent with him. His toothbrush had been chewed and well past its prime, so that had gone in the bin, and other than a few items of clothing and a book or two that had been taken upstairs, there'd been nothing of note. Even so, I found myself unzipping it now.

It was empty, as was the little compartment on the inside. But there was a pocket on the front I hadn't noticed before. I opened it now, and felt a flurry of something in the pit of my belly as I pulled out a folded white envelope. An acorn was printed on the back, the words *Tiny Acorns Preschool* in a child-like font beneath it, and when I turned it over, I saw what I'd longed for. An address. Not even that far from here by the look of the postcode.

I slid the letter from inside it and read the invoice, addressed to Chloe Phillips and someone called Scott Radley, and suddenly I knew what I had to do. I had to go and see the man who'd made my daughter into a single parent. I would find out exactly what had been going on in her life these past fifteen years.

I had a feeling I wasn't going to like it. Not one bit.

I'd anticipated that Chloe might have had to settle for a place rougher than her childhood home, but as I climbed the unlit staircase to the fourth floor of the grey tower block, avoiding puddles of unidentifiable liquid on the landings, litter and broken glass scattered in the corners of the steps, I realised just how much I'd underestimated the dire situation she'd been in. How could she have chosen to live in a place like this rather than come home to me? I wouldn't have stood for it if I'd been aware of how bad things were. She should have known there was nothing she could do that I would find unforgivable. I was her mother. And nothing was ever black and white.

I tensed, my hand hovering over the metal banister, not

wanting to touch it yet feeling my nerve rock as an echo of deep masculine laughter descended from above. Frozen, my eyes trained on the step beneath my feet, I waited as a group of five tall men wearing padded jackets and beanie hats came barrelling down, their voices loud and intimidating. They passed me without acknowledging my presence at all – a fact I was grateful for. I let out the breath I'd been holding, feeling shaky and sick. I shouldn't have come here. It wasn't the kind of place I had ever been before.

Self-consciously, I pulled my leather handbag closer to my body, then tucked my gold necklace into the collar of my jumper. It was impossible to imagine her here. To think of little Tommy having to walk these stairs day after day, seeing the kinds of men who'd just passed me, thinking of them as his role models in life. It was a recipe for failure. He didn't have a chance of becoming a decent man with a start like this.

I thought of Mirium, who would tut at me if I voiced these thoughts to her. How she would say that poor doesn't mean low standards, and tell me off for being judgemental. She'd said it once before, something about my narrow world view, and it had rankled because she was right. I hadn't intended to put myself in such a small box; I'd had dreams, goals, but life had other plans for me, and I'd made the best of them. I couldn't help if that made my opinions a little derisive at times.

With the voices fading into the distance, I resumed my climb, double-checking the door number on the envelope and stopping outside number 407. I knocked without hesitation, unwilling to back out now I'd come this far. I had to meet him. Understand what I'd missed in my daughter's absence. I needed him to tell me she'd been okay. That what she'd experienced with her brother hadn't sent her off the rails. Because right now, I wasn't sure.

I waited, my ankles pressed together, my hands clasped

tight in front of me. The low heel of my pale-pink satin court shoe tapped impatiently, and I felt my shoulders ripple with tension as I waited for him to come.

When the door remained closed, I knocked again, louder this time, *bang, bang, bang, bang, bang*. It was getting on for 10 p.m. I'd had to ask Floss next door to come and sit in my living room in case Tommy woke up – not that I imagined he would. That boy slept like the dead after his busy days. I was damned if I had traipsed all over town and put myself in danger only to be left standing on the doorstep, my questions unanswered. If I was going to help my daughter, I needed to see what she'd been dealing with.

With a flash of irritation, I gave a final knock, then, hoping to rattle the door some more, jiggled the handle. It slid down easily, and the door swung wide open. I stood on the threshold, wondering what to do. Was the flat abandoned? Or was Chloe's ex just so irresponsible he couldn't even remember to lock his front door when he went out?

There was the sound of footsteps below, a door opening and shutting, a cackling smoker's laugh. I wasn't sure which was more frightening: heading into the unknown of the dark, empty flat or back down there past *those* kinds of people.

Making up my mind, I sucked in a breath, squared my shoulders and stepped inside, pushing the door quietly closed behind me. It felt safer to be shut in here, out of the view of prying eyes. I reached to the side for the light switch, but when I pressed it, nothing happened.

As my eyes adjusted to the dark, I saw that it was every bit as awful in here as the stairwell had been. A part of me had hoped it would be a little oasis in the midst of the squalor, but as I took in the piles of unwashed plates on the kitchen counter, the smell of something rotten lingering in the air, my hopes went up in smoke. There was a sticky feel to the carpet as I walked slowly across it, pushing open a door that led to a bedroom. The mattress was bare, aside from one pillow and a pair of discarded boxer shorts lying in the centre, but the smell of cigarettes was too strong for me to consider it abandoned. Someone had been here recently.

I looked at the bed, the wall behind it, paint peeling and yellowed, the glass in the window blown, making the view of the night sky a blurred pattern, a hazy glow from the moonlight that must be shining beyond. I couldn't imagine her here. Couldn't picture it. There was no chest of drawers, no bedside table for me to investigate, though even if there had been, I couldn't be sure what it was I was looking for. Evidence, perhaps, that she had been okay. That the last fifteen years hadn't been hell for her, a self-inflicted punishment for her guilt. And I wanted to know that she wasn't keeping secrets. I was involved now, in her life and Tommy's, and I wouldn't send him off in her care if I thought for a second there were lies in what she was telling me. I had to be sure of that.

A sound came from behind me, and I turned as the front door clicked closed. A man, six foot tall, with an unlit cigarette clamped between his lips, stood watching me. He dropped a plastic carrier bag by his feet and regarded me with a hard expression. '*You* must be lost,' he said, his words soft, too smooth.

The way his eyes fixed on me made me feel exposed, vulnerable, and I glanced over his shoulder to the door, wondering what on earth I'd been thinking coming inside. It dawned on me that nobody knew where I was.

'What are you doing?' he asked, beginning to walk slowly in my direction. The way he moved was reminiscent of a tiger stalking its prey, calculated and confident.

I would not let myself be cowed by him. After all, this was exactly what I'd come here for. To confront him. Ask why he'd abandoned my daughter, his responsibilities. I owed her that much.

I pursed my lips, folding my arms across my chest, the strap of my bag still clamped tight under my arm.

'Scott, I presume?' I said, my chin jutting out. I considered offering a handshake, trying to be cordial, then changed my mind, not wanting to touch him.

His brow furrowed, and he paused, pulling a lighter from his pocket and holding the flame to the cigarette. He took a deep drag and then blew a cloud of smoke in my face. I stood frozen, stubbornly refusing to cough, to show him I was intimidated.

'Who the fuck are you?' he asked. He glared at me for a moment, then his eyes widened. 'No way! Don't tell me she's gone crawling back to Mummy? After everything she did to get away, she's gone back?' He shook his head. 'You look just like her. Only the face, mind. You've not got the body,' he sneered, his gaze raking over me, lingering a touch too long on my thick midsection. 'But bloody hell. Same eyes. Same mouth. The hair too.' He gave a smirk. 'It's like seeing into her future. Weird.'

I felt myself bristle. 'It seems to me Chloe's future is something you won't be privy to. You've clearly failed at providing for her and your son.'

'I never asked to be in that position. She knew what she was signing up for.'

I stared at him, feeling a crawling sense of hatred for the man who should have given my daughter so much more. She deserved the world. 'A lot of people don't ask to become parents. But they make the best of it. They step up. Why should *you* be any different?'

He flicked his cigarette, dropping ash on the carpet, and I grimaced, unable to fathom how Chloe could have let Tommy live like this. After her childhood, the clean clothes, the home-cooked food, the safety and security I'd bent over backwards to provide for her, how could she accept so little for her own child?

Scott gave an infuriating shrug, as if my words had no impact on him at all, and I felt my blood boil at the injustice of it. It wasn't fair. He'd got my daughter pregnant and then let her down. I could see now that in leaving him, she'd made the only sensible choice available to her. He was never going to be the kind of man who would step up, deserve a woman like Chloe.

'I want you to cut all ties. *I'll* make sure they have what they need. I don't want you in their lives. Do you understand me?' I said, feeling the adrenaline pulse through my blood as I squared up to the man who towered above me. I pointed my finger into his chest. 'You leave them alone. I don't know what you did to make her see sense and walk away from you, but it was the best thing she ever did.' I was fired up by my disgust at what she'd had to endure. 'You're not fit for her.'

I didn't see him move, didn't recognise the moment his body language changed, but all of a sudden I felt myself thrown back against the wall, his hand at my throat, his face inches from mine. His grip tightened, and I stared up at him, his expression terrifying as I realised exactly the kind of man my daughter had set up home with. It was so much worse than I'd feared. Panic coursed through me as his fingertips pressed into my skin, squeezing tight enough to render me speechless.

'I don't take orders from no one,' he snarled, his breath acrid and sour, tiny droplets of spittle landing on my face.

Even in my terror, I wanted to wash it away – couldn't stand the sensation of it soaking into my pores, a part of him infecting me, tainting me. It made me so angry I could barely think straight.

'Anything I did to her was because *she* made me feel like an animal in a fucking cage. You take a man's freedom from him and watch how it changes him. It's not right. She trapped me, and now you have the gall to turn up here and act like *I'm* the one at fault? You have no idea what you're talking about.'

His grip loosened slightly, just enough for me to suck in a breath.

'I'm not surprised she left you. You're a monster. A selfish, self-obsessed child!' I screeched, heedless of the consequences. He made me sick. Full of excuses, unwilling to take responsibility for the people he owed it to.

The slap ricocheted across my cheek, and I gasped, the stinging heat radiating outwards, making my eyes water. He stepped back, his chest heaving, and though I should have been scared, cowed, all I could think was how he had done this to her. He had made my strong, beautiful girl into a victim. I would not let him dominate me too.

'You walk away,' I demanded breathlessly, my hand pressed to my cheek.

He sneered and picked up his dropped cigarette from the floor, where a patch of carpet was beginning to smoulder. Stamping on it with his dirty trainers, he took a drag and gave a sardonic smile. 'If I could, I would. But I can't. That bitch has got me over a barrel and I'm stuck with her. Unless she has a change of heart. Or something happens to force a change of heart.'

His eyes had a dangerous glint as he spoke, and I felt my hackles rise at the implied threat. I wanted to ask what he meant, but he was already striding towards the door. He held it open pointedly.

'Now get the fuck out of my flat. And if you come back again, I'll give you a proper taste of what I gave her. That was just the highlights.' He met my furious stare, and had the cheek to wink.

It took all my willpower not to fly at him, claw at his face and punch him in the belly, sick to my stomach at what he was implying. I couldn't bear to think of it.

Without a word, I strode past him and rushed down the four flights of stairs. It felt as if I didn't take a breath until I burst out of the double doors into the night. I had learned precious little about Chloe's life since leaving home, but I knew one thing for certain. If she had been suffering with her mental health before she left, it would only have got worse in the conditions she'd been thrust into.

TWENTY-EIGHT

I watched from the bedroom window as Jeff put his golf clubs into the boot of his car, waving at Mirium, who stood at their front door, before driving away. It was a habit that had become second nature over the years. I never went to visit unless I knew he'd be out for a long while, never wanted to find myself trapped in an uncomfortable situation with him in the position of power.

I waited a few more minutes, scanning the street from the window, then called Tommy to come and get his shoes on, preparing to go across the road. I couldn't avoid Miri for ever, and the longer I stayed away from our usual meet-ups and routines, the more questions she would inevitably have.

'Will your friend's grandchildren be there today?' Tommy asked as he slipped his feet into his Velcro shoes, sitting on the bottom step.

'I think so. Do you want to play with them?'

'I don't know.' He looked down at his feet. 'I want my mummy.'

I pursed my lips, seeing his discomfort. It was likely the fact that we were going somewhere he hadn't been before that was setting him on edge. He was an anxious boy, and now, having seen the kind of environment he'd been raised in, I was beginning to understand why.

'I know you do, Tommy,' I said, holding out my hand, waiting for him to take it. I guided him to the front door, still talking, hoping to distract him enough to make it over the road without incident. 'Mummy told me she has some appointments this morning,' I went on, closing the door and continuing down the path. 'I expect she's off to get a new job. But she always comes here afterwards, doesn't she? And you'll have fun in Mirium's garden. She has a slide and a sandpit.'

I watched his eyes light up at the revelation, and before his enthusiasm could fade, I rapped on Mirium's front door. She opened it with a smile, though I hadn't told her to expect us. She never seemed to mind me turning up unannounced – said it gave her an excuse to avoid the housework.

'Clarissa! Hi, come in, come in,' she said, stepping back to let us pass. 'I'm glad you're here; I was planning to pop in on you later today and give you this.' She pressed a book into my hands. 'It's the latest choice from the book club. I know you missed this week's session, but I finished it yesterday so you may as well take my copy. Save you having to buy one. It's not very good, if you want my opinion, but I'll wait until you've read it before we get into all that.' She gave a little laugh and gestured for us to follow her.

Tommy was squeezing his hands into anxious fists by his sides, looking from me to Miri.

'Are Berty and Lola here today?' I asked, taking a seat at her kitchen table as she went to fill the kettle.

'Not until this evening. I'm having them overnight while Joseph and Emma go to a concert. All right for some, eh?' she said with a wry smile. 'I can't remember the last time Jeff took me somewhere on a date, but I suppose that's what you get after forty years together.'

I watched Tommy's shoulders relax as he listened, realising he wouldn't have to compete for the garden toys, and pointed to the back door.

'Go on, Tommy. Miri doesn't mind you playing out there.'

She looked up from the mugs and nodded. 'Help yourself. There's a bag of trucks and diggers next to the sandpit. You're lucky my two aren't here – they haven't mastered the art of sharing yet, but you're quite safe today.'

Tommy hesitated, and I got up, opening the door for him. 'Go on then. You don't want to hang around in here; it'll be boring.'

I saw him look longingly across the garden to the utopia Mirium had created after years of looking after her grandkids. Then temptation won out, and he rushed through the open door, running across the grass. I watched as he emptied the bag of plastic vehicles into the sand and lost himself in a game.

'He'll be happy out there,' I said. 'It's a wonder you ever get yours to come inside with all that to distract them.'

Mirium laughed, placing a mug of coffee on the table in front of me. 'That was the point. The more they're out there playing, the less exhausted I am at the end of the day. And it stops Jeff from losing the plot. He can't stand the noise. Oh, for a shred of their energy, am I right?' she said, plonking herself down opposite me.

I nodded. 'I have to admit, I'm burned out myself. But it's helping Chloe, so I don't mind. It's what grandparents are for, isn't it?'

She took a sip of her drink, regarding me over the rim of her mug. 'I saw her yesterday, as it happens,' she said.

I held her gaze. I'd been hoping they wouldn't bump into each other. It complicated everything. 'Did you? That's nice,' I replied, trying to sound as if I didn't mind.

'I still can't understand why you didn't correct me – why you let us believe the worst had happened.'

I had hoped she would have dropped this by now. I'd done my best to answer her questions when she'd come to mine the other day. How could I explain to her that it had felt safer to let people believe Chloe was dead? That I'd been trying to protect my daughter. That the last person I would want to know the full story was Mirium's husband. I dreaded to think what might have happened had *he* got wind of the truth. But I couldn't tell her any of that.

'I'm sorry you feel like I misled you. But I was in a bad place...' I took a sip of my coffee, finding it far too milky and not nearly strong enough for my liking. 'Did you have much time to talk with her? To catch up, I mean?'

She shook her head. 'No, not really. She was in a rush. A shame, as I'd love to have a proper chat with her. Hear how she's been over the years.'

I winced. I bet she would. I could only imagine how Chloe would feel being put on the spot, Miri's questions – as subtle as a bull in a china shop – peppering every other sentence. Perhaps if I gave her a little bit of background now, she'd be less forceful when she next saw my daughter.

I gave a sigh, putting my cup down. 'I don't think she's had the best time, if I'm honest. She seems to have got herself mixed up in a nasty relationship.'

'With Tommy's dad?'

I nodded. 'I met him last night,' I admitted, still feeling the after-effects of his slap, the bruise I'd carefully covered with make-up. 'Not that Chloe knows, so please keep that to yourself. He's a nasty piece of work. I think he's been physical with her.'

Miri raised her eyebrows. 'No! Not to Chloe.'

I nodded. 'And from what he was saying, he has no intention of leaving her alone. Tommy complicates things. She'll always be tied to him.'

Miri narrowed her eyes. 'What possessed her to have a child with a man like that?'

I shrugged, not wanting to put the blame on my daughter. She had made mistakes, but hadn't we all over time? 'The important thing is that she's been brave – she's left him now.'

'Yes, but if he won't leave her alone, she'll never be free. He sounds dangerous, Clarissa. You can't let him think he can treat her like that. What a piece of work.'

I nodded, but I didn't know what could be done about it. Chloe would have told me herself if she'd wanted me to know. She would be humiliated if she realised I'd found out how she'd been living.

'Do you think we should get Jeff to go and have a word? He can be intimidating when he wants to be.'

I stifled a laugh, wondering how she could be so oblivious, how she could manage not to see how true I knew that statement to be first-hand. 'No,' I managed, shaking my head. 'It would only make things worse. Honestly, Miri, he's not someone you want to involve yourself with. I'm just going to focus on getting my daughter back on track, make her see her worth. I'm going to help her move forward.' I thought of the way Chloe had stormed out yesterday, her unhealthy fixation with the past.

'I get that, but something needs to be done. Men like that never back down. He'll destroy her life if she's not careful.'

I stared out at the garden, watching Tommy ram a plastic bulldozer into his sandcastle, laughing as it crumbled into pieces, and knew that Mirium was right.

TWENTY-NINE

CHLOE

I couldn't stop fidgeting, pulling at the waistband of the skirt I was wearing, running my sweat-soaked fingers through my hair. I'd arrived at the house on Windsor Avenue far too early after a long, sleepless night spent thinking about the last time I'd seen my brother, and now I felt sure I'd made a horrible mistake in arranging the meeting without warning him what he was walking into. Every path my thoughts travelled took me to the same horrible conclusion. That if he hadn't said goodbye, hadn't cared enough to even leave me a note, explain why he was going, it had to be because it was my fault he'd left.

I knew something had happened that night – something awful. I'd known it the moment I saw my mother's pale, unsmiling face, so different from the warm, loving smile she always wore. Had I done something so bad whilst under the influence of a night terror that he couldn't forgive me? That he'd left without giving me the opportunity to apologise, to try to get help for my sleep disorder? And if that was the case, why would my mother tell me I'd killed him? Was it possible she'd kept his secret too, to protect him from me? The more I thought about it, the more ridiculous I knew I was being. It was impossible. She would never have lied to me, blamed me for something so heinous. He had to have convinced her too.

My brain felt as if it had been put on a spin cycle, my eyes throbbing, my heart racing painfully within the confines of my chest. Nothing made an ounce of sense, but there was one thing I was sure of – if I was right, if it had been my actions that had made him leave so suddenly, then he would be livid to find out I'd set him up now. He wouldn't want to see the sister he'd walked away from.

I stood on the pavement, glancing behind me at the red-brick mansion, wondering if we'd even make it inside, or if he would take one look at me and leave.

'Good morning, Annie!'

My head snapped round, and I saw him walking up the street wearing a well-cut charcoal suit and a dark-blue shirt. His face was freshly shaved, and that same expensive smell from yesterday was cocooning him as he approached. I smiled tentatively, my eyes meeting his, a rush of love, pain, regret hitting me. It was him. It was as if the past fifteen years hadn't happened. His face was a little fuller, and he was no longer a boy, but I would have known him anywhere.

'I hope you haven't been waiting long,' he said, holding out his hand and shaking mine in a firm, confident grip.

'I... Well, no, not long,' I said, still holding his gaze, waiting for the moment it clicked, for the recognition to appear in his expression.

'I'm glad. Although it's a beautiful day. Shall we?' he said, gesturing for me to go ahead as he fished out a bunch of keys from inside his jacket. 'The vendors have gone out, so we have the place to ourselves. It'll give you a chance to really picture yourself in the space.'

He followed me up the three concrete steps to the heavy-looking oak door, sliding a key into the lock and pushing it open. I waited for him to look at me again, but he gave me only the briefest of glances before stepping into the entrance hall. Speechless, wondering how it was that I couldn't take my eyes from him and yet he seemed oblivious to our connection, I followed him inside.

It was a dim, old-fashioned hallway, with a dark wooden staircase dominating the space, the windows obscured by heavy velvet curtains. There was a massive painting on the wall beside the front door, in the Renaissance style – a naked woman lying on a chaise longue with a toddler lounging over her belly, smiling up at her. It was lovely but overwhelming, and I felt claustrophobic, unable to focus.

'Don't let this put you off,' Rhodri said, noting my expression. 'I think it's a nod to the owners' love of history. He's a professor at the university apparently. But the rest of the house is far more modern. Let me show you the kitchen.'

I nodded, unable to speak. There was a sense of embarrassment lingering beneath the surface, now that I realised he wasn't going to break the ice for me. Though my thoughts had travelled to the darkest places in the early hours of this morning, there had also been hope. The fantasy that he would look into my eyes, grab hold of me and hug me tight. That he might even cry as he gave me a plausible explanation for all that had happened. I hadn't wanted to admit to myself quite how desperate I was for that moment with him, and now I felt deflated, flat and more than a little humiliated. Had I *really* meant so little to him? We'd never been the best of friends, but he was my flesh and blood. That meant something, at least to me.

'You see?' he said, striding into the kitchen, where the light made me squint after the gloominess of the hall.

'It's very different, yes,' I agreed, unsure how to respond, how far to take the pretence that I was looking to buy the place.

'Is it to your taste?'

I screwed up my mouth, looking at the lantern above the

pristine white kitchen counter. The pale-green range cooker.
The huge picture windows looking out onto an overly mani-
cured garden, not a single weed or wild flower in sight. It felt
churlish to say no when this place was a show home compared
to the mould-ridden flat I'd just moved into. It was a dream
house – one so far out of my reach it was laughable that I'd even
been allowed to set foot inside – and yet it felt sterile somehow,
the hallway too dramatic, too showy, and this room cold and
soulless in contrast. I would have loved to see evidence of the
family who lived here. See their children's drawings taped to
the fridge, maybe a photograph or something. But despite it
being worth over a million, it wasn't the place I would have
bought if I'd won the lottery.

He turned to me, a quizzical expression on his face, clearly
wondering how he might convince me of the merits of the
house. 'Of course, it's a blank canvas in here – you could really
put your own stamp on it. Some people like to rip everything
out and start from scratch when they're buying somewhere new.
Makes it feel like your own then, don't you agree?'

He was so slick, so salesy, and it seemed to come without
the slightest effort. I couldn't remember him being so smooth,
but then perhaps it was something he'd picked up over the
course of doing the job.

I met his eyes and didn't return his smile. 'You don't know
who I am, do you?' I asked, my voice quiet, trying to hide my
hurt.

'Who you are?' He shook his head. 'Would I have seen you
on TV?' he asked, clearly imagining I was some offended celeb
who'd expected him to ask for a photo.

'It's me... Chloe.'

'Chloe?' he repeated, sounding none the wiser. Was he
really so stupid, so distracted by the thought of his big commis-
sion that it still hadn't clicked?

'Yes, *Chloe*,' I snapped. 'Your sister. I'm your sister, Rhodri!'

Can't you see that? Don't you know who I am? What's the matter with you?' I yelled.

He stared at me, his hand clamped in a fist around the bunch of keys, his lips unmoving. I waited for him to react, to say something, my pulse racing, my cheeks hot.

Finally he cleared his throat. 'I'm afraid we need to get going. I have another viewing in a few minutes and I can't be late. Let me show you out, Annie... uh, Chloe, I mean.'

'But—'

He walked behind me, practically pushing me as he ushered me towards the front door and out onto the steps. He pulled the door closed and locked it, then, without meeting my eye, jogged down to the pavement. 'I'll let you get on then,' he said. 'Must dash.' And he walked briskly down the street back the way he'd come.

I stared after him, wondering how I'd messed it up so badly.

I was still reeling as I made my way through town, my thoughts swirling like a black hole inside my head, unable to fathom my brother's reaction. I'd braced myself for the possibility that he might be angry with me. That he would reject me all over again, though I'd hoped some small part of him would be happy to see me. But to not even be acknowledged – ushered out of the house without a sign of admission that he was indeed who I knew him to be – was shocking. It hadn't crossed my mind that he could have painted over his past so thoroughly that he wouldn't deign to accept I was a part of his history. I couldn't decide if I was more angry or hurt. Certainly confused, and I didn't know what I could do now to get my questions answered. I wasn't about to drop it though. Not until I knew what the hell was going on.

I was lost in thought as I rounded the corner, and didn't see the woman heading towards me until it was too late. I heard my

name called and glanced up, coming face to face with Irene,
Scott's mother. From the look in her eyes, I knew I'd have to
stop and make small talk. She was a painfully thin woman, with
brassy dyed copper hair, her wiry steel-grey roots several inches
long. Her face had a hollowed appearance, the wrinkles
covering every last inch of her sallow papery skin. Even her
cheeks looked as if they'd been scrunched up into a ball, the
lines criss-crossing in every direction.

I wondered if Scott had been to see her yet. Unlike me, he
had never lost touch with his mother, despite living on the
streets. I'd been surprised when he first took me to see her, especially given what I knew of his childhood. Irene was a cold,
cruel woman, so unlike my own mum, and I couldn't help but
blame her for the way her son had turned out. Unsurprisingly,
I'd never been keen on her spending time with Tommy, and it
was a sore subject between us, one she brought up often.

'I saw Scott yesterday,' she said, her expression betraying
nothing of what he might have told her. I wondered if she knew
how he treated me. If she cared.

'Right.' I nodded.

'I asked him when he was going to bring Tommy to see me,
and he didn't have an answer for me. It's not right to keep him
from his family like this. Not fair – on *him*, I mean. He's missing
out on having a grandmother.'

I sucked in my bottom lip. Clearly Scott hadn't told her I
had left. Was it because he was ashamed of what he'd done, of
forcing me into walking away? Or, I thought with a sinking
feeling in the pit of my belly, was it that he wasn't ready to let
me go? That he couldn't accept the power I'd seized for myself
in leaving him? I knew it would have irritated him, the lack of
control, the way I'd made the decision for both of us. I felt a
tremor travel up my spine, wondering what it meant for my
safety if he was still giving people the impression we were
together.

'Irene, I'm not sure if you're aware,' I said, glad of the busy street, the pedestrians all around enabling me to feel protected, 'but Scott and I are no longer living together. I've left him, and he's made the decision not to see our son.'

Her mouth dropped open, and I could see genuine shock in her eyes. 'He never said that to me!'

I shrugged. 'I won't go into the details, but you can ask him all about it. I'm sure you can understand how busy I've been with all the changes. I haven't had time to arrange social visits – I'm trying to put my life back together and take care of my son.'

'I don't believe Scott wouldn't want to keep in contact. Surely that isn't what he told you? And if he did, it would have been in anger, in the heat of the moment. You know he can be impulsive, harsh even, when he's feeling backed into a corner. But he wouldn't have meant it. Don't take his son from him, Chloe.'

I shook my head. 'Scott isn't my problem. He's brought all this on himself. I don't have time to pander to him; I have enough to do, and I've given him far too much of myself already.'

Irene took a pack of cigarettes from her back pocket and lit one, the tiny lines around her mouth deepening as she sucked in a lungful of smoke. 'Are social services involved? Do they know you've taken Tommy?'

It was voiced like a casual question, but I couldn't help feeling she was making a threat. 'No, Irene, they're not, and now that he's free of his father, there's no need for them to be. He's going to have a nice life. Safe. Secure. Unlike the one Scott was prepared to offer us.' I watched her face, wondering what she was thinking, plotting. If she might call them herself and create another layer of chaos in my life. 'Look, I can't stop any longer, I'm in a rush,' I said.

She grabbed my arm as I tried to pass, the cigarette still clamped between her fingers. I could feel the butt pressing into the skin by my elbow. 'You and Scott may have fallen out, but Tommy is my grandson. And I have a right to see him. I *want* to see him. Think about it, Chloe.'

I yanked my arm away, half tempted to lie and tell her I would arrange something soon, afraid of what she might do if I didn't, but then I hardened my resolve. I wouldn't let Scott or his toxic family push me around any longer.

'Bye, Irene,' I said, hitching my bag on my shoulder and walking away. I could feel her stare burning into my back and wondered how long it would be before she confronted Scott. And what he might do to me when he found out I'd told her the truth.

THIRTY

CLARISSA

I stifled a yawn as I pushed the hoover around the living room, my eyes itching with the need to close. I could hear Tommy upstairs as he talked to himself, busy working on the puzzle I'd picked up from the charity shop to keep him occupied. I had barely managed more than a few hours' sleep last night, and now I was irritable and longing for my bed. Every time I closed my eyes, I saw either my son or my husband, their faces burning into the frame of my mind's eye. And when I tried to bat them away, unwilling to fall into the trap of thinking about them, it was Jeff's cold, hard eyes that replaced them.

Over and over again, I'd begun to fall asleep, only to find myself in a nightmare I'd had to fight to escape, clawing my way back to consciousness before I could sink too deep into the horrors of my memories. It seemed silly, in the cold light of day, that I'd let myself get so worked up over the past, but the events of the last week had brought up a whole host of unwelcome thoughts and fears, and I was struggling to squash them.

Chloe's quite frankly absurd claim that she'd seen her brother was playing on my mind, bringing up questions and worries for her well-being. And though Jeff's behaviour was far from new to me, it was something I hadn't seen in years. Over-stepping. Pushing his nose into my family, my business, hyper-focused on Tommy in a way that sent chills through me and made me want to pack up and leave my house – the home that I loved. I couldn't believe I was considering letting that odious man push me out, but I was afraid of the consequences of stay-ing. Of what he might do.

I rammed the hoover beneath the coffee table, though the carpet was already clean, unable to stop the memories from flooding back. I could still conjure the smell of the aftershave the police officer had been wearing when he'd knocked at my front door to tell me my husband had died. Jeff had been the only person present when Reece had collapsed in his back garden. A heart attack, the coroner had said, though it had seemed so unlikely. He'd been forty-three years old, but they'd said it was becoming more common in younger people, espe-cially men. The stresses of modern living, they'd told me, and I'd felt as if they were blaming me, making it *my* fault somehow. Jeff had been with him until the end, and yet his twisted mind had tried to find a way to make *me* responsible for what had happened.

He'd never liked me. And if I'd considered his fixation unhealthy before Reece died, it was nothing compared to how focused he became on my son in the aftermath. If he got wind of Chloe's fantasy that she'd seen Rhodri, I could only imagine how it would fuel his obsession. Not for the first time, I wished I could call the police, have him removed from my life for good, but he was clever – too clever to ever enable me to do something like that.

I pushed the faces of my dead husband and son from my mind and closed my eyes as I tried to think of some way to get Jeff out of our lives and keep him from my grandson. There was a solution. There had to be. I just had to be clever too.

THIRTY-ONE

CHLOE

Burts. I stopped dead, my hand gripping the fridge door in a white-knuckled hold as the name hit me out of the blue. I'd been trying to remember it so hard, but to no avail, and now, having given up trying, my mind far too preoccupied with Rhodri's strange behaviour and Irene's threat of social services, it had finally come to the surface. My childhood friend had been called Annie Burts. Her mum had been Pat, her dad Bill, and she'd had twin younger sisters, Jessie and Poppy. Now that I'd opened the door to the memory, I could see it all so clearly.

They'd had a cat – a grey Persian who'd liked to cuddle on my lap when I went over to play and whom Annie had been completely besotted with. She'd brushed his fur every day after school, and he had slept on her pillow, his tuna breath hot against her cheek – something that had turned my stomach but she'd never seemed to mind.

I slammed the fridge door closed, pulled my phone from my back pocket and opened the internet browser, typing in the name hurriedly, fearful that it might escape me again. I paced the kitchen floor as the page loaded, then clicked on images one by one, staring hard at each of the faces. An old lady. A teenage

girl. A news story about a woman of the same name being
sentenced to fourteen years in prison for armed robbery. I
clicked the article, breathing a sigh of relief when I saw the
photograph and it wasn't her. I clicked back, scrolling some
more.

There was another article, just a photo of a cat, the silly
headline about an award for most disloyal feline giving me no
hope at all, but I clicked on it all the same, scrolling down, skim-
reading about the ginger tom that had run away from home
sixteen times in the past year and been found sleeping on every
neighbour's bed in the street. At the bottom of the article was a
tiny photo of the cat being cuddled by a woman with dark hair,
pale skin and a freckled nose. My stomach tightened as I
enlarged the picture, zooming in on her face. Her eyes were
crinkled as she smiled, and I felt a rush of warmth, a feeling of
coming home. I hadn't known I was missing her until I laid eyes
upon her, but now I felt as if I'd been lost without her all these
years without ever realising the hole she'd left behind.

At the bottom of the article was a link to a Facebook page
called 'The Adventures of Fat Tom', and I followed it. Two
things stood out to me. One, that Annie was still absolutely mad
about cats. And two, that she was no longer in Norway with her
family. The photos were quite clearly set in England. The green
recycling bin Fat Tom was preening himself on. The kitchen
counter he was sitting on looking longingly up at a larder filled
with tins all labelled in English. And to my joy, there was a
picture of the cat walking serenely down the middle of the
street he'd so unfaithfully paraded himself along, sneaking in
windows and through open back doors. A sign on the corner
was just visible in the frame, and when I zoomed in, I could
make out the words *Magpie Close*.

Heart racing, I navigated to Google Maps, my fingers
shaking as I typed in the street name. Five options came up. I
clicked on the first, instantly seeing a beachside road and

knowing it was wrong. I tried the next and spun the little cursor round, then clicked the tab to compare the map to the photo on the cat's page. *Bingo.*

I put the phone down on the side, my hand pressing hard against my mouth as I took in the fact that Annie lived in Bursledon. I could be there in twenty minutes on the train. I stared at the map, wondering what to do; then, making up my mind, I grabbed my keys and headed out the door.

The street was quiet, off the main road and lined with tall trees that cast shade over the small gardens fronting the terraced houses. Now that I was here, I felt silly and embarrassed for having come all this way without a plan. Not only did I have no idea which house was Annie's, but I couldn't imagine what she would think of my having tracked her down in such a round-about way. I should have tried to find a personal Facebook page, or sent a message via the cat's page, but at the time, I'd been so excited by the thought of seeing her again that I hadn't been thinking straight. I was regretting it now.

I walked slowly up one side of the road, looking at the unre-markable front doors as I passed, seeing nothing that might give me a clue as to which house was Annie's. Reaching the end, I crossed over and made my way back down the other side. There was nobody around, and this too made me feel like I'd acted in haste, thoughtless and stupid. Of course the street was deserted. It was the middle of the day. No doubt everyone was at work. Perhaps Annie too.

I closed my eyes, my head spinning from exhaustion after yet another sleepless night, and leaned against a postbox as I tried to organise my thoughts. I *wasn't* going mad. I was certain of it. I was tired, admittedly, and afraid – of Scott, of how I would keep my son safe, of not being able to get another job, and of the strange, confusing mess that was Rhodri and Annie.

But I knew I hadn't invented these stories in my mind. I knew the man who had walked out on me this morning was the same boy I'd argued with as a child over the swing set in the garden, the boy who'd been cheeky, naughty, but my brother all the same.

And Annie – I had no idea what I would say to her when I saw her, what I even wanted to ask. But a part of me thought that seeing her would remind me of her leaving and the imaginary friend who had stepped into her shoes. I needed to keep moving forward, figure out what was going on before I really did drive myself to the brink of insanity with all these unanswered questions.

I reached the end of the road, still clueless as to which house might be the right one. I had two choices. I could head back to the station, back to town, where I could go and cuddle up with my son at my mother's house, or I could swallow my embarrassment and start knocking on doors. She was the famous cat's owner. A neighbourhood sensation. *Someone* would be able to tell me where she lived. I tucked my hair behind my ears, squared my shoulders and walked up the path of the first house on Magpie Close.

I cleared my throat before rapping on the door. A moment later, it opened, an elderly woman staring at me expectantly.

'Hi, I'm Chloe Phillips. I'm here for the interview.' The words rolled off my tongue without my ever instructing them to, the lie spilling out as a plan morphed into action in a split second.

'I'm sorry, what interview?' the woman asked, her brow creasing as if she were trying to remember.

'About the cat? Fat Tom? I'm a journalist, you see, for the papers. I arranged with Miss Burts to come and talk to her. Is she here?' I said, craning my head to look past her shoulder into the house.

'Oh!' She broke into a smile. 'You mean *Annie*. You've got

the wrong address, love. She's at number nineteen, just there.' She pointed to a house on the same side of the road a little way up.

'Oh, really? I'm so sorry to have disturbed you. I have a new assistant and she's not very good. This is the second time she's sent me to the wrong place. Thanks for helping me out.'

'Not a problem.' She smiled, stepping back into the house. 'You can tell Annie from me, that cheeky beggar almost made off with my dinner last night. I left the chicken on the side while I popped to the loo, and when I came back, he was halfway through my kitchen window with his eyes on the prize. Gave him a squirt with a water pistol I keep just for him. I'm terribly allergic, but he doesn't seem to care.' She shook her head, still smiling.

I nodded, thanking her again as I walked back down the path, buzzing at what I'd just done.

When I reached number nineteen, I checked to make sure the old lady had gone back inside, then opened the creaking gate. The door knocker was a brass cat viewed from the back, something I should have noticed.

I lifted the tail and banged it against the door, shuffling impatiently from one foot to the other as I waited. I knocked again, hearing a muted miaow from within, picturing the fat ginger tom preening himself on the doormat, but nothing else happened. Irritated, I opened my bag and pulled out a pad and pen, leaning against the door as I scribbled a note.

Hi Annie,

I'm not sure if you remember me, but we were neighbours and good friends in junior school. I tracked you down via your celebrity cat and would love to catch up. I'm still in Southampton, never left – I'm sure you've seen a lot more of the world than me! I would love to hear how your life changed

after you moved abroad. Surprised to hear you've come back,
though they do say there's no place like home, don't they? I'll
leave my phone number and email address below. Be great to
hear from you.

Chloe Phillips

I reread the note three times, feeling self-conscious and
indecisive, wondering why I'd waffled so much; then, making
up my mind, I folded it in half, shoved it through the letter box
and walked away. It was in her hands now.

I spun the lid off the bottle of Chardonnay, pouring it into a
chipped coffee mug, wishing I had a proper glass to use
instead. The wine was acidic and warm, the bottle having
been won in a raffle several months earlier; I'd only managed
to keep hold of it because Scott couldn't stand wine in any
form. I'd have avoided it myself usually, but right now, I
needed something to take the edge off the delirium that was
creeping over me. My temples throbbed, my head pulsing with
adrenaline and exhaustion, the insomnia peaking, filling me
with that familiar sense of dread and terror that I'd learned to
expect. I couldn't stop my thoughts from travelling down dark
pathways, and as much as my stomach protested, my throat
closing at the paint-thinner quality of the drink, I forced it
down, needing the warmth to carry away some of my
anxieties.

I slumped on the sofa, clutching the mug in my hand as if it
was a shield. In another life, I could have happily given up...
given in to the gift of numbness that came with losing yourself
in a bottle. Blotted out the past, the future, concerning myself
with nothing but the goal of obtaining the next drink. It would
certainly have been easier. But I had a son to consider, responsi-

bilities to think about, and tempting as it was, I wouldn't let myself fall into that trap.

But right now, I thought, swallowing back another burning mouthful, Tommy was with my mum, and I was here alone, lost, fidgety with the uneasy fear paired with the hyper-colour memories that flitted across my mind, torturing me.

I'd called Mum on the way back from Annie's to let her know I was coming over, but she'd told me it wasn't convenient. To come tomorrow instead. She'd been explaining why, and I'd tried to argue, but the poor reception on the train made it impossible to communicate, and when I'd called again, she hadn't picked up. I wasn't going to give up though. I would wait an hour, and then I was going to head over to her house anyway. I needed to see my son.

I glanced at the wine, feeling guilty for indulging in the middle of the day, hoping Mum and Tommy wouldn't smell it on my breath, but not guilty enough to pour it away just yet.

I pulled my phone from my pocket, navigating to my emails, needing distraction. The summer newsletter had come in from Tommy's preschool, and I clicked on it, reading through the bulletins about parents forgetting to bring sunhats and late-pickup fees, followed by the usual descriptions about what the children had been up to this term. There had been the summer market held on the field behind the nursery, where they'd fundraised for a new soft-play room. Then the visit to the farm – a trip I'd kept Tommy off for as they'd wanted an additional payment of nine pounds, which I couldn't convince Scott to give me at the time. One of the staff had tried to persuade me to send him so he wouldn't miss out, but I'd brushed her off, and we'd spent the day having a picnic of cheap home-made sandwiches at the park. I hadn't mentioned the farm, relieved that he was young enough not to notice that he'd missed out on the fun. That wouldn't last for ever.

I remembered the WhatsApp group I'd been added to in

Tommy's first week, and went to find it now, seeing the stream of unread messages I'd left muted, hungrily scrolling in a toxic state of self-pity. I couldn't help but envy those parents who'd been able to treat their children to the day out, several of them having gone along as helpers too, despite the fact they'd had to pay the entrance fee themselves to do so, doubling the price. They were so lucky to have the means to do that.

Lots of them had shared photos of their children, accompanied by comments. *Freddy feeding a lamb*, his mum had written beneath a picture of a ginger-topped boy with a cheeky glint in his eye, a patchwork teddy clutched under one arm, the lamb's bottle in his free hand. A parent called Michelle had added, *Maddy didn't want to put the guinea pig down. So sweet!* I sighed, taking another sip of my wine, only half looking at the smiling faces, trying not to resent their happiness as I bent forward to put my drink down.

The last image was of a girl sitting on a little plastic stool, a tiny yellow chick clutched gently in her hands. The caption read, *Molly is in love. Shame we can't have birds – Fat Tom would dispose of them in seconds, feral feline that he is!*

I froze, then my mug banged down hard on the table, my fingers beginning to tremble, my thoughts suddenly racing as I gripped the phone close, looking at the name of the parent who'd posted. *Annie.* My mouth turned dry.

There was no photo of her when I clicked on her avatar, just a cartoon image of a kitten. What were the chances that another Annie had a cat of the same name? I zoomed in on the photograph of the girl with the chick, poring over her features. The pale skin. The smattering of freckles. The big round eyes. It couldn't be...

With fumbling hands, I navigated to the photograph I had saved of Annie and Fat Tom, clicking back and forth between the two pictures. The resemblance was undeniable. This was no coincidence. This had to be her child. Annie had a daughter at the same preschool as Tommy.

I sat back against the cushion, the realisation hitting me like a ton of bricks. Jeff had told me Annie had been outside my mother's house the night I killed Rhodri. Someone had been sending me threatening letters demanding justice for what I had done. One of them had come from within the nursery. It *had* to be a staff member or parent.

The wine threatened to come back up as I realised the implication. The letters weren't just an empty threat. Some practical joke that happened to have hit a nerve. Annie *knew*. She knew what I'd done. Which meant my mother had got it wrong. She must have been thinking of some other girl I'd turned into an imaginary friend. Because Annie was real, had been witness to my crime, and was about to ruin my life. And I couldn't let her do that.

THIRTY-TWO

By the time I reached my mum's house, my shoulders were aching, my head was pounding even harder and I was beginning to regret the wine. It had been an emotionally draining day, the new knowledge of who was sending me the letters bringing up more questions that I didn't have the strength to answer, and all I wanted now was to see my sweet boy. Hold him close to me, breathe in the smell of his skin, though lately the warm, biscuity fragrance of his neck had been replaced by a strong soapy smell – my mother had always been a stickler for nightly baths and hair-washing. Once I had him home, we'd revert to the gentle baby soap and weekly baths we'd always done prior to his stay with his grandma.

It was getting harder and harder to be away from him. And now, with maintenance sorted with Scott, and the redundancy package I'd wangled from my old job, I couldn't think of a reason not to take him home. I could continue my job hunt whilst he was at preschool. It was time.

I knocked on the front door, then rubbed my temples hard with the tips of my fingers, trying to disperse some of the tension. I didn't want to let Tommy see how much I was struggling. I had to protect him. I'd failed at it too many times in the past, and it was no longer an option.

I knocked again, wondering if they were in the garden and couldn't hear me. I hadn't bothered to call again. I was sure, whatever my mum was busy with, I could keep out of her way. If she had guests, I'd take Tommy out for a walk. It would be lovely to have him to myself for a while.

I waited, listening for the sound of footsteps, and when nobody came, I walked round to the side gate and let myself in. But the garden was empty, and when I tried the back door, it was locked. I felt like bursting into tears. I'd come all this way. I'd walked miles. I was exhausted and hot and dehydrated, completely fed up, and I wanted my little boy.

I pulled out my phone and called Mum's number, but it went straight to her answerphone, and I hung up without leaving a message, not wanting to snap at her. I couldn't expect her to sit in all day waiting for me, and yet to find them gone and not know where they were made me anxious and angry.

I stormed back to the front of the house, wondering how long they would be; whether I should wait or just give up and go home, put myself to bed and see if by some miracle I might actually fall asleep. I was so tired, and yet I knew it was pointless. It would be a few more days before I was able to crash and switch off. Before my body stopped fighting the process and gave in. Trying would only frustrate me. Lying in bed with my heart pounding, my thoughts racing, fearful of what would happen if I never slept again, was the worst thing I could do to myself. No, I would keep going until I couldn't any more. It had to be that way.

I stepped back and looked up at the bedroom window, then banged on the door again though it was useless. I turned, slumping back against it in frustration. As I did so, I saw a glint from the concrete lip of the porch above me. Reaching up, my fingers clamped around something small and metal. I opened them, a smile spreading across my face as I saw the key. I glanced across the road, seeing I was alone, then slid it into the lock and let myself inside, closing the door behind me.

The house was blessedly cool, the smell of furniture polish and bleach lingering in the air, taking me back to my childhood. I went straight to the kitchen, sticking my mouth under the tap and gulping down huge mouthfuls of tepid water, then straightened up and filled a glass, looking out of the window as I drank it down. Wiping my mouth with the back of my hand, I turned to the empty room, glancing around, wishing Tommy were here.

I put the glass in the sink, then went upstairs, into my old bedroom, where he'd been sleeping. It was tidy, the bed made neatly, the pale-green sheets too boring for my imaginative little boy. We would be sharing a room again when he came home with me, but I wanted to take him out to choose some pictures for the walls, a rug or something for his toy corner – whatever he liked that showed off his personality. This room was clean and tidy, but it didn't feel like my son's, and I walked out, closing the door behind me, feeling sad and disconnected from him.

I didn't know what prompted me to push open Mum's door instead of heading back downstairs to wait for them to return, but I found myself padding quietly across the thick cream carpet towards her dressing table. I sat on the little stool, lifting the lids of her various face creams, smelling them one by one, my eyes roaming around the room. Even in here, there were no photos. No old wedding picture, no snaps of her with me and Rhodri as children. No indication that she'd ever had a life other than the one she led now.

Curiosity got the better of me, and though I knew she would be annoyed if she could see me now, I couldn't help myself, couldn't seem to stop myself from peeking. It seemed so innocent. So simple.

I slid open the drawers one by one, finding neat rows of folded clothes. The bras and matching pants in various shades of beige were paired neatly together. The pop socks and tights balled and lined up in rows. There were no mementoes. No signs of her inner thoughts or workings. She'd always been a private person, never talking about her feelings, just getting on with the things that needed doing, as so many women of her generation had, but I longed to know what really went on in her mind. If she thought about my father. If she missed him still.

I squatted, reaching under the bed, my hand colliding with something hard. I slid out a shoebox, lifting the lid without much hope, expecting to find a pair of sandals or something equally boring. My eyes widened when I saw the stack of hand-written notes. The fat envelope with *Jessops* printed on the front, surely containing the photos I knew she had to have kept somewhere. It was a relief to hold them in my hands and know that she'd missed us – thought of us over the years. To picture her sinking onto her bedroom carpet, reading old love letters from my dad, her eyes damp as she spread the photographs on the floor around her, maybe speaking out loud the things she wished she could say in person. Did she, like me, talk about her day with the 2D images of her loved ones?

I smiled, tipping the pile of photos into my palm, seeing my own wide grin, tiny sparkling baby teeth peeking over rosebud lips, and big wide eyes – still so innocent and full of curiosity – staring back at me. I must have been only two or three in the picture. The next was me and Mum, the photo clearly taken by her – the original selfie. We were somewhere green, tall, leafy trees filling the background, her free arm around my chest, cuddling me close. We were both laughing, neither of us looking at the camera, instead focused on each other. We looked so happy. It filled me with warmth to remember now, all those things I'd let myself forget.

I shuffled through the photos, pausing to take in each image: my first haircut, the time I'd played Mary in the school nativity, the trips to the beach and the zoo. But as I continued to sift through the stack faster and faster, I felt my smile falter, then slide off my face. They were all of me. Me and Mum, or me alone. Not a single one of either my dad or my brother. Not even in the background.

I returned to the first picture, confused, then pushed the photographs back into their envelope, riffling through the shoebox to see if there might be another set. Perhaps she'd organised them so we each had a separate envelope? But there were no more.

Lying on my stomach, I peered under the bed to see if I could have missed a second box, but no... this was the only one.

I sat back up, frowning. Why would she only have memories of me? She was a mother of two. She had lost us both. Surely she wanted to see his face as well. Had there been some accident? A fire, perhaps, destroying her memories of Rhodri and Dad? It was baffling.

My hand sifted through the letters, and though I had intended to respect her privacy, never considered reading the personal love notes between her and my father, I found I had questions that couldn't be satiated without looking. Just one, I promised myself. Just a glance.

In another lifetime, I could imagine me and Mum sitting here together, her sharing the letters with me, talking about the man she'd once had a whirlwind relationship with that had led to marriage and children. But we weren't there right now. There was a block between us that hadn't been there before I left. Unspoken words, fears, apologies I wasn't sure how to make. And I knew she wouldn't want to talk about Dad with me. That even all these years later, it still hurt to have lost him.

I slid the yellowed paper from the small envelope with no name or address on the front. He must have left these around the house for her to find. It was impossibly romantic. Scott had never, even in his most loving days, done anything so thoughtful. I pictured her face, coming downstairs with baby Rhodri on her hip, tired after a night of feeding him, to find a little note by the kettle, encouraging her to keep going, telling her what a wonderful mother she was, how proud he was of her.

I wished more than anything that he'd survived. That I could speak to him now. That *I* had known him as she had. It was silly to be jealous of her relationship with him – she was his *wife* – and yet jealous was exactly the right word to describe the emotion I felt now, holding this secret communication between them in my hand. I longed for a note of my own to cherish.

I rubbed my thumb across the back of the folded paper, thinking of his strong hands pressing down along the crisp edge. Maybe she wouldn't miss one? I could take it, read it late at night when I was so alone, when it felt as if I was the only person still awake in the whole world. I could read his loving words and pretend it was *me* he was writing to. *Me* he was proud of.

I was about to open the note when I heard the sound of a car pulling up on the drive outside. Without hesitation, I shoved everything bar the letter in my hand back into the shoebox and kicked it under the bed, sliding my father's note into my pocket and running down the stairs. I heard the key in the lock and reached the kitchen just as the door swung open, steadying my breath and picking up the glass of water I'd left on the side.

Tommy came into the room carrying a shopping bag on his narrow shoulder, looking so grown up and serious as he helped his grandma. 'Mummy!' he yelled, dropping it to the ground and rushing over to me.

I scooped him up, kissing his cheeks, holding him tight. 'I missed you,' I said, breathing him in, forcing myself not to squeeze too hard and hurt him. I loved him so much it was hard to moderate it. I needed him home, needed him back where he belonged.

My mother came in behind him, a strange expression on her face as she saw me standing there.

'Hi, Mum.'

She shook her head. 'How did you...'

'I found the spare key. I hope you don't mind,' I said, shifting Tommy onto my hip, unwilling to put him back down yet. 'I didn't realise you'd be out, and I was so thirsty.' I held up the glass as if to prove my point.

'Right.' She frowned, then nodded, raising her eyes to mine and offering a bright smile that felt off somehow. 'No, of course I don't mind. I hope you haven't been waiting too long for us? We needed to pop to the shops. I'd forgotten how much young boys eat.'

'He likes his food,' I agreed, wondering why she was being weird. Her tone felt stilted, and I couldn't help but feel she was annoyed that I'd come inside without asking first. And that was without even knowing the truth of what I'd been up to, I thought, the letter burning a hole in my back pocket. 'I expect he's cost you a fortune in snacks. But I have good news.'

'Tommy,' she said, her tone curt, 'go upstairs and wash your hands. And change your shirt please – there's a mark on that one.'

I laughed. 'That can wait, can't it?'

'Tommy.' She raised her eyebrows, and I felt him slide down my body, heading for the stairs without a word.

'I'll see you in a minute, darling,' I called after him, feeling annoyed that she'd spoiled my moment with my son. I'd only just got him back in my arms, and she was already worrying about him being presentable. I'd seen him in far worse states, and I hadn't even noticed a mark on the bloody shirt!

I folded my arms, breathing in and counting to ten. I had to remind myself that she'd gone out of her way, dropped everything to help me out. It was hardly a surprise that she was feeling strained, tired. But after today, everything would get easier.

'Well,' I said, once I'd calmed down a little. 'What I was

going to say was that I'll be taking Tommy home with me tonight.'

'What?' She paused in the unpacking of the shopping bag, shaking her head. 'Have you got another job?'

'No, but I have enough money to get by. I was given some compensation from my last job, and Tommy's dad is paying support now. I'll be fine. I'll keep looking for a job while he's in nursery; it won't be long before something comes up.'

'So you're speaking to him? Tommy's dad?'

'Not exactly speaking, no... but we've come to an agreement of sorts.'

She stared at me. 'No.'

'I'm sorry? No *what*?'

'No. You cannot take Tommy home with you.'

I put the glass on the counter. 'Excuse me?'

'I'm sorry, love, but you aren't ready. I have to do what's best for Tommy. And that is not going home with you. Not yet.'

The wind was taken out of my sails; I was shocked and humiliated that she really thought so little of me.

'I'm his mother.'

'I know. But it's too soon.'

'I disagree. I wanted him to come here so I could get my finances in order and rent a flat. And I've done those things. There's nothing else I need to do. It's time.'

'No. I mean it, Chloe. You might have a roof over your head, but don't you think he needs more than that? For Christ's sake, you're seeing imaginary people! Rhodri is dead! He's dead, by your own hand, and yet you think he's walking around town as plain as day. I know you still think it! That he's out there alive somehow. Do you think I can't see right through you? You've always been easy for me to read. I *know* you, Chloe. Tell me I'm wrong. Look me in the eye and tell me you aren't having these hallucinations!'

'I...' I shook my head.

'And you *really* think I'm going to send you off with my grandson with you going through all that? Are you even sleeping?'

I looked down at my hands and saw they were shaking. What on earth was happening? I cast my mind back and couldn't think of a single time she'd ever spoken to me this way, ever made me feel like this – small and inept. Was she really so afraid of what I might do to my son that I'd driven her to this reaction? It frightened me, this uncharted ground, the way she was looking at me like a stranger, like she didn't trust me at all. Had I created this situation?

I tried to put myself in her shoes. She believed I'd killed my brother, and up until a few days ago, I'd believed that too. She knew I was going through a hard time. And she clearly cared deeply for Tommy. But she was wrong if she thought he wasn't safe to be alone with me.

I swallowed, steadying myself, though I could feel unwelcome tears burning the backs of my eyeballs at the shock of her harsh tone. 'I never sleep well without him,' I replied, my voice quiet, measured. 'I will when he's back. I know I will.'

She folded her arms. 'No, Chloe. *No*. You asked for my help, and I'm giving it. You need to sort yourself out. Get the silly fantasies you've been giving in to out of your head and get your focus back on what's real. And *then* we can talk about him coming home.'

I stared at her, unable to come up with an argument, though a voice inside my head screamed that Tommy was mine. She had no right to stop me taking him. But what if she was right?

She looked away from me, glancing towards the hallway. I could hear Tommy singing to himself in the bathroom, the occasional splash of water. He would have filled up the sink and mixed in the soap to give his hands a little bath, as he called it – his favourite way to get washed. She pursed her lips, and I wished she would hug me, offer the kindness and comfort I'd always been able to seek from her.

Instead, her tone was cold when she finally spoke. 'I think you should go.' She turned towards the shopping bag, continuing to unpack. 'It's nearly time for dinner, and I only bought enough for me and Tommy. You can come back tomorrow when you've calmed down.'

'But I've been waiting to see him! I need to spend time with him. I don't think you realise how much we're missing each other. How much we need each other!' I said, trying to appeal to her good nature. 'It's destroying me being apart from him.'

'And it's confusing for him when you keep popping in and out with no schedule, no warning. You don't get to see how hard it is for him to adjust when you leave – something *I* have to deal with every bedtime. Children need consistency, Chloe. Something he's clearly been lacking up until now.'

She took in my horror-struck expression as I absorbed the message that my son was struggling far more than she'd previously let on, and her face softened. 'I'm not saying it's your fault. I know you've done your best.'

'But it's not been good enough. Is that what you're trying to tell me?'

She stared at me, unspeaking, and I felt the tears well up again. This time I couldn't stop them from spilling over, running in a scalding stream down my cheeks. I didn't want Tommy to see me like this. His mother in tears had been something he'd had to bear witness to far too many times before, and I'd made a promise to myself after leaving Scott that it would never happen again. He needed to feel safe, and the last thing I wanted was to remind him of those awful times when his mummy had been bleeding and sobbing, and he'd felt helpless and scared.

I picked up my bag, knowing I had no choice but to leave. 'Tell him... tell him I'll be here tomorrow afternoon. And that

I'll be taking him to the park. Just the two of us,' I added pointedly.

'Let's see, shall we.' She walked towards me, placing her soft, warm hand on my forearm, and I saw a glimpse of the mother I had grown up with, the woman who had always known the right thing to say to make me feel better. But this time, there were no words that could help. 'Get some rest, Chloe. You look burned out.'

I gave a curt nod, then walked away before I could say anything I might regret. I closed the front door quietly, hating that I was leaving without a goodbye for Tommy, and for the first time since he'd arrived here, I couldn't help but feel I'd made the wrong choice.

THIRTY-THREE

CLARISSA

I stood stiff as a board as Jeff stretched out his long legs on my sofa as if he'd bought and paid for it, his eyes challenging me to complain, to make a scene in front of Mirium. She'd said she would pop round with a bottle of wine after Tommy was in bed – a chance for me to unwind, she'd claimed – but she'd turned up at nine with a bottle of red, a Victoria sponge and Jeff looming over her shoulder, his smug smile making me want to slam the door in their faces. She'd poured three glasses, exclaiming how nice it was for us all to catch up, and I'd had to bite my tongue hard to stop myself from disagreeing, upsetting her.

'We saw Chloe leave in a hurry again earlier,' Jeff said, pressing his damp, rubbery lips to his glass. It made my insides recoil, and I made a mental note to throw that one in the recycling bin. 'She didn't stay long after you got home, did she?'

'She was just dropping a few things off for Tommy. He's going to be staying a little longer, so she wanted to make sure he had everything he needs. She's such a good mother to him,' I said, keeping my tone sweet, as I replayed the image of him standing in Tommy's bedroom door just days ago. How good he was at hiding his true colours, I thought, picking up the knife and turning to Miri. 'This looks lovely. Shall I serve?'

'Oh, yes please. You'll have to save a couple of slices for Tommy and Chloe. I remember how much she used to love my cakes. Always had a sweet tooth, didn't she?'

I nodded, cutting into the powdery sponge, though as far as I could recall, Chloe had never shown any particular preference for sweets.

Miri leaned back in her chair, making herself comfortable. 'We had Joseph and the grandkids over for dinner yesterday while Emma was out on a girls' night. Told him that Chloe's back on the scene. Obviously it came as quite a shock to him... He had a lot of questions,' she said, taking the plate I passed her and picking up the slab of cake without bothering to reach for a fork.

'I'm sure,' I replied non-committally. 'How's the garden, Jeff? Roses coming along okay?' I asked, feigning interest for Mirium's benefit.

He raised an eyebrow but didn't offer a response. 'It sparked quite the debate over the dinner table,' he said, picking up on Miri's comment as if I hadn't spoken. I fizzed with anger at the cheek of him. 'We were remembering all sorts, weren't we, Mirium? About Reece... Rhodri. God, that boy was a green-fingered lad if ever I saw one. He always pruned my roses to within an inch of their life, and yet they never seemed to die. Interesting, that.'

'Really.' My tone was sardonic, and I took a sip of my wine, wishing I could tell them to leave. It had been an exhausting evening, with tears from Tommy after Chloe's dramatic departure, and now I just wanted a long soak in the bath followed by bed. I was drained, both emotionally and physically – even my bones felt tired – and I didn't want to play nice with a man I hated just to keep the peace with my best friend. Why had she brought him here? There were things I wanted to talk to her about. Things I certainly wouldn't say with Jeff listening in. Did she really not see how he was goading me, taunting me by bringing up the past? Did she not realise what he was doing?

She finished her cake, wiping crumbs from her mouth, and stood up with a smile. 'Just going to pop to the loo, then I'll make a cuppa. I always fancy one after pudding. I'll have that after,' she said, nodding towards the glass of red on the table.

'I can make the tea,' I said, leaning forward to place my wine on the table, keen to make my escape before she left me alone with Jeff.

'No, don't be silly. I know my way around the kitchen, and you've been rushed off your feet with the little one all day. Sit. *Relax*. Jeff, why don't you fill Clarissa in on your plans for the flower show?' She flashed me a smile. 'I'm so proud of him – he's got some gorgeous ones for the competition this year. I know he's going to get first place.'

She walked out, and I tried not to cringe as I made unintentional eye contact with her creepy husband.

'He's still here then.'

I didn't need to ask who he meant. And I wasn't prepared to answer his question. It was none of his business. 'Tell me about your flowers, Jeff,' I said, my tone flat and uninterested.

'Reece used to be good in the garden, I recall,' he mused, taking another swig of his wine. I noticed he hadn't touched the slice of cake I'd dumped on a plate for him. I didn't know if he was trying to offend me – perhaps he'd forgotten his wife had been the one to bake it. I couldn't care less if he sat there hungry, trying to spite me.

'Why don't you head off?' I hissed, mindful of Mirium overhearing. 'I told you to stay away from us. Away from Tommy.'

'And I heard you.' He gave a smile that flashed his yellowed teeth, then propped one foot on the coffee table. He was still wearing his shoes, and I seethed inwardly as his mud-caked sole pressed into the polished wood. He was trying to force me into a reaction, and I wouldn't give him the satisfaction.

'Fine,' I said, standing up. 'Stay, if you must. I'm going to help Mirium with the tea.'

'She told you she would do it.'

I glared at him, then turned away, trying to compose myself as I walked through to the kitchen, wondering how long I would have to endure his company before he gave up and left. Mirium was standing with her back to me, hunched over something on the table, and I paused in the doorway, realising she hadn't heard me come in. I watched, wondering what she was doing, then saw what she had in her hand. Tommy's backpack was open, and I caught a flash of white paper.

'What are you doing?'

She visibly jumped, turning to face me, the letter from the preschool clamped tight in her hand. 'Oh, Clarissa, I didn't hear you. I... Well, this is awkward...' Her eyes darted from the letter with Scott's address printed on the front to me.

'What are you doing with that?' I asked quietly, holding out my hand for it.

She didn't hand it over. 'I should have asked, but of course I didn't want to accuse little Tommy. Berty has lost his tablet and he thinks Tommy might have... well, might have taken it home with him after you came to visit. I wanted to have a quick look myself. Thought it would create a fuss if I asked you.'

I shook my head, not believing a word. 'Mirium. Give that to me.'

'What? Oh, of course...' she said, a blush creeping over her cheeks as she handed the letter over.

'Did you look at it? *Read* it?'

'No, I told you – I was looking for the tablet.'

'You were looking for an address.'

She shook her head. 'I don't know what you mean.'

I felt sick. 'I don't want you to do anything stupid, Mirium.'

'I don't know what you're talking about.' Her eyes met mine, and we held each other's gaze, locked in a silent battle for what felt like minutes.

I was the one to break the deadlock. 'I actually have an awful headache coming on,' I said, making my tone light, apologetic. 'I'm so sorry, but I need to go to bed. Do you mind if we cut tonight short?'

She hesitated just a fraction of a second, then smiled, mirroring my carefree expression, and stepped forward, pulling me into a hug that felt stiff and awkward. 'I'm sorry you're not feeling well,' she said, holding me tight against her. 'We'll get out of your hair. Everything will be fine soon.' She pulled back, smiling. 'Tomorrow is a new day after all.'

It was a phrase I'd heard her say before, one that sent chills up my spine, and I couldn't decide if she was trying to frighten me, *warn* me.

I didn't get a chance to ask. She patted me on the shoulder and then strode past, calling to Jeff. In a moment, they were gone, and I was left alone in the kitchen with a sinking feeling that she knew where Scott lived. And that couldn't be a good thing for any of us.

I locked the front door, then double-checked the back, sliding the bolt across at the top and patting it, reassured by the heavy thud it made. Carrying a mug of tea, I trudged up the stairs, glad to finally be alone again. I was too tired for a bath now. All I wanted was to get into bed and close my eyes.

I peeked in to check on Tommy, then pulled his door closed and padded into my own room, flicking on the lamp and moving to draw the curtains, needing the privacy. If I left them open, even the tiniest crack, I couldn't help but feel a crawling sensation of being watched. Couldn't stop myself peering out into the darkness at Jeff and Mirium's house, wondering if a pair of eyes was pinned on me at the exact same moment.

I pulled the heavy curtains tightly closed and then frowned, my eyes falling on my dresser drawer, the corner of a nightdress peeking over the side. Had Tommy been in here messing around with my things? Or... My blood ran cold as I suddenly thought of a second possibility. Had Chloe come in here when she'd let herself inside earlier? Had she snooped in my room, in my private things?

I felt my mouth go dry, my heart pounding as I dropped to my knees, feeling under the bed for the box. It was in a different place. I *always* kept it at the back by the wall, and it had been moved, shoved recklessly in a diagonal position beneath the middle of the mattress.

I yanked it towards me, flipping off the lid, seeing instantly that things had been tampered with, moved. The photos had been on the top, but now a stack of letters lay half over them. My heart was racing as I gripped the lid in my hands. Had she read them? And if she had, why had she kept quiet during our argument today?

I tipped the box upside down, spreading the letters out across the carpet. There had been thirteen. I knew that as well as I knew my own date of birth. I had read them a thousand times over. And yet, only twelve were here now.

I dropped the lid of the box, slumping against the side of the bed, my spine pressing hard against the wooden frame. 'Oh, Chloe,' I whispered, closing my eyes as if I could somehow make things right. 'What have you done?'

THIRTY-FOUR

CHLOE

I sank my fork into the bowl of noodles, twirling it around before shoving it into my mouth, tasting nothing. Once I'd left my mum's house, I'd been unable to stop myself from giving in to the ball of emotion I'd been suppressing with every last scrap of my energy. The moment I'd walked through my front door, I'd burst into tears, sobbing until my throat hurt, my ears ringing, snot trailing down my face, choking me, making my chest pound and my stomach churn. I'd been unable to prevent the image of disappointment on my baby boy's face when he came down from washing his hands to find me gone from searing into my mind. I was letting him down again and again, and I hated myself for it.

Now, cradling the only thing I felt capable of eating, I sat in drained silence, an empty hollowness swallowing me up from the inside out. I was angry at myself for not doing more, not arguing with her, but I had never had to do that before. Even in the days following Rhodri's death – *disappearance* – I'd never felt that she was angry with me. But today, I'd seen something that brought fear and panic to the surface of my emotions. I couldn't help but wonder if her reaction was a mirror to my

actions. Was she right? Was I stupid to even consider bringing
Tommy home with me?

My phone rang, and I grabbed it, hoping to see her name,
hear her soft, gentle voice as she told me she'd been overanxious,
that I should come back now, though realistically I knew it was
far too late for Tommy to be awake.

Disappointment and fear flooded through me as I saw
instead Scott's name. The lit screen glowed in the palm of my
hand, and I dropped the phone as if I'd been stung, watching
until it stopped ringing, turned dark. What did he want? There
was nothing left to discuss, nothing we needed to say.

I looked down and realised I'd dropped the bowl, noodles
spilling out over the arm of the sofa, my fingers pinching the
bare skin on my inner thigh as if the pain could help channel
my fear, force me to stay calm. Sometimes it worked. I
wondered if it was a subconscious reaction to the expectation of
pain that came with thinking of him. That I tried to get in first
to make what was coming – what he was going to do to me – less
frightening, desensitising my fears and breaking that anxious
buzz of nerves.

I looked at the bruise that had formed beneath my fingernails, and then, startling me, the phone rang again. I didn't want
to look, but I had to know. I glanced across the cushion and
swallowed a wave of nausea, bile creeping up my throat past the
solid lump that had wedged itself into my windpipe, stealing my
breath away. Scott.

I curled my legs up beneath me, wanting to turn off the
phone, to reject his call, but too afraid to move. I watched as it
happened again and again, the phone going dark, silent for a
few seconds, before flashing to life once more. I was trembling, I
realised. I unfurled my body, leaning across the sofa, and placed
a cushion over the phone to muffle the sound, still unable to
bring myself to touch it.

A sudden knock at the door had me recoiling into a tight

ball again. Had he found me? How could he have figured out where I'd gone? I thought of all the times I'd felt as if I was being followed recently, and realised just how easy it would have been had he really wanted to seek me out.

I closed my eyes, memories flashing in still images across my thoughts – his hand on my throat, his knuckles colliding with my cheekbone so hard I couldn't fathom how it didn't shatter. I caught my reflection in the dark glass of the window across the room – timid, weak, pathetic – and was rewarded with a rush of shame. What had I become? What had I let him turn me into?

Sucking in a breath, I set my jaw, making up my mind. I would not let that man scare me. Not now that I'd found the courage to leave. I couldn't let him continue to have this hold over me.

With a flash of blinding rage, I grabbed the phone, switching it to silent.

The knock sounded again, louder this time, and I stood up, walking on bare feet towards it, leaning forward to look through the peephole. For a second, all I could see was a masculine shoulder, but then the figure stepped back and I stared hungrily at the man who stood waiting. I opened the door, looking at him wide-eyed.

'Rhodri.'

His mouth twitched as if he might argue with the name, but then he shrugged. 'Can I come inside? I have to talk to you.'

I stepped back wordlessly, watching in stunned silence as he walked past me, casting his estate agent's eye around the space with undisguised horror. 'Wow... if I'd searched your address after you called, I never would have let you book a viewing for that house. Damn, Chloe, this is... quite a step down from where you started.'

It felt as if he'd slapped me across the face. Stunned by his rudeness, I jutted out my chin, folding my arms across my chest. 'So, you know who I am now, do you?'

He had the grace to look sheepish. 'Yeah, well, I suppose.' He ran his hand through his slicked-back hair, struggling to maintain eye contact. 'Look, I shouldn't have left like that. It was the last thing I expected you to come out with. And it's been a long time since I went by that name.'

He took a step towards me, and I rubbed the tops of my arms, consciously trying to keep my stance strong, to not shy away in fear. I glanced at the sofa, wondering if Scott was still calling. If Rhodri would stand up for me against him if it came to it, or if he would just walk away again.

He gave a wry laugh.

'What?' I asked, frowning.

'It's just, looking at you now, it's hard to understand how I missed it before. You look like her.'

I nodded. I knew I was a younger version of my mother, though I'd yet to put on the weight she'd always carried. Sooner or later, genetics would creep up on me, no doubt. 'And *you* look like Dad.' I walked to the wall, where I'd already hung the framed photograph of my father. Easing it off the hook, I walked back over, handing it to him, watching his face as he took in the image of the dark-haired twenty-something man in a leather jacket. He was leaning against a wall, his brown eyes sparkling, his mouth open in a laugh as if someone had just told him a joke. He and the man in front of me could have been the same person.

Rhodri's mouth pursed as he looked down at the photograph, then he handed it back to me with a short nod.

'Why did you leave?' I asked.

He glanced at me as if he hadn't been expecting the question. 'Like I said, you caught me off guard. I wasn't expecting it.'

I shook my head. 'Not then. Not at the viewing. Why did you leave *home*?' I asked quietly. 'Did you *mean* for us to think you were dead?'

He breathed in, his nostrils flaring as he moved towards the sofa, perching on the back of it. 'It would have been better for everyone if that was the conclusion they arrived at.'

'How? How would that have been the right thing to let us believe?'

He shrugged infuriatingly. 'It was a long time ago, Chloe. I only came here because I wanted to check you were okay. When I realised you were living *here*, of all places, it made me worry about you. How did you end up somewhere like this? You were always so good at school. I thought you'd make something of your life. I would have expected you to be living it up in London or Dubai, not—' He broke off as the bare light bulb overhead fizzed and crackled, flickering for a few seconds before evening out again. He gestured at it as if it had made his point for him.

I held his gaze defiantly, unwilling to delve into my personal history with a man who was a complete stranger and who was making it more than clear that he didn't intend to rekindle any kind of sibling relationship between us. It hurt, and it made me want to put up my own wall in petty retaliation. 'Life happened,' I said, annoyed by the sulky undertone to my words.

'You left home. When?'

'Not long after—' I broke off, realising I'd been about to say *after you died*. 'After you,' I corrected.

He opened his mouth as if to ask something, then snapped it closed as his phone rang. ''Scuse me a sec,' he muttered, pulling it from his pocket and turning his back on me as if it would give him some privacy.

I listened to what was obviously a work call, him reassuring someone on the other end of the line that the vendors were still considering their offer and that he would call them back tomorrow with an update. I wanted to ask why he had let me spend the last fifteen years believing I had killed him. I wanted answers for why our mother thought he was dead too. It made my head pound with the strain of it.

He turned back to me, sliding his phone into his pocket, pulling out a tiny notepad and pen in its place. He scribbled something on it and handed the scrap of paper to me.

'My personal phone number,' he said. 'In case you need something, you know, in case of emergency,' he added, and I knew he meant just that. Not for social calls or emotional reminiscing sessions. Emergencies only.

I gave a curt nod, folding my arms again, somehow unable to find the words to ask for the answers I deserved. There was a coldness in the way he spoke, and it made me feel shy and uncomfortable, as if we weren't the long-lost siblings we both knew we were.

He stared at me, an awkward silence hanging between us. 'Right then,' he said at last. 'I'll leave you to get on.' He walked back to the door, pulling it open. 'Good to see you again, Chloe. And' – he glanced over my shoulder, and I tried not to cringe as I saw the judgement in his eyes – 'good luck for the future.'

'Yeah, thanks,' I replied.

I closed the door, bolting it shut behind him, and wondered if I'd ever set eyes on him again.

THIRTY-FIVE

The bus pulled into the stop, and I got off, fanning my face with a magazine someone had left on the seat across from me. After all the tears I'd shed last night, followed by the visit from my brother, which had only served to drain me further, I had somehow fallen into a deep, dreamless sleep on the sofa. I'd woken at gone seven this morning as if I were emerging from a ten-year coma – dribble dried onto my cheek, my hair plastered to my face – and despite the initial shakiness and disorientation that had hit me on waking, now I felt stronger, steadier than I had in weeks. I'd showered, eaten a bowl of porridge and sent some emails about jobs I'd found online. I had three interviews set up for later in the week and was buzzing with the energy that always came from finally getting the rest my mind and body so desperately craved.

I crossed the road, lingering on the corner opposite the preschool, watching the familiar faces of the parents arriving to drop off their little ones for the day. My blood pulsed with adrenaline as I searched the crowd waiting for the doors to open, hoping to spot Annie amongst them. I'd barely let myself consider the pros and cons of coming to confront her this morn-

ing. If I went back to her house to try to see her there, there was
no guarantee she'd let me in, let me talk to her, but here, dropping off little Molly, she'd have no choice. I would give her no
choice, I thought, setting my jaw in determination, a grim sense
of certainty taking over as I narrowed my eyes.

I'd racked my brains trying to understand why she was
coming for me now, after so many years had passed, but perhaps
the simplest answer was the most likely. She hadn't known
where I was after I left home. Hadn't known if I was dead or
alive even. Perhaps by sheer coincidence, she'd signed her
daughter up to the same nursery as Tommy, spotted me picking
him up and tracked me down. It wouldn't have been that hard
for her to follow me home from here to the flat I had shared
with Scott. I wished she had just come up and spoken to me
instead. Asked me to explain. Though I had to admit, it was a
mess even to me. I was being threatened because of a murder I
couldn't have committed, because the victim had walked into
my flat last night.

I chewed the loose skin at my cuticles, feeling tense, trying
not to let myself open the box in my mind I was trying to jam
shut. It was baffling, and a part of me wondered if I was really in
my right mind. *Could* I have imagined it all? Conjured up this
man in my imagination in order to whitewash the past, make
myself out to be innocent, absolve me of the guilt I could no
longer stand to carry? It would explain why my mum was so
concerned over my well-being, over my desire to take Tommy
back. How I was going to go about explaining any of it to Annie
was still unclear, but I was sure that as soon as we got talking, I
could make her see sense. We'd been friends once. I would help
her understand that she'd got it all wrong. That whatever she
thought she'd heard that night was a mistake. Rhodri was *fine*. I
was innocent.

But, I thought, watching the nursery doors open, the children rushing forward, tiny backpacks swinging from their

narrow shoulders, what if she wouldn't drop it? What if she continued to pose a threat to me, to my family? *Then* what?

I shook my head, determined not to catastrophise before it was necessary, my eyes scanning the street, wondering why she hadn't arrived yet. The parents had all gone inside now, but still there was no sign of Annie or Molly. I wished she would just reply to the note I'd posted through her letter box. Realise that this whole thing could be sorted out if only she would call me.

I leaned against a tree trunk, waiting, watching, feeling the adrenaline build with each minute that passed, until I was ready to explode with the pressure of it pulsing through my body.

The street that led from the bus stop to my mother's house was lined with pretty gardens overflowing with flowers in full bloom, and I cringed away from them, unable to stop myself from making the comparison with the bleak path that led to my flat. I wished I'd been able to provide more for my son. He deserved to walk home past brightly coloured hollyhocks and sweet-smelling honeysuckle, as opposed to the graffitied walls and broken bottles we'd had to learn to ignore. I was hot and irritable as I walked, my temples throbbing, my shoulders already sunburned despite it not yet being mid morning.

I'd waited for more than an hour outside the nursery, and then, when Annie still hadn't arrived, had reluctantly left, feeling frustrated that the situation was still unresolved. Now, putting her to one side, I had an even more pressing issue to deal with. How to have the conversation I needed to have with my mum about Rhodri. A part of me wanted to just put my head in the sand and pretend it wasn't an issue. The past few weeks had drained me, and all I wanted was to take my son home, shut the door and cuddle up on the sofa with a pile of storybooks. But as much as I wanted to escape from reality, I knew I wouldn't rest until I understood what had really happened. How I could have spent so long blaming myself for a crime I couldn't have committed.

I'd thought long and hard about how to approach the situation. I had so many questions still. How had Rhodri managed to convince my mother of his death? And furthermore, how had she come to believe *I* was at fault? I realised I didn't have a clue what had happened while I was sleeping that night. Who had called the ambulance? What story had been told in order to protect me from what she believed to be the truth? Had someone else been involved? Had Rhodri been wheeled out on a stretcher for the neighbours to see, then sat up and disappeared into the night?

As I let myself sink into the rabbit hole of questions that only seemed to lead to more confusion, I realised I had no choice but to bring it up with my mother again. I needed the details, the full story, and *that*, I knew, would be an uncomfortable conversation for both of us. As little as she'd said before, I knew how desperate she was to brush the past under the carpet and ignore the elephant in the room. It was going to be hard for me to convince her of what I knew.

I thought back to my childhood, the mornings I'd woken groggy and confused with her sitting beside me on my bedroom floor, her face pale, dark circles beneath her eyes, her rollers half hanging out of her curls as she asked softly if I was okay, told me I'd had another one of my episodes. I felt certain that she wouldn't believe me if I told her I'd spoken with Rhodri, that he really was alive, and living a short journey from where we'd grown up. She would continue to think I was ill, crazy even, and if she believed that, she wouldn't let me take Tommy home. With that in mind, there was only one solution. I would have to wait until my son was back under my roof before I could broach these difficult conversations. It was for the best.

I turned the corner, continuing towards my mum's house.

Up until now, I'd forced myself not to think about the confrontation we'd had yesterday, but with every step closer, I felt the tension building, wondering if she would be waiting with an apology, an explanation for the way she'd spoken to me before throwing me out of her house, or if I was heading into another argument.

It wasn't as if I hadn't seen this side of her in the past. I could recall her being overprotective when I was small – the way she would shield me from conflict when children were unkind at the park, or how she would always want to talk about every little incident, trying to understand how it had impacted me, how I felt deep in my heart. I'd found it stifling at times, though as I grew older, I appreciated the ability to look deeper than surface level and analyse my true feelings. But the difference now was that she was using her protective nature to shield my son, with me cast in the role of the bad guy.

I had never considered that she would take her responsibility for him quite so seriously. I'd wanted a temporary babysitter, not a substitute parent, and yet it almost felt as though she'd washed her hands of me and chosen him instead, completely neglecting to factor in that *I* was her child; *I* had feelings too. And right now, those feelings were that she was overstepping, trying to push me out of Tommy's life.

I hoped she'd told him I was coming. I couldn't wait to take him on the bus to the little park I'd discovered five minutes' walk from our new home. It had been a wonderful find, a huge, well-kept children's paradise obviously there for the benefit of the families who lived in the big Victorian houses on the tree-lined roads surrounding it, yet within easy reach of our grotty tower block. Tommy was going to love racing around all the play equipment and making friends. Hopefully we would meet some nice families out enjoying the sunshine, make a proper fresh start. It was all I wanted.

And afterwards, I thought, smiling to myself, I could take

him to see the new flat, show him the reading nook I'd created, and then, rather than drag him all the way back here in the rush-hour traffic, keep him home with me. I would send my mum a text to let her know the change of plan, then in a few days' time, I could drop him at preschool and come back here to pick up his things. It would be good for her to have a break from seeing him as her responsibility, and it was more than apparent that I was going to have to be assertive in proving I was no longer a child; that I was a mother now, and as much as I appreciated her help, I was in control – in *charge* – of my son's care.

I didn't want to hurt her feelings of course, and when I considered it from her point of view, I could understand her struggle. The last time she'd known me, I'd been barely out of childhood myself. It was going to take time for me to become a woman in her eyes, but I would have to make that happen. Things couldn't go on the way they were; she couldn't keep doubting me.

'Chloe!'

Torn from my thoughts, I glanced up as Mirium, standing at the end of her driveway, waved me over. 'Oh, great,' I muttered under my breath, pasting on a smile.

I crossed the road, making my way towards her with reluctant slowness. 'Hi again, Mirium. Everything okay?'

'Oh, you know, getting by. Jeff's gone to pick up the grandkids. Your lovely little chap has met them a few times now. I think they're a bit rambunctious for him. He's a gentle soul, isn't he?'

I smiled more warmly now, relieved that Jeff wasn't about to show his face and glad that Mirium had noticed Tommy's lovely character. It made me proud that she'd seen it for herself. 'He is.' I nodded. 'He's a sweet boy.'

'He reminds me so much of your brother.'

Her eyes met mine, and I saw something in her expression,

an intensity in her eyes that made me wonder if there was an ulterior motive for her bringing up the resemblance.

'Does he?' I replied, though I knew that as a child, Rhodri had been as blonde as Tommy was now. I wondered when it had changed.

She stepped forward, gripping my arm suddenly, her fingers vice-like around my wrist, digging into the skin so hard I knew she'd leave bruises. 'Leave him with us. With me and Jeff.'

'Mirium! Stop! You're hurting me.'

She continued speaking, her grip growing even tighter. 'It wasn't Jeff's fault. What happened with Rhodri. If that's what you heard. I have a second chance, and I won't make the same mistakes as—'

She broke off, releasing me so suddenly I stumbled backwards. She stepped away from me swiftly, and I steadied myself before grabbing my wrist, rubbing it hard as I tried to comprehend what had just happened. What the hell was she talking about? How could any of it be Jeff's fault? I frowned, wondering if Jeff had been involved in the letters after all, though I'd ruled that out after learning about Annie. It would make sense that his wife would know. Was *that* what she meant?

I followed her gaze and saw that my mother was crossing the road towards us, her grey-streaked auburn hair set in neat fifties-style curls, her rose-coloured dress buttoned high over her ample bosom.

'Clarissa, hi!' Mirium's smile was effortless, as if she hadn't just lost the plot. 'How's the headache? Gone now, I hope?'

Mum returned the smile but didn't reply immediately, instead looking towards me. 'Hi, Chloe,' she said. Her expression was warm, but I could still feel a sense of tension between us after yesterday. I gave a curt nod and she turned to Mirium.

'My headache has gone, but now poor Tommy seems to have got it. He's had to go back to bed.' She looked my way again. 'Sorry, darling, I called to let you know, but I think your phone was off. He's not fit for the park. He's had a big drink of water, and he's fast asleep. I'm sure he'll feel better when he wakes later.'

'I'll go and see him. Does he have a temperature?' I asked, feeling anxious.

She held up her hand as if to stop me. 'No need to disturb him. He's had a rough morning and just needs rest. He'll be fine by dinner time; I'm sure of it.'

I shook my head, about to argue, but Mirium spoke first.

'Oh, look, here's Jeff back now,' she announced, her voice weirdly high-pitched as the car pulled into the driveway. There was a burst of noise, the children in the back arguing loudly over some toy as they clambered out.

'Go in and put the telly on,' Jeff said, walking round the car to where our little group was standing. 'Worn me out already,' he muttered as he came to a stop beside his wife.

I pulled my phone from my bag, squinting at the screen beneath the blinding sun, unable to stop myself from checking. I'd switched it off last night when Scott had continued to call, but it had been on all morning, and I was sure I would have heard it ringing. As I navigated to my recent calls list, it rang and, distracted, I answered, instantly regretting it when I heard Scott's voice on the other end of the line.

'Chloe?' he said. His tone was filled with rage, and I felt my shoulders coil inwards, instinctively making myself small, my whole body primed for danger. 'Where the hell have you been? I've been calling since last night!'

I took a step away from the prying eyes of the group, turning my back on them. 'You need to stop calling me, Scott,' I whispered through gritted teeth. 'There's nothing left to say.'

He made a horrible snorting noise, and I pictured the hatred in his expression. 'Well, you seemed to have plenty to talk about with my mum, didn't you? Where the hell do you get off telling her I walked out on you and Tommy? You're the one who left!'

'I never said you'd walked out. I said you'd abdicated responsibility for him. Which you have. You don't want to see him. You said as much yourself,' I reminded him in a low voice. Glancing over my shoulder, I cringed as I realised that not only were all three watching me, they weren't even trying to hide the fact.

'I'm paying for him, aren't I?' he demanded. 'And how do you think it makes me look when you tell my mum I'm not interested in raising him? You're trying to make out you're some fucking hero of a single mother when we both know that couldn't be further from the truth. You're a fucking joke, Chloe! Mum's on about calling the social – she wants me to go for full custody now, because you've terrified her, made her think she's never going to see her grandson again!'

His words sent a jolt of terror through me.

'You've made a mess, and you need to fucking fix it. Get yourself and the kid round to her and make amends. Or I'll come and get him from you myself,' he yelled, his voice reverberating in my ear.

He hung up, and I let my hand, still gripping the phone in a white-knuckled fist, drop to my side, my mouth dry, my heart pounding through my ribcage. Slowly, I turned to face the three silent onlookers, sure they'd heard every word of his rant. It was humiliating that they knew what a mess my life was, the poor choice of a father I'd made for my son. My mum looked disgusted, her eyes wide, and I realised she'd had no idea just how low I had sunk.

I stared at her, willing her to break the tension, to tell me *he* was the one at fault and I'd done well to walk away from a man like that.

Instead, she sucked in a breath, looking over her shoulder at the house. 'I should get back to check on Tommy.' She turned and walked away without so much as a word, and I was too shaken, too stunned to speak up.

I felt like bursting into tears. She'd never been so cold in my life, never failed to give me a cuddle and make me feel better. What had changed? I stared after her, wanting to tell her to stop, that I was coming to check on Tommy, but no words came. I bit my lip, trying not to give in to the tears that were threatening to fall, humiliated to be standing here with all my failings on view for the whole world to gawp at.

'You look like you've had a shock, love,' Mirium said, seemingly oblivious to her part in the bewildering events of the last few minutes. 'Come in and I'll make you a cuppa. Jeff made eclairs this morning. They look like they've been dropped from a very tall building, but they taste divine.'

'No... no thanks,' I mumbled with a shake of my head. I looked back at my mum, watching as she headed inside and closed her front door without so much as a backwards glance, and wondered if I should follow, insist on seeing Tommy. But the strength I'd carried with me all morning seemed to have evaporated, replaced by fear, by the terror of what was coming. Would social services be at my door when I got home? Would Tommy be better hidden if I left him here? I didn't know, but it no longer felt like the right moment to take him back. Not today.

Feeling sick and light-headed, I ignored Mirium's encouraging smile and, turning away from her and Jeff, walked back down the street to await the bus that would take me back to my empty, damp-ridden flat.

THIRTY-SIX

CLARISSA

I poured the wine into my glass, not stopping until it was in danger of overflowing. I hadn't drunk regularly for years, but since Tommy's arrival on my doorstep, I had found it a necessity to get through the evenings. It brought back memories of the early years of being a mother. The sleepless nights, the constant feeling of being stretched paper-thin, of being in danger of ripping wide open at any given moment. That glass or two of wine of an evening had been my saviour back then, the only thing that carried me through to the next day, though I'd frequently woken with a banging headache and a furry tongue, wondering how I would make it through another day as I pasted on a smile and went to make the children's breakfast.

I lifted the glass of Merlot to my lips, drinking deeply, then carried it through to the living room to stand at the window, watching... waiting. The sun was setting, the sky a blaze of orange and pink, framing Miri's house like a picture. I knew her grandchildren were always late to bed – it was half past nine now, and it wouldn't have surprised me if they were still jumping on the mattresses, asking for stories and snacks. For all the qualities she possessed, discipline had never been a strength of hers.

I took another sip of wine, enjoying the warmth as it travelled down my throat, the burn in my belly. My stomach muscles clenched as, across the road, Mirium's front door opened and Jeff walked outside. Instead of crossing over towards me, though, he carried a black bag down the path, dropping it into the wheelie bin and lowering the lid softly before turning and heading back indoors.

I closed my eyes, letting the relief wash over me, but it was short-lived. When I opened them, she was standing there in his place, her eyes finding mine across the empty street, her expression hard and unsmiling. She pulled the front door closed behind her, wrapped a shawl round her shoulders, which struck me as odd on a balmy night like tonight, then, her eyes not leaving mine, walked across the road. I didn't bother to move from the window to let her in. She would come round the back, as she always did. I stayed frozen to the spot, squeezing the stem of my glass tightly between my fingers.

The door creaked, and my shoulders tensed beneath the cotton of my dress, which suddenly felt far too tight, irritating the hot skin beneath. I let out a slow breath, waiting for her to speak.

'Where is he?'

I didn't turn to face her in the doorway behind me. 'In bed. Obviously.'

She snorted. 'That was some real cruelty today, Clarissa. Not letting Chloe come and see him. A headache, you say?'

I spun, glaring at her. 'You don't want to get involved in this, Mirium,' I said, hearing the harshness of my tone. 'You don't have a clue what's going on with Chloe. I'm *trying* to help her. It's more complicated than you realise.'

'It always is with you, isn't it?'

She walked slowly forward, plucking the glass from my

hand and drinking from it. There was a crusted white patch of dried saliva in the corner of her wrinkled lips, and I shuddered internally, willing her to wipe it away. Seemingly oblivious to my disgust, she offered the glass back to me. I shook my head.

'Suit yourself,' she said, taking another sip and lowering herself into her usual armchair, fixing me with a piercing stare. 'You're trying to stop her from taking him.'

It was phrased as a statement rather than a question, and that alone rankled. '*No*. I'm simply holding off until I know it's what's best.'

'For who?'

'Excuse me?' I folded my arms, feeling a surge of anger towards her.

'Best for *who*? Not Chloe. And certainly not Tommy. Don't you think he should be with his mother? His life has been thrown into chaos, he's lost his father—'

I let out a burst of laughter. 'You heard him on the phone to Chloe today, right? It's no great loss, I can assure you. And he's hardly dead; he's just another absent father. Ten a penny these days. Tommy won't miss him.'

'I bet you can't stand it, can you? That she ended up with a man like that?'

'What mother could?' I retorted, bristling.

She gave an infuriating shrug, and I walked out of the room, back to the kitchen, yanking another wine glass from the cupboard and slamming it down on the side. I poured a healthy measure, downing half of it in one go before storming back to the living room, where Mirium was still sitting. She smiled up at me with an expression of absolute serenity, though I could hear the cogs of her brain ticking. They never stopped, despite the impression she liked to portray to the world.

'So, what's your plan? What are you intending to do to help Chloe?'

I glared at her. 'I don't like your tone, Mirium. And what

happens between me and my daughter is quite frankly none of your business.'

'So you're just going to string this out? Keep the boy here?'

'If it's what's best.' I took another sip of my wine.

'Give him to me.'

I smirked. 'First Jeff and now you, Miri. How predictable you are. Don't you think I've given you enough already?'

Her mouth dropped open, and I felt the mood shift; knew I'd seized back control of the situation.

'Did Jeff come to you?' she asked, her eyes wide.

'Of course he did. For a couple who've been married so long, you really don't communicate, do you?'

She leaned forward, and her usually soft expression was suddenly filled with anger. 'Clarissa,' she said, her tone a low warning.

I knew I was treading on dangerous ground. I didn't want to bring up the past, the secrets we'd sworn to keep for one another, but she was forcing me into a corner, and I felt the fight rear up inside me, a caged bear being prodded too hard, too deep to remain calm.

I held out a hand, cutting her off. 'Stop inserting yourself into my business. You can tell your husband that too, if you can manage a conversation with him. Because if you don't, I have plenty of things I could share with him that you don't want him to know.'

She gave a tinkling little laugh of disbelief, though I could see the tightness around her eyes, the narrowed pupils weighing up my threat. 'We both know you wouldn't say a word.'

'*Do* we? Don't you think you have more to lose than I do?'

I watched her face, hoping she wouldn't call my bluff; saw the moment she realised I'd won as my message sank in.

She placed her glass on the coffee table and rose to her feet. 'You're unbelievable, Clarissa.' She walked slowly to the door, pausing as she reached it, her hand lingering on the frame. 'If you won't send him to us, send him home.'

'I'll hear no more on the subject. We'll see you tomorrow at the community centre. I'm bringing a lemon cake.'

She pursed her lips, and I saw her fighting with herself, wanting to say more. Then she spun around, and I heard her leave through the back door. A moment later, I followed, bolting it behind her, my heart thumping hard in my chest, my hands trembling. I leaned my head against the wood and wondered what on earth I'd got myself into.

THIRTY-SEVEN

CHLOE

The key had gone. I ran my fingers back and forth over the ridge above the porch, then lifted the pot plants lined up along the external wall, searching beneath them fruitlessly. Straightening up, I turned to stare at my mother's house, feeling a sense of inexplicable fear deep within my gut. I'd called repeatedly since arriving home yesterday afternoon, needing an update on how Tommy was doing, worrying myself sick that what she'd thought was a simple headache could be any number of awful childhood illnesses. She hadn't answered my calls, and despite my arriving here just after half past eight this morning, unable to wait a moment longer to see my boy, now I found that the house was empty, my mother gone and my son with her.

For the tenth time in a row, I unlocked my phone, pressing call on her name, listening to it ring until it cut out. What was she thinking taking him out when she had to have known how much I wanted to see him? How desperate I was to take care of him when he was ill. He *needed* me. I couldn't shake this awful feeling that she was actively trying to prevent me from taking him home. That I'd made the worst mistake of my life in sending him here in the first place. It was unreasonable, I knew, my emotions running wild because I'd been away from him too long. And of course, after my one night of decent sleep, last night had been right back to square one, pacing, fretting, worrying about Scott and Irene, her threats to go to social services. Thinking about Tommy and having to actively force myself not to get a taxi and come and collect him, bring him back in the middle of the night.

The only thing that had stopped me was the thought of how crazy, how unhinged I would look in doing that – precisely the impression I was trying not to give. I felt as if the world was crashing down around me, and I didn't know what to do. All I'd wanted was to give my son a safe place to stay while I set up our new home and broke free from Scott, but now I feared I'd given my mother too much power, and in doing so had relinquished control of the situation. I'd stayed awake until three in the morning, trying to come up with a solution, then woke at just gone six with no recollection of falling asleep, feeling just as wired and unrested as ever.

I looked at the closed living-room window and, with a reckless feeling of desperation, wondered fleetingly if I should put a brick through it. Break in. But what would be the point when I knew they weren't there? I should call the police, then. But say what? That my mother had taken my son out somewhere and I couldn't get hold of them? They'd quickly realise I'd sent him to stay with her, and then, if Irene did call social services, it would only complicate things further having the police involved. And it was silly. I was just getting dramatic and worked up. I had to be calm.

I lowered myself to sit on the rough doormat, my eyes trained on the driveway, waiting.

My phone rang in my hand, and seeing the word *Mum* emblazoned on the screen, I answered it without hesitation, pressing it to my ear.

'Mum?' I asked, my tone urgent.

'Chloe, it's Irene,' came the scratchy, husky voice of Scott's mother.

I glanced at the screen, realising it said *Scott's Mum*, something I'd missed in my hurry. My heart sank. 'It's not a good time,' I replied. 'I can't talk now.'

'Wait. Please, Chloe, listen. Scott's in hospital. I don't think he's going to make it. I... I think I'm going to lose him.'

'What?' I sat up straighter, wondering if this was some trick, and yet somehow I didn't think so. She sounded so broken. 'What are you talking about? What happened?'

'They're saying he took an overdose. I went round at half past six this morning on my way to work to give him some cash, and found him in a pool of shit and vomit. He wasn't breathing, Chloe... He looked dead...' Her words were lost in a choked sob.

I frowned, confused. 'An overdose? Of what?'

'Heroin. But I told them that wasn't possible. He doesn't do heroin! He's always saying it's a one-way ticket to misery. You know he won't touch the stuff, Chloe – you know it!'

I nodded silently, my thoughts racing. She was right. He might have smoked the occasional spliff, but he'd always been scathing of anything harder, mocking the addicts we'd met in the squat, saying they were like animals, unable to think of anything but the next hit. He'd been disdainful of anything that required commitment, and a drug habit was the ultimate bind in his view. I couldn't think of a single reason he would turn to it now when he finally had the freedom he'd wanted.

'Are you with him now?' I asked.

'I've just stepped out to call you. He's in intensive care. They had to shock him to restart his heart. It was horrible, Chloe. He still hasn't woken up, and they don't know what damage has been done – how long he was without oxygen.'

I pictured the man who had dominated me for the past four years. Who had transformed from my saviour to my abuser, destroying the dream of the life I'd longed for us to share. The little farmhouse in the country, the animals and children, the fresh air and a home full of love. I'd wanted it so much it burned a hole through my soul, and he'd snatched it from me, leaving me scrambling for pennies, having to rely on my mother to care for my son. He'd stolen so much from me because he was selfish, unable to care for anyone but himself.

I closed my eyes, thinking of the way I'd learned to flinch every time he came close, the pain he'd seemed to feed off, the love I'd thought he'd had for me entirely absent as he caused untold agony and trauma to the mother of his child, the woman he should have protected at all costs. I found I couldn't decide what emotion I felt now. I was numb. He might die... might be gone for ever. And I didn't know if I could admit out loud that I wouldn't feel the loss that Irene would.

'Will you come and see him? He'd want you with him. I know you aren't together any more, but you're important to him, Chloe. Even if he doesn't show it as well as he should. He loves you.'

I shook my head, wondering if she'd made the same excuses to herself about her poor parenting. If she'd told him she loved him after laying into him as a child. 'I don't think so... I don't know, Irene. I—'

'Just think about it,' she cut in. 'I'll be here all day. I'll text you the details for where to find us. Think about it. The doctor's coming now – I have to go.'

The line went dead, and I leaned my head back against my mum's front door, my mind spinning, a feeling of sick dread pulsing through my veins along with the awful sense that somehow this was my fault.

THIRTY-EIGHT

CLARISSA

Tommy was curled into a ball on Chloe's lap on my sofa, his arm snaking around her waist as if he thought she might sneak away, his eyelids tinged red, closed tight in sleep. He'd burst into tears when we'd arrived home to find her waiting in the porch, and she'd scooped him up without so much as a word to me, following me indoors and settling herself down to console him.

I had tried to explain that he'd tripped and scraped his knees on the way back from the community centre, hence the heightened emotions, but Chloe was acting like his reaction was somehow my fault, offering curt one-word answers to my questions and giving me the cold shoulder. I supposed I'd half expected it after the way we'd parted yesterday, but still, she had to know I was only doing my best. Parenting was never easy – not if you wanted to do it right.

I picked up my tea, casting a glance over to the pair of them now, wishing she would wake him. He would never sleep tonight having napped for so long today. She seemed in no hurry to disturb him though, her fingers stroking his tousled blonde head, her eyes trained on his face.

I plonked my mug on a coaster. 'Here,' I said, picking up the untouched plate from the table, passing her the ham salad sandwich I'd made for her. 'Eat. You look like you need it. Honestly, you're wasting away, Chloe,' I said.

From the flash in her eyes, I could tell she'd taken it as a judgement on my part, a condemnation of her ability to take care of herself, though in truth, I was just worried. She was far too thin, and whether that was down to money, stress or something entirely different I couldn't be sure. I glanced down at my hands, and when I looked back up, I saw with relief that she'd picked up half the sandwich and had taken a bite. She chewed slowly, then swallowed, her eyes rising to meet mine.

'Something's happened. To Tommy's father.'

'Oh?'

'He's in hospital. They're saying it's an overdose.' She put the sandwich down on the plate, picking at the crust with her fingernail. 'He might not make it.'

I felt the room distort, my heart stuttering in my chest, my fingers knotting tightly together in my lap. I swallowed, took a breath, then spoke. 'You never said he was into that kind of thing.'

She shook her head. 'He isn't. He hates hard drugs. Belittles people who can't control themselves around them. It doesn't make sense.'

I regarded her carefully, watching her expression. 'So, this is out of character for him?'

She nodded.

'But he's still alive? They think he'll wake up?'

'I don't know.'

My thoughts were racing, but I kept perfectly still. 'It wasn't your fault, Chloe. You couldn't have known.'

She looked up at me sharply. 'Of course it wasn't my fault!' Tommy stirred in her lap, and she lowered her voice to a harsh whisper. 'I haven't even seen him. I've cut all ties.'

I stared at her and knew we were both thinking of the phone call he'd made only yesterday. The threats he'd uttered about taking her son from her. 'It seems sinister somehow,' I said slowly.

'You're not suggesting *I* had anything to do with it?' she demanded.

'Of course I'm not. But...'

'What?'

'Never mind.'

'Mum, what? What is it? If you know something, you have to tell me.'

'It's silly. Just me being paranoid, that's all. He'd never...' I drifted off, glancing out of the window towards Mirium and Jeff's house.

'Who? Who would never? What the hell are you talking about?' she said in a hissed whisper.

'Jeff... I just... Oh, never mind. Ignore me – I'm being ridiculous. Too many late-night crime documentaries.'

Chloe shook her head. 'What would make you bring Jeff into any of this? How could he possibly be involved – he doesn't even *know* Scott.'

'He has a history of... being overprotective. Some promise he made to your dad long ago that he's taken to heart in an unhealthy way. We've fallen out over it plenty of times in the past. He's overstepped his boundaries, with you and with Rhodri. It just got me thinking, what with him overhearing Scott being so unpleasant to you. He wouldn't have liked it.'

'But I'm not his responsibility. And why would he make a promise like that to Dad? It wasn't like Dad knew he was dying. He had a heart attack, didn't he?'

I looked away, regretting ever having spoken. I didn't want this to turn into some reminiscing session about Reece, the past, all the things I'd long since buried.

Chloe sat back, and I could see her thoughts turning over in her mind.

'Forget it. I'm being a silly old woman. And I'm sure Scott will pull through. Maybe he's taken your break-up harder than you expected. These things can be tough on a man's confidence. And if he's inexperienced with drugs, I'm sure it can be only too easy to get the measures wrong. The doctors will take care of him. You're not thinking of taking him back, are you? If he pulls through, that is?'

'No.' She shook her head. 'That's over. No matter what happens to him. I won't go back.'

I nodded, relieved.

She was silent for a moment, scraping crumbs from the sandwich, piling them on the plate. I wished she would just pick the thing up and eat it, but I didn't dare comment on it again.

'I wanted to talk to you,' she said, not looking up. 'About this arrangement with Tommy. I want to take him back... today.' She continued without pause, her words coming in a breathless rush, and I could tell she'd been building up to it. 'I'm grateful for everything you've done – you know that – but it's time for us to start afresh together, and I don't want to put it off any longer. Tommy's coming home with me today, and I won't negotiate on that. I'm his mother.'

I'd known it was coming. It was only to be expected, and yet the thought of stepping back was daunting. I didn't know if she would manage, if she would be a good parent to Tommy, though I would never have said as much to her face.

I took a deep breath and nodded. 'Okay. You're probably right. You *are* planning to visit me though? You're not going to disappear into the unknown for another fifteen years?'

She broke into a smile, and I realised she'd expected me to argue. 'Of course we're going to visit. All the time.'

'Good. That's a relief. Well' – I looked at my watch – 'I promised Tommy we would go to the garden centre this afternoon. He wanted to help me choose some seeds for the vegetable patch, and I don't want to let him down. Why don't we wake him up now, and he can have his lunch, then I'll take him as promised. You can pop off and get some nice bits for your dinner and then come and collect him around four to take him home?'

Chloe gave a deep sigh. 'Thank you, Mum.' She stroked Tommy's hair again. 'I know I've been a bit difficult, but I *am* grateful to you. And I know you'll miss him being here.'

I nodded, wondering if I was about to make a mistake I wouldn't be able to undo. 'Yes,' I replied, my knotted hands squeezing tighter together. 'I will.'

THIRTY-NINE

CHLOE

The stairwell was empty as I dashed up to the third floor, wishing there were more windows to help me feel less claustrophobic in here. I could never get past the feeling of being followed, watched, and it was always a relief when I finally made it to my front door.

I was breathless as I headed up the final flight of stairs, but I didn't slow my pace. I wanted to get back and pop the groceries I'd bought for dinner in the fridge before I went to collect Tommy from my mum. I'd bought all his favourites for a picnic tea. Pears, blueberry muffins, vanilla yoghurts, crumpets and cheese. I'd even got the little cartons of smoothie he always asked for and I always said no, they were too expensive. But today, I didn't care.

I was going to lay out a blanket on the living-room floor and do everything in my power to make his welcome home really special. After a week of him eating my mum's home-cooked food, I had a lot to compete with. I couldn't bear the thought of him looking around and wishing I'd left him there, though in my heart, I was sure he'd be happy to be with me again.

I reached the top step and stopped in my tracks as I came

face to face with two policemen standing outside my front door, my eyes wide, a deer in headlights as I realised they were looking right at me.

'Chloe Phillips?'

I wondered if I could shake my head and keep walking, pretend the officer had got the wrong person, but my bravado faltered, and I felt myself nod silently, wondering why he was here. Had Annie done this? Finally made good on her threats?

'Can I help you with something?' I said, keeping my voice casual as I hitched the shopping bag higher onto my shoulder.

He met my eyes, his head tilting towards the door. 'Can we come in for a moment?'

I shook my head. 'No. Sorry, but I'm not comfortable with having two strange men in my flat. We can talk out here, or not at all.'

The two of them glanced at each other. They were both young, the one furthest away good-looking, his stance confident, the one who'd spoken to me less so, and I could see them silently communicating, wondering whether to push it. There was truth in what I'd said. I didn't want to put myself in a position of vulnerability. But on top of that, I didn't want to encourage them to stay any longer than was absolutely necessary.

'What's this about?' I asked, folding my arms.

'Are you aware of what's happened to your ex?'

'Scott?' I said, raising an eyebrow. It was still jolting to hear him referred to as my ex, when it had only been recently that I'd still hoped for a future together. 'Yes, his mum called to tell me this morning. Is there an update?'

'I'm not in a position to share that information with you at the moment. Are you sure we can't step inside?'

I shook my head.

'If that's your decision, we'll talk here then. Where were you last night, Chloe?'

'Where was I? Here of course.'

'Can anyone confirm that?'

I thought of Rhodri, his visit, yet something stopped me from speaking his name out loud. The tiny niggle of doubt in my gut that I might somehow have got it all wrong. I didn't want them to go away and check what I'd told them, find out that my brother was dead so couldn't possibly have come.

Before I could make up my mind what to say, the second PC chimed in. 'Specifically, between the hours of four and six a.m.'

I stared at him, about to say that I'd been in bed, where any normal person would have been at that hour. Only, I couldn't claim that, could I? I recalled waking on the sofa at just after six. The groggy feeling of disorientation, unable to remember how I'd got there, the deep, dreamless sleep that had been so out of character.

My stomach clenched, a painful spasm of fear rolling through my gut as I was reminded of those awful mornings from my childhood. Hearing that I'd been sleepwalking, that I'd left the house, that I'd done things I had no recollection of. It was a disembodying feeling, knowing you'd taken on another life whilst your mind switched to autopilot, acting without instruction. I thought of the blood on the carpet, my mother's pale face – that awful night that had ruined my life – and for a moment wondered if I might have done something without meaning to. If Scott might be in hospital because of me.

'Chloe?'

I licked my lips, moistening them, though my tongue was sticky and dry. 'I was here, asleep. Where else would I be?' I stared at him, daring him to challenge me.

He breathed in, his nostrils flaring. 'Well,' he said finally. 'If you remember anything else, give us a call.' He handed me a small white card, and I looked at it so as not to have to meet his eyes. 'Anything at all. We have reason to believe this wasn't self-inflicted,' he finished with a wry smile.

I nodded, fishing my key from my bag, holding it tight as I waited for them to descend the stairs before darting inside, slamming the door closed behind me.

I hitched the bag containing wine and chocolates for my mum onto my shoulder, crossing the road back to the bus stop. I'd ignored three calls from Irene, the voicemail notification flashing up on my phone every hour or so since we'd spoken this morning. I found I couldn't bring myself to listen to her messages. Despite everything he'd put me through, I didn't want to hear her say the words that Scott had died.

Had *she* been the one to send the police to question me? What had they discovered to make them suspect foul play? I could only imagine how my mum would react if I told her they'd come to my flat today. It would put us right back to square one, make her reluctant to send Tommy home, though of course I hadn't done anything. I couldn't have. But if Scott died…

I swallowed a wave of bile as it rose, burning against the back of my throat. The very idea of it sent a chill through me, made fear swell up in my gut, a noose around my neck, stealing my breath away with the uncertainty of what it would mean for me and Tommy. So the notifications from Irene remained on my screen, a glaring reminder of a past life I was desperate to erase, as I shoved the phone to the bottom of my bag – out of sight, out of mind.

Instead, I concentrated on running through my to-do list in my head. I mustn't forget to collect Tommy's books, his teddy. I had to call the preschool and let them know he'd be returning next week.

The bottle of wine I'd bought my mum as a thank you for

dropping everything to take care of him clinked against the plastic tub of chocolates in the bag, and I smiled, feeling relieved that we'd finally come to an agreement, that the fears I'd let myself be drawn into had materialised into nothing. I had always been blessed with an overactive imagination. The Scott stuff was silly. It would all work itself out in the end.

The bus pulled up and I climbed aboard, taking a seat near the window, itching with pent-up excitement as I thought about tucking Tommy into bed tonight. Cuddling together to read stories, talking about all the wild daydreams he'd been having – he too loved to get lost in his own world. There had been a sense of disconnection between us lately, a side effect of never being fully alone. Mum tried her best to make her presence discreet, but she was always near, always listening, and it made both Tommy and me less open with each other. I couldn't wait to get him on his own and re-establish the close bond we'd always shared.

We hadn't even talked properly about my having left his dad yet. He would be fine, relieved even, of that I was certain. I suppressed a shudder as I pictured Tommy's terrified expression as I lay on the ground at his father's feet, broken and bloody. But the confusion he must have been feeling lately weighed on my mind. The sooner I got him home and into a healthy routine, the better. For both of us.

I saw my stop coming up and pressed the bell, standing and making my way down the aisle, trying not to knock anyone with the bag balanced on my shoulder.

Instead of taking the main road to my mum's, which would lead me straight past Mirium and Jeff's, I went around the back way to where a tiny alleyway led between the main road and the far end of the cul-de-sac. It meant a five-minute detour, but it would enable me to get there without a fanfare, which was far preferable to another unsettling interaction with Mum's strange neighbours.

I still couldn't understand what Mirium had been talking about when she'd accosted me on the street – how Jeff could have *possibly* had anything to do with Rhodri's disappearance. Once Tommy was home, settled, I would have to find the courage to broach the topic with my mother again. I had to let her know that her son was alive. I'd find a way to bring the two of them together, get to the bottom of it all and work out how it was that I had got the blame for something that hadn't even happened.

I was trying not to linger on how that made me feel. There was a cauldron of bubbling emotions inside me growing wilder by the minute, but still, I forced a lid over it and pretended not to notice. It would only distract me from what I needed to focus on now. My son. He was all that mattered.

As I reached my mum's driveway, I glanced across the road, glad to find Mirium and Jeff's front garden empty, their car missing. *Good.*

I knocked on the front door, already fishing around inside my shopping bag for the magazine I'd picked up for Tommy. I couldn't really afford it, but I'd wanted to treat him, and I was buzzing with excitement at the thought of watching his face light up when he saw the little train toy that came with it. There was a double page where you could cut and colour your own track – something we could do together after our picnic tea if I could find a pack of crayons at home. Simple pleasures I'd missed so much since he'd come here.

I looked up, smiling as the front door opened, then frowned, seeing my mum peering out through the two-inch gap she'd created. I laughed. 'You've left the chain on, silly.'

'I'm well aware of that.'

'What's going on? Are you having trouble? Is it stuck? I can go round the back way and—'

'He's not coming. I'm sorry, Chloe, but I have to make the right decision for Tommy.'

'What? What are you talking about?' I asked, shaking my head in confusion. An icy trickle of dread began to filter through my veins, a throbbing pulse pounding in my eardrums. I had the sudden unsettling fear that I might be hallucinating and blinked hard, gripping the wall for support. 'Where's Tommy?' I asked, trying to push the door wider, though the chain held firm.

'You can't see it yet,' she said, her tone calm, controlled, 'but you aren't well. I've been worried from the moment you turned up. Sending little Tommy on his own in a taxi to arrive on my doorstep.' She gave a twist of her mouth. 'You need help, love. You're not in your right mind. First that stuff imagining you'd seen your brother, and now Tommy's father.' She lowered her voice. 'I *know* you did something to him, Chloe. We both do.'

'What? No! You're wrong. I—'

'The papers have picked up on it – the story was in today's tabloids. There's speculation the police suspect someone else was involved. Have they questioned you yet?'

My mouth dropped open, no words emerging as she nodded knowingly.

'Nobody has more of a motive than you, do they?' She took a deep breath, glancing over my shoulder as if she couldn't bring herself to meet my eyes. 'Look, you know I love you. I'm your mother; I will *always* love you, but I cannot send a four-year-old child into your care whilst you're struggling with reality. Don't you see you're a danger to him?' Her tone was gentle, cautious, yet the words cut like a knife.

I stared at her face, willing her to back down. 'You can't think I had anything to do with Scott's overdose? Why would I?'

She shrugged. 'Because you needed him gone. Out of the picture so his mother couldn't make good on her threat to help Scott go for custody. I heard every word of that phone call, Chloe. And don't forget, I *know* you. I know how you think.

You can't fool me. You might be able to pretend to the rest of the world, but not to me. I see everything. I always did.'

I stepped back as if she'd slapped me, panic racing through my veins, its tendrils wrapping tight around my heart. 'Give me my son,' I said, my voice low, dangerous. '*Now*. Or I will break down this fucking door. I mean it. Give him to me.'

'You're going to kick down the door and terrify the life out of him? For what? To take him away to a home where he'll be cold and hungry? Where he'll never feel safe and where you can't protect him from yourself let alone the rest of the dangers lurking close at hand? Go home, Chloe. I'm not discussing this now. Get yourself some help, then we'll talk about Tommy's future.'

She slammed the door in my face before I could think how to appeal to her, and I stood trembling, half determined to carry out my threat and break down the door, half wanting to crumple to the ground and sob, to scream his name and make such a scene she would *have* to return him to me.

I did neither. I stood still for so long my toes began to tingle. Finally, with a sense of clarity that numbed the roar of emotions in my mind, I pulled my phone from my pocket, scrolled to the number I needed and pressed call.

'It's me,' I said, my voice strangely calm. 'I need to see you now. It's... it's an emergency.'

Rhodri leaned back in his chair, his mug of coffee steaming on the little circular table in front of him, his expression blank as he appraised me. He glanced at his watch, clearly waiting for me to speak, and I felt frustration well up inside me, annoyed that he'd insisted on meeting here at this packed café near his work, clearly making the point that he didn't have time to go out of his way for me.

I'd waited more than half an hour for him to show up,

defending the chair I'd saved for him as I drank my Americano, forcing down a Danish in the hope that it might help the trembling. It hadn't. Now, it lay heavy in the pit of my stomach, competing with the fear that churned relentlessly inside me.

'So?' he said, reaching for the mug. 'I wasn't expecting to hear from you so soon. You said it was important.'

I nodded, knotting my fingers in my lap, wishing we were somewhere quiet. It was hard enough without having to worry about people listening in on our conversation. 'I have a child,' I said quietly. 'Did I tell you that? You're an uncle.'

'Really? No, you didn't mention it. How old?' he asked, though his eyes drifted to the door, his expression glazing over with obvious disinterest, as if he thought I'd brought him here to make small talk.

'Four... Do you have any? Kids, I mean?'

'Nope. Not something that's ever appealed to me, if I'm honest.'

I waited for him to go on, to ask if I had a boy or a girl, to say he wanted to meet him, but he didn't. He took a sip of coffee and then looked pointedly at his watch again.

I took a breath, struggling to find the words, to know where to begin. 'My ex and I, we aren't together any more. He wasn't the best boyfriend, and he was a terrible father.' I felt the tears begin to fall.

There was a look of horror on my brother's face. 'I'm not here to judge you. You don't have to explain yourself to me.'

'It's not that... It's... He's in hospital. They said he took an overdose – he might not make it – but he's not into that kind of thing. It doesn't make sense, and now Mum's blaming me... She's accused me of being unstable. She thinks I have something to do with it, but—'

'Wait, hold on a minute. You're still in touch with her? You never said.'

'I wasn't. I hadn't seen her in years. I left after... after what happened with you. But we've been back in touch for a few weeks, and I think...' I broke off, not wanting to say the words on the tip of my tongue: that I'd made a mistake in letting her get so close to my son.

Rhodri pressed his lips together, and I could see him deliberating over his words. It annoyed me. I was sick of the secrets, the lies. I just wanted honesty. Was that too much to ask for?

'What is it?' I demanded. 'Just say what you're thinking.'

He met my stare and gave a short nod. 'Fine. Is she right? *Did* you have something to do with your ex ending up in hospital?'

'What? No! For fuck's sake, what the hell is wrong with everyone? I have spent the last fifteen years blaming myself for *your* death when it's clear to me that you're alive and well, and now you want to pin this on me too! It's crazy!'

'What are you talking about, *my death*?'

I rubbed my knuckles into my eye sockets, feeling a headache coming on. 'I wish I knew. You fake your own death for God knows what reason, and *I* get blamed for it because of my night terrors. You have no idea what you put us through. What you put *Mum* through. I don't even understand how you did it. Or why. But you ruined my life. You're the reason I walked away from every opportunity I had ahead of me. Why I decided I deserved the abuse Scott doled out to me. You let me think I was a murderer!' I sat back in my chair, wiping harshly at my damp cheeks, aware of several pairs of eyes watching from the nearby tables.

Rhodri looked uncomfortable. He leaned forward, lowering his voice. 'I never imagined you would think... I thought you'd be all right... that you would have an amazing life. You were doing so well in school. You were happy. I never expected to hear that you'd been living with this much guilt. Did you really leave straight after me? When you were fifteen?'

I nodded. 'Mum was so broken. And I knew... well, I *thought* it was all my fault.'

'But where did you go? Not family.'

'The streets.' I shrugged as his eyes widened.

'Shit.' He put his head in his hands, his shoulders slumping. 'I thought... I thought you'd be okay. If I'd known, I never would have left.'

'But why did you? You were twelve! A child. I know you were always so much more free-spirited than me. Naughty, wild, hard to keep in check.'

I remembered how little we'd had in common back then. He'd been a handful, Mum had always said. Never following the rules, always getting grounded and punished, though it never seemed to make the slightest bit of difference. I'd prided myself on being good. On making Mum's life easier, getting my homework done early, keeping my room tidy. I'd enjoyed being the golden child, and wondered time and again why he didn't see that life was easier if you did what was expected of you. I tried to picture the little boy I remembered, but it was hard. We'd spent so little time together, never playing as siblings.

'You were so dismissive of the rules, so desperate to be grown up,' I went on. 'But where could you possibly go, a boy of twelve? And don't tell me you were living rough too – you'd have been picked up and taken home. Besides,' I added, my gaze raking over his expensive suit, 'you don't look like you've been living hand to mouth, begging for your dinner. You've had the means to make something of yourself, unlike me.'

He opened his mouth to reply, then closed it, looking over my shoulder to the door, where a pretty, dark-haired woman stood, waving him over. He stood up, nodding to her in response, and I felt my heart sink, disappointment flooding through me.

He shrugged apologetically. 'I have to go. I'm late for a meeting. Look, I really am sorry, Chloe, and I hate that you've had such a rough time of it. I would have done things differently had I known. Let's just say you and I had very different child-hoods, and I believed you would be okay.'

'But I haven't explained everything. I—'

'There's no point dredging up the past,' he said, pushing his chair under the table. 'It's best to look towards the future. See you around, Chloe.'

He squeezed my shoulder as he moved past me, in what I assumed was a gesture of affection – or was it apology? – and then he was gone. I watched him walk briskly away with the woman, both of them looking at their phones and talking animatedly, the problems of his estranged sister already forgotten.

It was clear to me that he wasn't going to help me. I would have to take matters into my own hands.

FORTY

CLARISSA

I was trapped in a stand-off with a four-year-old, and despite my best efforts, it felt as though I was losing. If he'd been my child, it would have been different. *My* two had been brought up in a different time, when respect for parents and teachers was still the norm. Going by the cheekiness of Mirium's grandchildren, these were values that had dwindled considerably over the years. Cutting Tommy's sandwich in half, I glanced at his little red face as he watched me from the table. Although if I were honest, it wasn't just Berty and Lola that Mirium struggled with. She hadn't had much more control when it came to their father, Joseph, either.

I walked round the counter, placing the plate in front of Tommy. He didn't reach for it, and I sighed. I was emotionally drained after the argument with Chloe earlier. It had been the last thing I'd wanted to do, and I knew I'd upset her by sending her away without even letting her through the front door. But I'd had no choice.

After telling her she could take Tommy home today, I'd been sick with worry that I'd made the wrong call, that it was too soon, that she couldn't handle the pressure of raising her son. And now, seeing this stubborn streak in him, I was sure I'd made the right choice. She wasn't strong right now; she'd been through so much, needed to get back on her feet before being thrown into the reality of parenting full-time again.

Tommy jutted out his chin, and I pushed the plate closer. 'Eat up. I know you're hungry.'

'But why can't Mummy take me to the park?' he said in a plaintive voice. 'I heard her talking to you before.'

I frowned. 'You were listening?'

'She said she was coming this afternoon to take me home. You said she could!' His bottom lip wobbled.

I sighed. 'You shouldn't listen to people's conversations, Tommy. It isn't polite.'

'Mummy doesn't care about that.'

'Well, she should. It's her job to teach you how to be a good person. Kind, well mannered. Mummy and I were having a grown-up conversation, and you've upset yourself by listening in and misunderstanding.'

He folded his arms in a sulky gesture and leaned back in his chair. 'I want my mummy.'

I closed my eyes, feeling suddenly too old for all this. I had raised my children. I'd done the homework with them. Made the healthy dinners and the packed lunches. Brushed their teeth and hair and taught them how to tie their shoelaces. I had dedicated myself fully to the role I'd been given, and I'd done a damn good job of it. But it had taken its toll, required all my energy, my focus, my strength. And now I felt as if I were back at square one, only this time I didn't have a child who was a blank slate, who knew my expectations. I had one who had countless traumas under his belt and a distinct lack of regard for my rules.

I lowered myself into the chair beside him, running my fingers through my hair, distracted by how wrinkled the skin on the back of my hand was, how paper-thin it had become without my noticing. When did I lose my drive? Become this person who couldn't cope with the challenge of overcoming a difficult situation? I'd always been able to adapt to my circumstances.

I leaned forward, meeting his eyes. 'Mummy isn't very well. It's why I had to send her away. She needs to spend some time resting before she'll be ready to take you home.'

Tommy scratched at the table with the tip of his finger, his legs swinging beneath him, still too short to reach the floor. 'Mummy doesn't need rest. She doesn't like sleep.'

I sat back, surprised that he'd noticed. 'What do you mean?'

'When I wake up for a wee at night, she's always sitting up with the lamp on. She reads at night. She hardly ever sleeps. She says you don't need to when you're grown up.'

'Well, that's not completely true. And Mummy's mind is starting to struggle without it. She needs to learn how to rest, and then maybe she'll be able to come and take you to the park.'

'But I want to go now. I want—'

'*Tommy.*' I took a deep breath, and he looked down. I could tell he was trying not to cry. It was an impossible situation.

My phone began to ring from the other room, and I stood up, glad of an excuse to take a break from the conversation. 'Eat your lunch. I need to see who's calling.'

I strode through to the living room, tension pulsing through me as I wondered if it would be news about Tommy's father. I hadn't been able to stop my mind from wandering back to him over and over again since hearing that he was in hospital. I couldn't help wondering if he would live or die. It was a dreadful situation.

My phone was on the windowsill, and when I picked it up, I saw Miri's name emblazoned on the screen. Irritated and in no mood to speak to her, I waited for it to stop, then put it back down.

I was still standing at the window, wondering how to deal

with Tommy, when I saw the door across the road open, Jeff
stepping out, his eyes fixed on me. *Damn.* I should have just
spoken to her. Now she'd sent him over to check on me. Make
sure I wasn't doing anything she didn't approve of.

I needed to leave this place, these people. I couldn't cope
with their suffocating presence in my life, not now there was
another child involved. As long as Tommy was here, they would
never stop, never relent. They would do anything to sink their
claws into him.

I rushed back into the kitchen, seeing that the sandwich was
gone, Tommy having wolfed it down in the way only young
boys seemed capable of.

'Go to your room, Tommy. I'll be right up.'

He stood, his expression silently challenging, as if he were
going to ask about Chloe again. I strode past him, checking the
bolt on the back door and drawing the curtains, casting the room
into a dim orange glow. When I looked around, there was no
sign of him. I heard the creak of the floorboards as he crossed
the landing above. Seconds later, the back door handle rattled,
followed by a hard volley of knocks.

'Clarissa, open up.'

Jeff's voice was demanding, expectant, but he had no right
to tell me what to do. No right to harass me like this.

Stepping away from the door, I opened the larder, pulling
the biscuit tin down from the top shelf and lifting the lid. I took
a piece of flapjack and placed it on a plate, then, ignoring his
shouts and knocks, sat down and bit into it. I wasn't going to let
them try to control me any more. Enough was enough.

FORTY-ONE

CHLOE

'Are you going to order something else? Because this is a business, you know.'

I looked up at the teenage waiter, who was glaring at me, his lips twisted in challenge.

'Excuse me?'

'It's a *café*. You need to let someone have the table if you aren't going to order something. You've finished your coffee. And people are getting annoyed,' he added in a snarky tone, gesturing to the group of customers by the door.

I sat back in the chair. 'Fine. I'll have another coffee, and a tuna melt.'

He raised an eyebrow, obviously having been expecting me to leave with my tail between my legs, then gave a short nod and walked back to the counter, writing down my order on a pad. I wasn't hungry, wasn't thirsty, but I didn't want to leave. I had nowhere to go.

Rhodri had left ages ago, and I'd remained in my spot by the window, feeling lost, scared, desperate. I didn't want to overreact, be seen to be unhinged, as my mother so clearly thought I was, but to do nothing, let her pick and choose when and how I got to see my child, was out of the question.

I half considered calling the police but ruled it out almost immediately, still afraid of Irene's threats, unwilling to look out of control and unstable if it came to a fight for custody. Besides, talking to the police again after their unwelcome arrival on my doorstep and their unsettling questions about Scott was the last thing I wanted. I wouldn't invite them back into my life unless I'd exhausted every other option.

My phone rang, and I answered immediately, hoping it was Mum, my heart racing as I pressed it to my ear. 'Hello?'

There was a beat of silence, and I held my breath, waiting, then glanced at the screen. It was a withheld number. Probably a double-glazing salesman or some such rubbish. I was about to cut them off when I heard a voice.

'You got my letters.'

I stared at the phone, bringing it slowly back to my ear. 'Annie?'

'How did you know it was me?'

I let out a long breath, closing my eyes, memories flooding back at the sound of her voice, so familiar. It was as if I'd found an old jumper, threadbare and soft, smelling of home, cocooning me, reminding me of cosy winter days in front of the fire.

A sudden image filled my mind – the two of us rollerblading on the street, pink knee pads and iridescent purple helmets, gripping onto each other for support, half holding each other up, half pulling each other down. I batted away the memory, swallowing down a ball of emotion.

'I pieced it together,' I said. 'I wish you'd spoken to me in person, Annie. You didn't need to write those notes.'

'I needed you to take responsibility. Although they didn't have that effect, did they? You still haven't gone to the police.'

I shook my head. 'There are things you don't understand.

It's complicated. You don't know the full story.' I glanced out of the window, not admitting how little of it I understood myself. I hated how cold, how distant she sounded. I wanted to ask about her life, how she'd been. If she'd married, if she had the life she wanted, or if like me it was a tangle of blessings and curses. I wanted to know what she'd seen that night and why she'd moved away. How her daughter had come to be at Tommy's preschool.

'I want you to go now. *Today*. Go to the police and confess what you did.' I heard the crack in the back of her throat. 'He was like a brother to me, Chloe. Did you know that? Did you even care? I was closer to him than you ever were. He confided in me. Said you were your mother's favourite. That he didn't trust you. That you'd do anything to make her happy. I always stood up for you, but I shouldn't have. I was wrong, wasn't I? I loved him like he was my own flesh and blood, and you killed him!'

I flinched, glancing over my shoulder, hoping the other diners couldn't hear her shouted accusations through the phone.

'I believed karma had caught up with you. Your mum told me you were dead.'

I pressed my lips together, stifling the rebuttal that was itching to escape. I wanted to call her a liar, say that no matter how upset she'd been, my mum would never make such a bold statement, wouldn't tempt fate with such an awful lie, but hadn't Jeff and Mirium claimed the very same thing? Had my mother really been so sure I wouldn't return that she'd told people I was dead? I blinked as hot tears blurred my vision. She would have been protecting me. It was an awful thing to admit to myself, but I knew that she would have gone to the ends of the earth to stop the finger-pointing, the hushed whispers and questions directed at her daughter. *Of course* she would have been forced to lie. But it hurt all the same.

Annie was still talking, her tone filled with malice, accusation. 'Everyone was saying what a tragedy it was for her to lose both her children one after the other like that. She wouldn't talk about it, but I was sure you'd killed yourself. If *I* had done what you did, I couldn't have lived with myself... It was poetic justice. The only end I could accept. You weren't the person I believed you to be, but in death you'd paid a price, and I could deal with that. But when I dropped my daughter off at her new preschool and saw you there, talking and laughing with the receptionist like you didn't have a care in the world...'

She made a spluttering sound, and I closed my eyes, wishing she'd pause for breath so I could correct her.

'I don't know how you did it, Chloe, how you just vanished like that, but if you think enough time has passed that what you did to Rhodri doesn't matter, you're sadly mistaken. You don't deserve your freedom. The fact that I have to be the one to tell you that is frankly unfathomable. Your poor mother. Does she even know you're alive?'

'Yes,' I whispered. 'Annie, what did you hear that night? Why do you think I...?' I broke off, glancing at the woman drinking hot chocolate at the table beside me. 'What makes you think I did anything?' I finished, my voice soft as I pressed the phone closer to my ear. I needed to know from her perspective what had happened, why both she and my mum were so certain I was to blame for a death that I had proved to myself never even happened.

I heard her sigh. 'I don't want to go through it all, Chloe. What's the point?'

'*Please*, Annie. I need to hear it.'

There was another long silence. 'Fine. But after this call, you have twenty-four hours to hand yourself in, or I'll be going to the police to tell them everything I know. I wrote it all down that night. I have every detail recorded. I only wish we'd had CCTV back then.'

'Tell me what you know. Then do me a favour and listen to what I have to say before you hang up. Let's get everything out in the open, okay?'

'If it makes you feel like you've got control of the situation.' Her tone was sarcastic, cold, and it made me sad to hear her speak with such obvious contempt for me. 'Like I said, I'll give you a day. *One* day.'

'Go on,' I pushed.

She sighed again, and I could picture the frustration on her face, the way her nose used to wrinkle, her freckles merging together into one, whenever she was annoyed by anything. 'I was out that night. You remember that boy I was seeing? Rick?'

I tried to put a face to the name but couldn't.

She continued without waiting for a response. 'I'd snuck out to see him at the park. He walked me back to the end of the road but not to the house – I didn't want my parents to see us together, so we said goodbye on the corner. I was heading up the path when I heard it... screaming, coming from his room. It was like nothing I'd ever heard before. Like something animal. It terrified me.

'I was about to cross the road to knock on your door when our neighbour Jeff came outside. I was too afraid of what was happening to even worry that he'd tell my parents he'd seen me out past midnight. I was just relieved there was an adult there to make a decision on what to do. He asked what I'd heard, and I told him: just the screams.'

'Rhodri's screams?' I asked, keeping my voice low.

'No. It was you, Chloe.'

I felt nausea churn in my belly as I absorbed her words, nodding silently.

'We waited for a while, but there was just silence after that. A few minutes later, the light went off upstairs and then one came on in the living room.'

I nodded again. That was what Jeff had told me too. I opened my mouth to say as much, but she continued speaking.

'I said it could have been one of your nightmares. We all knew about them. I'd seen you sleepwalking down the road like a ghost in that creepy white nightdress you had. Your mum rushing after you, bringing you home, your eyes glazed, *gone...*' she said, her sentence drifting off.

'What happened next?'

'Jeff stared at the house for a long time, then agreed with me. He told me to go to bed and went back inside. But I didn't. I couldn't. Those screams... they'd stayed with me... I couldn't banish the echoes of them from my mind. It didn't *feel* like just a nightmare. It was too real, too raw, and every instinct in my body was telling me something was really wrong. So,' she continued, taking a shaky breath, 'I crossed the road. I went round to the side – you know that little window that we used to climb through that led into the utility? Your mum was always forgetting to shut it. I climbed in and pushed the door open a crack, and I heard what she was saying.'

'My mum?'

'Yes... She was trying to calm you down, Chloe, and then she said it. She said she didn't blame you. That you couldn't help it. And then *you* said, "I killed him. I really killed him!" You started crying, and I was suddenly so scared of what it might mean for me if I was found hiding... listening. You were a murderer, and you might go to any lengths to keep me quiet.'

'Annie...' I whispered, feeling close to tears. I shook my head, hating that she'd ever been afraid of me. The idea that I would have hurt her was simply ludicrous.

'I snuck home, and the next morning I woke up hoping it had all been a bad dream. But then my mum was there, telling me that Rhodri had died in the night. That Clarissa was in bits and that it had been something to do with his heart, some undiagnosed condition. It was a bare-faced lie. I should have known she'd protect you, but you were fifteen; you weren't a fucking child, Chloe. You should have spoken up, told the truth. But you were too much of a coward. And now, *now* I find out you've been living in the shadows all these years, hiding from the consequences you should have faced. Your mum might have chosen you over him, but I can't. I won't. I will stand up for him, and I won't stop until I get justice for what you did.'

I sat back, shaking, her words tearing through me, bringing back the awful memories of that night. I hadn't remembered screaming. I must have blocked it out, unable to bear replaying the horror of the moment when I'd been told what I'd done. 'I don't understand...' I said. 'I don't get it. I can't—' I broke off. 'Annie, Rhodri is alive. I didn't kill him.'

She gave a biting laugh that was too loud against my eardrum. 'Oh, *of course*. Is this really the path you want to go down? You want to play games with me?'

'No, no, I'm not. Please, just listen. Are you near a computer?'

'What? Yes, but I don't see—'

'Type in Emerald Estate Agents.'

'Chloe—'

'Just do it, okay?' I snapped, my tone sharp, desperate.

I heard the clicks as she complied, relieved that she was cooperating.

'Done. And what was the point to this?'

'You see the tab that says "Meet Our Staff"? Go to it and read the first bio.'

There was no reply, but I listened hard as she breathed; heard the moment her breath stopped.

'What is this? Who the fuck is Paul, and why do I care?'

'Look at him! Zoom in on his face. Don't you see it, Annie? It's him. It's *Rhodri*. He's alive!'

The woman beside me cleared her throat, glancing at me over her mug, but I didn't care any more. Let her listen.

'But... I don't understand. He died. Your mum was distraught. He was gone. He wouldn't just leave. Not without talking to me. To never get in touch...'

'How do you think *I* feel?' I retorted, letting my irritation rise up, though I'd fought to keep it contained. 'I don't have any answers for you. I've spent the last fifteen years believing my brother died, that I was somehow responsible, though I had no memory of doing anything to him, and now I find him strutting around in a suit selling mansions to millionaires and doing quite all right actually.'

'You've seen him? In person?' Her tone was incredulous, as if she still didn't quite believe me.

'Yes. And before you ask, he hasn't enlightened me as to why he let us believe such awful things. Be my guest and drop in on him. The address is right there on the website. But I doubt you'll get any clarity.'

I felt my nostrils flare as I spoke, the anger and frustration I'd been holding on to fizzing and popping like fireworks in my chest. I forced myself to relax my jaw, breathe a little slower, calming myself down before I spoke again.

'Look, I get it. I understand why you believed he was dead. I did too up until a few days ago. But we were close, weren't we? When you saw me at the preschool, you could have spoken to me. I'm still the girl you used to ride bikes and play dolls with.'

I heard her swallow and wondered if she might be crying.

'I'll call him. Or visit. I don't know... It's... This is a lot to take in. But you're right, I should have spoken to you. The letters were the wrong approach. I was just so upset. Seeing you standing there brought it all back. I don't think I ever fully processed the grief. It was too sudden. And we were so young.'

I nodded, reflecting on how different my life might have

been if I'd had her to confide in. The way she would have been there for me in my darkest times, if only circumstance and lies hadn't torn us apart.

'Maybe we'll catch up one of these days?' I said, hope clawing at the edges of my casually tossed suggestion. I felt vulnerable the moment I spoke the invitation, but it was too late to take it back.

'Actually, I'd like that. I'll call, in a few weeks, after I've had time to think... process it all, you know.'

'Of course. Annie, just one more thing before you go,' I said, suddenly thinking of something. 'Did I ever have an imaginary friend when we were younger? I don't suppose you remember... did I ever pretend someone else was around? My dad? Another child?'

There was a pause, and I waited nervously.

'I don't think so. I can't remember anything like that.'

'Right...' I said, wishing she'd had a different answer for me. 'Well, I'm glad we cleared things up between us. No more notes, okay?' I said, the jokey tone coming out stiff, awkward, despite my best efforts.

'No more notes,' she agreed. 'Bye, Chloe.'

She ended the call, and I found myself staring at the screen as it turned black.

'Here's your order.'

I looked up, feeling dazed, surprised to see the surly waiter with a tray balanced on one hand. He dumped the plate in front of me but wasn't brave enough to do the same with the coffee, placing it down more carefully.

'Thanks,' I said, pushing both aside.

He huffed and walked off, leaving me to reflect on the call. I wanted to go straight round to my mum's house and demand she tell me what had really happened. Why so many of the things she'd told me had turned out to be wrong. Had she intentionally lied to me, or had she just been mistaken? The relief I should have felt at clearing things up with Annie was conspicuously absent, my only thought being how I was going to get my son home, convince my mum I was a good mother, that I could raise him alone, without her help.

The smell of the tuna panini on the table was making my stomach churn, and I felt suddenly fidgety, desperate to move, to do something. I'd spent too long being a victim to put up with this now. Good as my mother's intentions might be, I'd had enough. I had to embrace the awkwardness and tell her that she'd overstepped the mark, despite my never having disagreed with her in the past. And if she wouldn't listen, wouldn't let me in, then yes, I *would* break down the door. I would take my son back by whatever means necessary. It was my only choice.

I stood up and reached into the pocket of my shorts for my purse. As I pulled it out, something floated to the ground. Bending to pick it up, I recognised the letter I'd taken from the hidden box beneath my mother's bed. What with all the drama going on with Scott, Mum, Rhodri, I'd completely forgotten I'd taken it.

No longer in the mood to reminisce, I opened it half-heartedly, not bothering to sit back down as I scanned the surprisingly short note. I reached the end, then read it again, sure it couldn't be right.

I'll probably be dead by the time you read this. I can't see a way out, a way to escape her. She's going to kill me, I know it. I would leave, but I can't abandon my son, can't save myself without sacrificing him. I never knew I could feel so much hatred for another person; it boils inside me, a poison running through my veins. I know I'm weak. I'm lost. And more than anything, I know she will destroy me. My greatest regret is meeting her. If you can help me, you have to find a way. I'm begging you. You're my last hope.

I gripped the page, my hand shaking as I stared at the words of someone clearly in fear for their life. This wasn't the love letter I'd been anticipating. This was terrifying.

I yanked open my purse, fishing out a five-pound note, though I wasn't sure it was enough, and slammed it down on the table, then practically ran through the café, knocking into chairs and customers as I barged my way through and out onto the street. I broke into a run, crossing the road, forcing a bike to swerve round me, knocking into a man with a gym bag and not stopping to apologise. Sweat prickled under my arms, trickled down my back, the humid air making my clothes stick uncomfortably to my skin, but I didn't slow down.

I ran around the corner, down the road, my heart pounding hard, saliva pooling beneath my tongue, finally coming to a stop outside the estate agent's and bending over to catch my breath for a moment. Looking up, I saw the closed sign on the door, Rhodri, the dark-haired woman from the café, and a handful of other smartly dressed men and women all sitting self-importantly round a table towards the back. Without pausing to question my actions, I pushed open the door and strode inside, still holding the letter in my sweaty grip.

'Sorry, we're closed,' the brunette said, looking in my direction.

'What the hell is this?' I yelled, holding up the crumpled piece of paper.

Rhodri, recognising my voice, looked over his shoulder, his face a picture of horror. I was sure the last thing he wanted was for his fancy colleagues to know this mess of a woman was his sister.

'Chloe! What are you doing here?' He stood up, coming over to me, trying to guide me back outside.

'Do you know what this is? Who wrote it? Who is it about? Read it, Rhodri.'

The man who'd been sitting opposite him rose to his feet. 'Uh, Paul, do you need me to call the police?'

Of course. Paul. His fake little life. How easy it must be for him, erasing his past, pretending we didn't exist.

He shook his head. 'No, no, it's okay. Just give me a minute,' he said, his cheeks flushing, his eyes panicked. 'Chloe, come out the back with me. We can talk.'

'I won't let you fob me off again! I need to know the truth!'

He pressed his lips together in a firm line, then grabbed my arm and guided me forcibly past his bewildered colleagues and out to a small kitchenette. He shut the door and turned to me. 'What the hell are you thinking? This is my business, Chloe. You can't come in here screaming and making demands. Are you fucking deranged?'

'No, I'm not deranged. I'm scared! I don't understand what's going on! I don't know what to think. Read the letter,' I demanded again, thrusting it at him.

I watched his face as he read, waiting for the moment when he understood my panic, but it never came. Instead, he nodded, a resigned expression taking the place of the horror I'd expected. He passed it back to me.

'Well?' I pushed.

'I don't know what you want from me.'

'I found it in a box under Mum's bed. Who do you think wrote it? Could it have been our dad?'

'Just leave it.'

'No, I won't just leave it. What did you mean earlier when you said you and I had very different childhoods? Were you talking about Mum?' I felt sick as I asked the question, wishing any part of this made sense.

'Look, I've left my past firmly where I want it. I suggest you do the same. And I don't think this is going to work,' he added, gesturing to me. 'I'm not the brother you want or need. We should say our goodbyes. We were never close anyway; it'll be no great loss to either of us.'

I shook my head, trying not to show how hurt I was by his words.

'It's all toxic,' he continued. 'Walk away from it and start afresh somewhere new. Don't go raking all of this up.' He jabbed a finger at the letter.

'She's our mother! She's never done anything wrong. Besides, she's got my son. I can't just—'

'Wait? You have a *son*? I just assumed you'd have a girl. I pictured a little mini version of you.' He pushed his hands to his face, making a sound that sent a shiver through me.

I stepped back, pressing against the kitchen counter, instinctively wanting to create space between us.

'You let her take your son?' he whispered, lowering his hands. 'You need to get him, Chloe. You have to go and get him now.'

'But—'

'I'm not joking. *Go*. He's not safe there. Trust me.'

I stared at him, seeing the fear that had been so conspicuously absent when he read the letter now filling his eyes, the colour drained from his previously flushed face.

'Come with me. Please,' I said. 'Let's all sit down and figure out this mess. We need to get everything out in the open. I need answers, Rhodri; I feel like I'm going mad.'

He shook his head. 'No. There's no way.'

'Rhodri—'

'I said no!' he yelled, his voice loud and terrifying in the tiny room.

I felt myself cower, covering my face, expecting the blow to fall as it would have had it been Scott in his place, but nothing happened. Slowly, I lowered my hands, looking cautiously across at him. He was staring at me, a questioning look in his eyes, but I didn't dare to speak again.

'Go and get your son, Chloe. I hope things work out for both of you.'

I nodded, too afraid to say another word in protest, then walked through the door as he opened it for me, past the group at the table and out into the street, more in the dark than ever before.

FORTY-TWO

I stood outside the house, unsure whether to knock, to try the back door or to do something different. My head was pounding, my eyes streaming from the pain of it, and my heart kept skipping a beat – a consequence of the horrific insomnia I'd been experiencing. The few hours of deep sleep I'd managed over the course of the week weren't enough. Not by a long chalk. I rubbed my temples, Rhodri's haunting warning playing on repeat in my head. *Go and get him... He's not safe.*

Despite everything I knew, the love I had for the woman who had raised me single-handedly without ever so much as raising her voice to me, I couldn't explain why those words had resonated so deeply, why they'd hit a nerve. She was a good person, a fantastic mother. She would never pose a threat to Tommy. So why did I feel so scared right now? Was it because I knew I was about to engage in a conflict with her that might cement her concern over my mental health? Because no matter what, I *would* be taking my son home with me this evening. It had gone on too long, and there were too many secrets popping up that had me feeling unsettled. I wanted my child with me, and there would be no argument that could make me walk away without him.

I headed up the path to the front door, trying the handle first, then, finding it locked, knocking hard on the stained-glass panel. I half expected it to go unanswered, but I heard footsteps beyond, and a moment later, the door swung open, my mother staring back at me with flushed cheeks and wide eyes. I didn't give her an opportunity to block my path this time. I pushed past her without a word, heading straight for the kitchen. Finding it empty, I went to the window to scan the garden.

'He's not here. He's with Miri and Jeff while I get dinner sorted. Her grandkids wanted him to come and play.'

I turned to see her standing in the doorway, her arms folded across her chest. She looked self-conscious, embarrassed almost, the bluster and bravado of earlier gone.

'Right. I'll go over there then.'

I turned to walk back out, my need to see him far deeper than my desire for answers to my myriad questions, but she grabbed my arm.

'Chloe, wait, I want to apologise for earlier. I was unreasonable, unfair on you. I didn't mean to make it sound like you're a danger to him. I just wanted to do the right thing, and it's not always easy. I feel torn between what I should do and what everyone demands of me, and I don't always explain that well.'

She reached out to cup my cheek, but I stepped back, still too angry with her, too confused to forgive so easily.

She gave a sad smile. 'You know how much I love you. How glad I am to have you back in my life. You have no idea how much I missed you after you left. I didn't expect you to go. You never gave me an opportunity to change your mind, never even said goodbye. It was devastating for me, waking up to find your room empty, waiting night after night for the sound of a key in the door. I don't want to lose you again.'

I stiffened my jaw, determined not to back down this time. I had spent so much of my life doing the right thing. I'd been top of my class at school. I'd never disagreed with any of the boundaries I was set. I'd moulded and stretched myself to become the woman Scott desired and let myself feel shame and guilt when he told me how I'd ruined his life, somehow believing it was my fault. But I was stronger now. I'd been pushed to the brink, and I wouldn't let my son suffer because I didn't have it in me to fight for him. He deserved my strength, and though he would never know it, it was the look of fear, shock, *disappointment* on his little face when he'd seen his father beat me that stuck with me more than anything, made me determined to be better for him.

I saw the sadness in my mother's eyes and wanted to tell her it would all be okay, that I forgave her, but I wouldn't take the easy path. I was taking my son home today whether she agreed or not.

I'd opened my mouth to say as much when a knock sounded behind me. I looked over my shoulder to the back door to see Rhodri standing there.

Mum's mouth dropped open, her hand reaching for the counter as if to steady herself. 'Don't let him in,' she whispered.

'This is ridiculous!' I strode to the door, twisting the key in the lock and stepping back. 'You came,' I said, managing a smile for him.

He nodded, then stepped inside. Slowly, he raised his eyes to our mother's face, an unreadable expression crossing his features. 'Hello, Mum,' he said.

I frowned, detecting a mocking, disingenuous tone to the greeting, as if he knew he wasn't welcome here.

She didn't respond, didn't even look at him, and I was afraid it was all too much for her, that his sudden reappearance had sent her into shock.

'I tried to warn you,' I said gently. 'I told you I'd seen him. I know none of it makes sense, but well, now he's here, we can get to the bottom of what happened.'

Rhodri shook his head. 'I'm not here to play happy families. I just wanted to make sure you were all right. Where's your son?'

'He's across the road.'

'Good. Grab his things, and we'll go and get him.'

I frowned. 'You aren't even going to have a conversation? After all this time?'

He looked at me blankly.

I shook my head, turning to Mum. 'Aren't you surprised to see your son here, alive and well?' I asked. 'Aren't you going to say hello?'

I watched her, not seeing the reaction I'd anticipated. Not seeing any reaction whatsoever. Admittedly, she'd been stoic, calm on seeing me again for the first time in fifteen years, but that was different. She'd never thought *I* was dead. Surely any mother would be a sobbing wreck if the child they thought they'd lost for ever came back from the grave? But then... she'd been the one to call the ambulance. She'd dealt with having him taken away. She'd lied to the police to cover up for me. His reappearance wasn't just unlikely. It was impossible. Perhaps she couldn't believe what she was seeing. I could relate: it had been a shock for me too when I'd first seen him. But she didn't look shocked now. She looked angry.

'Explain this to me, Mum. You said—' I cut myself off, not wanting to say the words: *that I killed him.* I took a breath, steeling myself. 'You told me Rhodri had died.'

Rhodri snorted. 'Yeah, I've been thinking about that since you told me. It makes perfect sense. She wouldn't want you asking uncomfortable questions, would she? Couldn't risk you trying to contact me and learning the truth. So much more convenient if everyone thought I was dead. Isn't that right, Mum?'

She bustled past me, picking up the kettle and filling it with water, and I felt as if I'd been dropped into some surreal alternative world where nothing made sense. How could she just be making tea when her son – the son she'd believed was dead – stood silent and sullen beside me?

She didn't look up. 'It was all so long ago. Let's leave the past where it belongs,' she said, echoing his words from earlier.

'How?' I shook my head. 'I don't understand.'

Rhodri touched my shoulder lightly. 'I'm not up for this. If you don't want my help, I'm going,' he muttered, his fingers already grasping the door handle, not even bothering to glance in Mum's direction.

'Don't you dare!' I exclaimed, shocked that he would consider leaving so soon. 'I can't let you go again. Not until you explain.'

I spun to face my mother. 'Why did you tell me he was dead? Why lie to me?'

'Chloe.' She stepped forward to put a hand on my arm, trying to soothe me. 'You weren't yourself that night. You're getting things muddled. It was a long time ago – it's not your fault, darling.'

'No!' I cried, stepping back, breaking her hold on me. I was angry with her, I realised. An emotion I couldn't recall ever having felt about her before today. She'd never been the type of mother to make me feel trapped. She'd been someone I could rely on for anything, but now, looking into those soft, imploring eyes, I knew she was keeping something from me.

'I'm not muddled, not confused. Do you really think I would ever be able to erase the memory of that night from my mind? You told me as clear as day that he'd died. That I had killed him, then passed out in his bed. Do you think I could mistake your words? They broke me!' I cried. 'I've had to live with the guilt of what I did every day of my life since then. I have *hated* myself! And yet somehow, here he is, quite clearly alive. And that means, whatever really happened that night, you hid the truth from me. You put that on my shoulders, the weight of a murder that never took place, and I haven't put it down for over a decade.'

Tears flowed down my cheeks as I thought about the life I'd let myself be dragged into. The squalor I'd considered my punishment. The boyfriend I'd allowed to beat me. I could have walked away after the first time. Could have gone to a refuge with my son. But deep down, the moment Scott turned against me, I'd experienced something that felt like relief. Retribution. Because I didn't *deserve* an easy life. Had lost the privilege of achieving my dreams, having the little farmhouse, the hens, the happy children with mud under their fingernails, scraped knees from climbing trees in the fresh, clean air. I'd lost any right to any of it the night I killed my brother and let my mum lie for me; protect me.

I'd never questioned her. Never gone to the police. She'd taken care of everything – there hadn't even been a funeral. It was as if she'd brushed the whole thing under the carpet, and despite my age, my unerring trust in her, I should have known better. Should have had the courage to admit to what she'd accused me of. Because there was no get-out-of-jail-free card. In lieu of any real punishment, the trial I should have faced, I'd been unable to move forward with my life – the guilt had gnawed away inside my belly, and though I hadn't seen it at the time, I realised now that I had done everything I could to atone. I'd sabotaged my own happiness, and it had all been for a lie.

'I could have been so much more than I am... could have made a success of my life.' The words came as little more than a whisper as I looked out of the kitchen window at a spot in the distance. 'I was clever. Doing well at school. I wanted to do so much, and that lie, that *awful* lie ripped away my future. So yes, I want you to tell me the truth. Both of you.' I stared at Rhodri, sure that he was to blame somehow. That despite her lies, she had been protecting me, misguided though she may have been. 'There was blood on the bedroom carpet,' I said. 'I remember it. Not much, but enough. And it wasn't mine.'

Rhodri sighed. 'It was mine.'

I nodded. 'So I *did* hurt you.'

'No, Chloe. You weren't even there—'

'Rhodri,' Mum interrupted, a warning look in her expression. His eyes narrowed, and I saw a look pass between the two of them that made hairs rise on the back of my neck.

I folded my arms tight across my chest. 'I was in your room,' I said softly. 'In your bed. Did you... did something happen?'

The very thought of it made me feel sick, but I had to know. It had been an idea that had been growing, rolling over and over in the depths of my mind ever since I'd discovered he was alive. What other reason could there have been for my mother to lie? For him to disappear without a trace? Had she caught him doing something unspeakable with me? Something that had forced her to send him away, humiliated and scared to the point that he'd never once tried to get in touch over the years? I watched his face closely, reading his expression as I spoke. 'Did you touch me? While I was sleeping? Did you—'

His reaction was instant: revulsion, shock, anger. 'Fuck! No, Chloe! What the hell? Of course not. I told you, you weren't even in the room. She must have put you there after I left.'

'That's enough! I want you to go!' Mum's voice was shrill, cold, and I was taken aback at the lack of warmth in her face – a face I'd never seen as anything but safe, loving, kind. In this moment, she looked like a different person.

'No, not until you both explain what happened that night. Why Rhodri sent me back here in a panic to collect my son. Why you've been so controlling, taking over like you're Tommy's mother instead of me. I want the truth!'

Rhodri sneered, his expression hard and cold as he watched Mum continue to fuss around making tea. 'Go on, Clarissa – tell her. Tell her what kind of a person you really are. How you treat the men in your life.'

For the first time since Rhodri had arrived, Mum met his gaze. For a moment, they just stared at each other.

'I hoped I would never see you again,' she whispered, almost to herself. 'That you really *had* died.'

'Mum!' I gasped, stunned by her malice, but she didn't seem to hear me.

'Ditto,' said Rhodri.

'You were always such an ungrateful child. Never realised how lucky you were. So reckless, so disruptive.'

He shook his head. 'You and I both know that's a lie.'

'I know nothing of the sort. You were your father's child through and through.' She turned to me, a regretful expression on her round, lined face. 'I wanted to protect you. I didn't want you mixed up in all the nonsense he brought home with him. He was out of control. You have to understand, I was raising him by myself and it was hard. I did my best.'

Rhodri shook his head. 'You were cruel. Evil.'

'If you felt like that, it was only because you brought it on yourself. Your sister never felt that way. She was well behaved. *You* needed far more discipline. And look, you've made something of yourself. Fancy suit. Expensive shoes. You wouldn't be where you are now without me setting you straight every time you rebelled against the rules.'

He snorted, eyes wide. 'You think my success has anything to do with you? I made it *despite* you. Despite everything you put me through. I was a child, a little boy, and you were never a mother to me.' He stepped closer, holding her gaze, a dangerous energy pulsing around him.

I watched, horror-struck.

'I *did* make a success of myself, *Mother*,' he said, spitting the word like it was dirt in his mouth. 'I have a business. Friends. And a girlfriend who's the polar opposite of you. Do you know what she does for a living?' He gave a wry smile. 'She's a thera-pist. I have *her* to thank for helping me become the man I am today. For making me see that what happened to me as a child was nothing to do with me being a *bad boy*, as you so often told me, but entirely down to you being the worst kind of person, unfit to raise a child. At least a male one.'

I listened in shock to his callous accusations, unable to accept his words. 'She did her best, Rhodri. And you were naughty. I remember you being in trouble so often.'

He gave a cold laugh. 'Really? You don't have a clue, Chloe. Not one. You didn't see what she did, and do you want to know why? Because on the nights I was punished, you were sedated. She didn't want her precious little princess tainted by it all. Didn't want you to see her true colours.'

'Sedated? What are you—'

He cut me off with a wave of the hand. 'Why do you think you had those night terrors? You were drugged up to the eyeballs on her prescription meds! You missed the whole show. You weren't there when she body-slammed me through the patio doors, cutting my head open in the process. You weren't conscious when she jammed my hand in the door or pushed me down the stairs. You didn't see the aftermath of her pouring the kettle over my arm because I forgot I'd dropped a piece of sweetcorn on the table and she thought I was treating her like a servant,' he yelled, yanking up his shirtsleeve to reveal a shiny patch of skin the size of a pack of cards. 'Your perfect childhood was only that way because you were lucky enough to be born a girl. You never had to suffer her hate, her so-called punishments for daring to be male.'

I stared at him, too stunned to speak.

Mum turned with a tut and began to wipe the counter as if he hadn't spoken. 'I think it's time you both left. I've had quite enough of this drama for one day. Come back tomorrow, Chloe, and you can collect Tommy then.'

I stared at her, struck by a sudden feeling of relief that at least Tommy was with the neighbours, that I knew he was safe. 'Aren't you going to say anything?' I asked. 'Is he telling the truth? *Did* you drug me? Did you do all those terrible things?'

I reached for Rhodri's arm, and he flinched as, with gentle fingers, I rolled back his sleeve to look at the burned skin again. I touched it with the tip of my finger, then raised my eyes to meet his rigid expression. There was so much emotion behind it. Fear. Determination. It had cost him to tell me. And despite everything I knew about my mother, I couldn't help but feel he was speaking the truth.

'Mum!' I insisted, shocked that she was saying nothing to defend herself. 'Tell me! Did you drug me?'

She spoke without turning, her words matter-of-fact. 'Anything I did was to protect you. You didn't need to see. You were always such a sweet girl. I couldn't bear for you to be tainted by his behaviour. It was out of love,' she insisted, running her cloth under the tap and wringing it out.

I stepped back, recoiling into my brother for support as I tried to fathom how she could possibly try to justify what she'd done. I looked up at him, understanding now why he'd been so reluctant to come back with me. 'Why didn't you tell me what she was doing?' I asked him softly. 'Why disappear? I was older than you. You could have trusted me to help.'

He shook his head. 'You always took her side. You'd never have believed anything I had to say against her. You were always so blind to it, her precious princess, the girl who could do no wrong.'

His tone was bitter, and it hurt to hear how he'd viewed me.

'I couldn't trust you. I didn't know how much of her you'd inherited. If you had the same warped views. She was like a worm in your ear, always whispering about my faults, putting down any man who came into our lives. Not to mention that as good as you think she was to you, she was trying to convince you that you were mad. The number of mornings I heard her telling you that you'd had another episode, that you'd been sleepwalking, that you'd hurt yourself. You were always falling out of bed or down the stairs; you even ended up getting out of the house once. She brought you home and completely neglected to mention that it was the drugs she'd slipped into your bedtime milk that were the cause. She wanted you to be afraid of your own shadow so you would never consider leaving her. She wanted to trap you.'

I shook my head, remembering the way she'd made me a cup of hot milk sprinkled with cinnamon before bed every now and then. She had sat on my bed, and we'd talked about school, our plans for the weekend – happy things – as I sipped the drink and she stroked my hair. I'd never put two and two together and seen the connection between those perfect evenings and the horrific mornings that followed.

He pursed his lips, looking over my shoulder towards our mother, who was pretending we weren't there. He looked back down at me, speaking in a low voice, though it was clear she was still listening. 'I assumed the drugging would stop if I was gone. She'd have no reason to do it any more. The night I left, I thought she would kill me.' He untucked his shirt, and I saw a long, thin scar running across his belly. 'I had to leave. I think she thought she'd really done it. She had a knife...'

He took a deep breath, and I saw the way his eyes glazed over, the pinched skin around his mouth. He suddenly looked ten years older.

He glanced out of the window as he went on. 'I'd spent too long across the road with Miri and Jeff's son, Joseph. He was my best friend, and I loved him like a brother. I never told him anything about what went on here, but it helped to have them over there – to escape this house and be normal for a while. Mum couldn't stand that I was spending time with them. She'd told me I couldn't see Joseph again, and, I don't know, I guess it was the final straw. Something I had to push back on, because without him, I didn't think I could keep on living. So I went there after school and she caught me.' He looked down at the ground, and I gripped his hand. 'She was out of control,' he finished softly. 'And she knew she'd gone too far.'

'You *pushed* me too far!' Mum cried.

Both of us looked up.

'And you're doing it again! I won't have this disobedience. Not under my roof. And this *is* my roof. *My* house! You never change, do you, Rhodri? You're just like your father. Is it any wonder I hated the bones of you?'

She slammed her fist on the kitchen counter, and I watched in horror as the woman I'd loved my whole life transformed into a monster I couldn't reconcile with the mother I'd thought I knew.

FORTY-THREE

CLARISSA

'You should never have come back here! Do you think I want to bring up the past? It's buried, over! I won't have you strolling into my house and rewriting history, making accusations when you've no right to be here!'

I clutched my chest, grabbing a handful of material from my dress, squeezing tight. I couldn't stand the smug expression on Rhodri's face, the way he looked at me as if he wasn't fazed by anything I said. He'd always been that way, even as a small boy. I would tell him off, try to explain where he'd crossed a line, and he would smirk, silently challenging me with a condescending air of disinterest. No matter the punishment, nothing seemed to break through the surface to make him take notice and try harder. It was apparent that he was rotten to the core, just like his father. It had been a nightmare trying to parent him, and it had only been Chloe who had given me the strength to keep trying.

I turned to her now, horrified by the way she was watching me, the look of distrust in her eyes. 'Chloe, please, let's you and me sit down over a cup of tea and talk. *You* can go,' I added, hearing the chill in my tone as I was forced to address her brother.

'Absolutely not.' She folded her arms, and I felt my mouth drop open in surprise. 'He's not leaving. I want to hear the rest. I want you to explain to me your side, because the half I've heard is appalling.'

I shook my head, meeting her eyes. 'You're trusting the wrong person. He's lying to you, Chloe. He was always so good at that.'

Rhodri gave a harsh laugh that sounded dangerous to my ears, and instinctively I gripped my hands into fists.

'If I was good at lying,' he said, his voice no less grating than it had been all those years ago, 'it was because you forced me to be. Don't you recall, Mother, the way you'd test me, get me to make up stories to explain how I got so many bruises? Couldn't have me going to my teachers, could you? And if I wasn't believable enough, what happened?'

'Shut up!' I cried, pressing my hands to my ears. 'What is the matter with you? You need to leave!'

He gave that smile again, the one that made me want to slap it off his evil little face, then turned to Chloe. '*Bleach.* She would dip my toothbrush in bleach and force me to brush my teeth. It was not the most pleasant experience,' he added, twisting his mouth as he looked down at the ground, playing the victim.

Chloe was shaking her head, and I was glad. She could see right through him.

'She wouldn't,' she whispered, and I hid a smile, relief flooding through me. If he cost me my daughter, I couldn't put a limit on what I would do in retaliation. I wouldn't lose her a second time.

'She did. It only took a couple of times for me to figure out the game. The mouth ulcers were unbearable, and I threw up so much afterwards I was afraid I would never stop. But I did in the end, and yes, I miraculously became a far better liar after that. It's been handy over the years. Got me jobs here and there. So yeah, you can take credit for that if you want. The worst parts of my character. But as for the rest, it's *despite* your parenting that I'm the man I've become.'

I shook my head. 'You sound just like you always did. A smug little shit who thinks he's so fucking smart. You were an evil little boy, and you're no different now!'

'Mum!' Chloe stepped forward, grabbing Rhodri's arm as if to comfort him.

I had never spoken this way in front of her. I'd done everything in my power to shield her from the awful impact her father and brother had had on me, never wanting to show this side, to let her see me struggling, for fear it would frighten her. If she had stayed longer, we would have talked more about the way men could be. How she needed to be careful of their traps, their manipulative energy that would wrap her up and destroy her if she didn't look out for herself. If she'd stayed under *my* roof, she never would have fallen prey to someone like Scott.

'No, Chloe!' I said, breathless with anger. 'No. I didn't want to do this; I didn't want to be the one to have to tell you the truth, but you've backed me into a corner. Your brother was a terrible child. He was just like his father, so sure of himself, so convinced the world owed him something. What is it with men thinking they're entitled to more just because they were born with a penis? Do we get the same? Of course not! We're expected to bend over backwards for them! Birth the children, feed them from our own bodies, give up every tiny piece of ourselves – fuck *our* dreams, our goals. It doesn't matter what we want! It's all about them! Do you think I *wanted* to give everything up and be a stay-at-home mum? A wife? Of course not! I was nineteen when I met Reece. It was only ever meant to be short-term. You know he was thirty-eight, right? He told me he was ready to settle down, and I said it wouldn't be with me. I wanted to travel. To have an adventure, a fucking life!'

I remembered how full of hope I'd been back then. I'd made it clear to Reece that I didn't want commitment. He knew all about my previous boyfriend, who'd taken me to Paris and proposed in the most disgustingly clichéd way imaginable at the top of the Eiffel Tower; how I'd walked away, leaving him in tears, surrounded by tourists. Cut him out of my life and never spoken to him again. I had hoped the story would make things crystal clear to Reece about what his expectations should be.

'He knew I was planning to leave him. It was only ever meant to be a fling. Someone to see during the long winter evenings – to entertain me. I had a job lined up in a hotel in Tuscany as a cabaret singer in the spring, and I couldn't wait to go. But he ruined all of that. He replaced my contraceptive pills with sugar pills. Make no mistake, he knew exactly what he was doing. He'd planned it all out, schemed and plotted, and by the time I realised I was pregnant, I was already fourteen weeks gone. I couldn't bring myself to end the pregnancy. I was trapped.'

'Is that how you felt?' Chloe's voice was small, and I saw her sadness as she took in what I was saying to her.

'When you were born, I loved you straight away. It didn't feel like a prison any more. I was more than happy to put aside my dreams for you. You were like a tiny version of myself, and we understood each other right from the start. We're so alike, Chloe.' I smiled. 'You have no idea how much of myself I see in you. I have never wished you hadn't been born, darling. You were a gift. But' – I let my gaze slide briefly to Rhodri – 'with him, it was different. By then, your father and I were on such rocky ground. I tried to make the best of it, allowed him to organise a wedding so I'd have security at the very least, but I couldn't forgive him, could never trust him again.

'To begin with, he gave me an allowance, money of my own,

but then, when things became...' I paused, trying to think of the right words. I didn't want to admit that he'd caught me giving baby Rhodri a cold bath for biting me. I took a composing breath. 'When things became less amicable, he cut me off. He made sure I had no money of my own so I couldn't leave. He wanted me with him, despite knowing how much I hated him. He was so proud of having a young, beautiful wife, because I *was* beautiful back then. I could have been a model, a famous singer, anything. The world should have been mine to take.'

I shook my head, thinking back to the life I'd dreamed of having. 'Men are so simple. If I'd been ugly, he would have let me go, but I was a prize as far as he was concerned, and he thought he deserved me. My wishes were irrelevant.'

'You think *that's* why he held on to the marriage?' Rhodri interrupted. 'You really are delusional. It was because he didn't trust you! He'd seen the other side of you by then. He understood how much danger I was in and so he couldn't leave.'

'What do *you* know about it? You were two when he died. You have no idea what happened between us!' I cried, furious that he would dare to try to sway Chloe with his toxic lies.

'Jeff told me. When I was older, when we used to talk. He knew something was going on, and he was scared. He told me everything Dad had said, how he was sure Dad was afraid of you, how you were crazy, and even though I was too scared to ask for his help, I knew he was telling the truth because it was exactly how *I* felt about you. You killed our dad, didn't you? You killed him as a punishment for trapping you. Even though all he ever wanted was a loving family, a normal home. He made a mistake in picking you, and he paid with his life!'

'Don't be so dramatic! I didn't kill anyone. I just paid him back with the same trick he'd played on me. He swapped my contraceptives for sugar pills. I tampered with his blood-pressure medication. I just had to open the capsules and tip the contents down the sink. It worked surprisingly quickly.'

'Oh, and you didn't fill them with something else?' Rhodri fixed me with an intense stare. Above the collar of his crisp white shirt, his skin was flushed and blotchy, a pulse hammering visibly, giving away just how rattled he was. 'I bet he never even touched your pills. You got pregnant and somehow decided it was his fault because you can never be wrong, can you? I know first-hand how you switch up the story to make your mistakes the fault of others – you did it to me countless times! You killed my dad because of a lie you'd convinced yourself of! What did you put into those pills, Clarissa?'

I ignored the question, not deigning to speak to him. 'I didn't expect him to *die*. I just wanted to teach him a lesson. Just a little heart attack. He was only forty-three. I didn't expect him to keel over so easily.'

It was a lie, but they didn't need to know that. At the time, I'd wanted nothing more. It had been something I'd come to realise in the months following Rhodri's birth, how my life had been infiltrated by these males, how I couldn't bear to live with their energy, their selfishness. My dear husband had thought he could change me, mould me into something I'd never had aspirations to be, and Rhodri... well, from the very start, he'd been manipulative, demanding, never satisfied no matter how much of myself I gave to him. He wouldn't stop, wouldn't rest even after he'd stripped away any part of myself I could recognise.

I'd seen quite clearly the limited options at my disposal. I couldn't leave – not without resigning myself to a life of poverty as a single mother, because despite what they thought of me, I would have taken Chloe with me. I would never have walked away from her. I knew Reece had had to take out life insurance in order to be approved for the mortgage on the house. And I saw an opportunity for me to get my freedom, to finally cut him out of my life and regain my independence. What did it matter now about the details? The contents of the pills. It was such a long time ago.

'Oh my God.' Chloe's words came out as barely more than a whisper, as she seemed to lean against Rhodri for support. His arm went round her, and the two of them shared a look that made me suddenly afraid I'd said too much.

'I'm sorry,' he said, not to me, but to her. His arm tightened around her waist as he looked down at her. 'I should never have left you behind. But I wasn't thinking about you. I was barely twelve, and I was just desperate to survive. Jeff had given me the address for Dad's sister a few days before, and that night when I left, that's where I went.

'*She* knew exactly where I was,' he said, giving me a cold glance. 'Auntie Louise called her when I arrived on her doorstep in the middle of the night, insisting that I was going to live with her now. There was no big secret. Dad had told his sister enough that she was more than willing to take me in. There was paperwork involved; Auntie Louise needed guardianship so she could register me for school. Mum signed it all. She never for a second believed I was dead. And I never thought you would be blamed for me disappearing.'

Chloe looked at me. 'You never told me I had an auntie. I never met her. Why not?'

I turned away, sickened by Rhodri's version of events, the way he was trying to make it sound like everything was my fault, when it was *his* behaviour, *his* disobedience that had brought it all about. Chloe would see through him soon enough. She was my daughter. She would always be my girl.

'We didn't get on,' I told her. 'She was never my kind of person.'

'You mean she never trusted you after what she heard from Dad,' Rhodri said.

Chloe wiped the tears that had begun to fall on her blanched cheeks. 'I've heard enough. Get me Tommy's bag,' she said, her voice unsteady, her eyes unable to meet mine. 'I'm going to collect him from Mirium and take him home.'

I stood still, knowing I couldn't let her do that but not wanting to anger her, not after all she'd heard today.

'Darling, I—'

I broke off as I heard the familiar creak of the gate, then felt my stomach drop as both Jeff and Mirium appeared, walking past the kitchen window. They stopped at the closed back door and knocked, a perfunctory show of manners.

Rhodri, seeing their faces, looked as if he might burst into tears, and Chloe moved to let them in.

'No! Chloe, wait! Don't!' I yelled.

But it was too late.

FORTY-FOUR

CHLOE

Ignoring my mum's shout to stop, I flung open the door to Mirium and Jeff. Seeing Rhodri, Mirium gasped, her hands going to her mouth, her eyes wide, while her husband made a sound of disbelief, striding into the room and grabbing him in a bear hug. Rhodri gripped him tightly, an audible cry coming from within the tight circle of their arms.

Slowly, Jeff pulled back. 'I thought I was going mad when I saw you on the path just then. Mirium said I must be imagining things, that it couldn't be you... but here you are! How—'

He broke off, and I watched in shock as the man I'd always thought of as strange and unlikeable broke into gut-wrenching sobs that made goose pimples rise on my skin. He stared at Rhodri, still grasping his arm as if to prove to himself that he was really here. 'I thought you were dead. I thought she...'

Rhodri, crying too, gripped Jeff's shoulder. 'I'm sorry. I didn't know. I had to leave, to make a fresh start, and I never built up the courage to come back.' He swallowed, and I felt as though I was watching a film, the moment between two men who'd had no connection as far as I could remember so surreal to me, forcing me to re-evaluate my whole history.

'I grieved for you. I called the police, but they weren't willing to do anything. I couldn't understand it. I was sure she'd killed you.'

Rhodri shook his head. 'They came to my aunt's house where I was staying. Mum sent them, but I didn't know she was telling people I'd died. My aunt wouldn't let me in the room while they were talking, but I listened outside the door – I was terrified they were going to force me to come back here. I overheard the police saying that Mum had told them she'd had to send me away because of a predator on the street. She said he was harassing me, and I was sure she meant you, that she wanted to get you in trouble. I knew she hated you. I went into the kitchen and told them you were a good man and you hadn't done anything wrong. I guess that's why they didn't come back and tell you the truth – they didn't know if you were trustworthy. Didn't want to give you information about my location. I thought they would explain it all to you. I never meant for people to think I'd died.'

Jeff shook his head. 'So *that's* what she meant. She told me time and again that she would ruin me if I kept on about Reece's death. I never trusted her; I knew she was dangerous, but that lie...' He suppressed a shudder. 'To come up with a story like that takes a truly despicable mind.'

I looked down, recalling that I'd made the very same threat to Scott to get what I wanted. It sent a wave of revulsion through me to see the similarities between us.

Jeff met Rhodri's eyes. 'It wasn't your fault. None of it.'

Rhodri continued as if Jeff hadn't spoken, unable to break his flow. 'And now,' he said, 'now she's just confirmed what you and I suspected all along. She tampered with Dad's pills. She *did* kill him!'

Jeff set his jaw, as if he was trying to hold back a reaction, but I could see the anger radiating through him. 'I knew it... I said, didn't I, Mirium? I told you she was an evil piece of work.'

Mirium, her eyes still fixed on Rhodri, looked as if she was about to keel over. She didn't speak, didn't move, her hand frozen in an outstretched position, as though she thought that if she reached out, she might touch nothing but thin air – the memory of a ghost, cold against her skin.

I shook myself. Tommy mustn't hear any of this. It was too frightening for him; I needed to get him away.

I looked past Mirium towards the doorway, wanting nothing more than to hold him in my arms. 'Where's Tommy? You haven't left him alone?' I asked, striding to the door and peering out into the garden to see if he'd already run off to play.

Jeff raised a questioning eyebrow. 'Left him where? He's not with us.'

Icy fear snaked around my heart, spreading slowly through my chest as I turned back to my mum.

'You said he was across the road? You said he...'

Her gaze slid away from me, down to the floor, and I felt as if I was going to be sick. An awful silence filled the room as I began to shake, all the words I'd just heard clamouring for space in my head: *punishment... entitled... smug... evil little boy.*

'Where's Tommy?' I asked, my voice quiet, measured. 'Where is he?'

'You can't take him away. You're not strong enough to parent him, Chloe. He needs proper discipline if he's got any hope of breaking the mould of the men in his family. And with a father like Scott, it will be all the more difficult.'

I blinked, wondering what she could mean. I hadn't told her anything about my life with Scott. How could she possibly have an opinion on him?

'It's in his blood,' she continued. 'He's already proved to be more of a challenge than his uncle.' She glanced with malice at my brother, who looked as if he might explode with suppressed rage. 'I can't let you take him. You're weak – at least when it comes to raising a boy. I've seen it from you already on too many occasions. You don't have the stomach for what's needed.'

'Oh my God.' I felt the room sway around me, my hands shaking so hard I couldn't control them, the fear of what might have already happened to my son too much to cope with.

Before I could speak, react, a blur of movement passed me, knocking me aside. Mirium stepped closer, gripping my hand, squeezing tight as Rhodri grabbed my mother by her shoulders, shoving her forcibly against the wall. I heard the slam as her back collided with the brick, and winced involuntarily. He was shaking as much as I was, but where I felt I might faint, he'd grown braver, a cornered animal ready to fight. He was no longer a timid little boy. He was a man, and in this moment, he was dangerous.

'Where the fuck is the boy? Tell me right now, you poisonous old witch!'

She glanced down at her feet, and I felt a surge of hope, but then she raised her head so her face was inches from his, a slow smile spreading across it.

She clicked her tongue. 'You never *could* understand who was the boss. Who was in control. You might be all grown up, but you still don't have any power, and under this roof, you never will. This is *my* house. I make the rules here. I won't answer to a man, not ever!'

Rhodri's hand balled into a fist, and I saw the physical reaction vibrating through his core, the way he pulled back, intending to hit her. I couldn't believe I was standing here about to watch the brother I'd thought I'd killed punch the woman I'd loved with my whole heart all my life; the woman who had tucked me in and taught me to bake and been everything to me. And my only objection was that if he did hit her, she might not be capable of telling me where to find my son.

I moved without thinking, grabbing his arm and yanking him back. 'No, Rhodri, stop!'

'Thank you, darling,' she said, seemingly unruffled.

'I'm not your fucking darling,' I hissed as I rushed past her into the hallway.

I ran up the stairs, into the bedroom I'd slept in as a child. The bed was made, empty, and I couldn't help but think of all the mornings I'd woken here, bruised, disorientated, believing I'd had another night terror. The fear I'd developed of letting myself give in to sleep, the insomnia that had plagued me ever since. And it had all been inflicted on me by her. She'd made me think I was mad. A danger to my child.

Scott had sworn he'd never seen any evidence of the night terrors, and I hadn't trusted him, had thought he must have slept through them, but now I realised he hadn't seen them because I hadn't had them. Not since leaving home, since the drugging had stopped. The insomnia I'd developed had been a result of fearing something that was never even an issue. And all because she wanted me out of the way so she could hurt my brother, for the simple crime of having been born a boy. It was too much to bear.

'Is he here?'

I turned to see Mirium in the doorway, her face a picture of anxiety, Jeff and Rhodri behind her.

'No.' I ran to my mum's room, looking into the en suite, the walk-in wardrobe. The scream came without me even realising it was building, and I gripped my knees, the terror of what could have happened to my darling boy filling my head, making me want to run, move, do anything, but I was paralysed, unable to find a solution.

I straightened up, yanking my phone from my pocket. 'I'm calling the police. He's been missing too long already. Fuck!' I screamed again.

Mirium dashed forward, taking my phone from my hand. 'I'll do it. Let me call them. You keep searching.'

There was something about the look in her eye that made

me hesitate. Perhaps it was just paranoia on my part after all the revelations I'd heard today, knowing how many lies I'd been subjected to, but my gut was screaming at me not to trust her. I reached for the phone. 'No, I'll do it. I need to do it.'

Her fingers tightened around the phone, and she pulled it away, tucking it behind her.

'Mirium!' I exclaimed. 'Give it to me! We're wasting time!'

'Don't call the police. This whole situation will get completely out of hand. You're upset, Chloe, and understand-ably so, but this is a family matter.'

Jeff strode forward. 'What the hell are you talking about, Miri? We're discussing *murder*. Kidnapping. Child abuse, for Pete's sake! Of course we need the police. I called them the moment the child arrived here – I knew it wasn't safe for him. They fobbed me off of course, and now I see it's because of the web of lies she fed them about me being some sort of child predator, but this time she won't get away with it. She's gone too far.' His face was puce, a thick blue vein protruding from his temple. 'Give Chloe her phone. She's right – we're wasting time.'

Mirium stepped back against the wardrobe, and I felt anger swell up inside me, seeing the refusal written on her face.

'I can't do that. I—'

I lurched forward, slapping her before I even realised I was planning to do it. Her face ricocheted to the left, and she gave a cry, dropping the phone to the carpet, both hands coming to her cheeks as if she couldn't believe what had happened. I picked it up, my fingers trembling as I keyed in my passcode.

'Wait!'

My head snapped up to find Rhodri standing in front of me. 'Not you too! What is the matter with—'

'I know where he is. Chloe, he's *here*.'

I glanced around, seeing nobody, shaking my head.

'No, listen. I just remembered... It was the worst punishment, worse even than the belt, the bleach... Chloe, he's in the loft.'

My eyes rose to the ceiling above me, and I gave a cry of dismay. Rhodri was already moving, rushing across the hall to the small room that had once been his. The long wooden pole used to reach the hatch was propped against the wall, and he grabbed it, looping the hook through the little brass ring and pulling. A ladder unfurled, and I stood at the base. Rhodri stepped back.

'I... I can't go up there... I can't...' He pressed his hands to his face, and I wished I could comfort him, but I had to keep moving.

I thrust the phone into his hand, then began to climb, my thoughts tunnelling in on the idea that my son might be cowering within the dark, cobweb-filled loft, scared out of his wits and wondering what he'd done wrong. I couldn't stand it. I was going to get him back, and then, I was going to kill her. With my bare hands if it came to it.

I climbed through the hatch, squinting in the darkness. Spotting a switch on a pillar, I flicked it, and a dim light emerged from a single light bulb overhead.

'Tommy? Tommy, are you up here?'

Rhodri's voice echoed from below. 'He won't be in the main part. Go right to the back, straight ahead. You'll see what I mean.'

I opened my mouth to ask a question but changed my mind, not wanting to waste another second. Picking my way through the heaped piles of boxes and bin bags, I moved as quickly as I dared, the light fading the further I got from the hatch. Terror pulsed through my veins, but I couldn't let myself give in to it. I had to save him.

Reaching the back wall, I yelled again. 'Tommy! Where are you?'

'Look for the door!' Rhodri called up.

Squinting, I ran my hand over the wood panelling, splinters snapping off into the soft skin of my fingertips as with an increasing sense of panic I searched for a handle of some kind. Why wasn't Tommy responding if he was up here? The reason for his silence was too unbearable to consider.

I glanced back across the expanse of the loft, a tremor vibrating through my body as I had the sudden awful feeling that this could be a trap. I could be made a prisoner up here, and then I would never be able to find my baby boy. I wished I knew where my mum was right now, what she was doing, if she was plotting something worse than all the terrible things she'd already done. Knowing that Jeff and Mirium were waiting in the room below made me uneasy, and as much as I was sure Rhodri was on my side, placing myself in this vulnerable position was putting that to the ultimate test. I only hoped he wouldn't let me down.

Turning back to the wall, I slammed my hand against the panel in frustration. There was a click, and it sprang open, revealing a tiny space no bigger than an understairs cupboard, with a bundle lying at the far end.

'Tommy?' I said softly, my heart racing. I didn't want to go in there, and yet I knew I had no choice. 'Tommy, darling? It's Mummy.'

I walked slowly forward, then crouched down over the bundle, pulling back the sheet and instantly bursting into tears. It was him. His skin was so pale it was almost translucent, his eyes closed tight, a bruise on his right cheek that looked fresh. But he was breathing. I pulled him into my arms, cupping his face in my hands. 'Tommy, wake up, darling, wake up!'

His eyelids fluttered, and he gave a groan, the kind he always made when he didn't want to get up for preschool on a winter morning. It made a fresh wave of tears well up in my eyes.

'Mummy?' His voice was croaky, the word sticking in his

throat, but as his eyes struggled to open, fluttering a few more times then finally managing to focus on my face, he broke into a smile. 'I missed you,' he said, wrapping his arms around my neck so tightly I could barely breathe.

'I missed you too, baby. So, so much. And I'm taking you home with me to our new flat.'

'You mean I don't have to stay here any more? Grandma says you're too ill to take care of me. And that I have a lot of lessons to learn.'

I pulled him against my chest so he couldn't see the impact those few words had on me, the images they'd conjured up in my mind. He would need a lot of love and support to get over what had happened to him in this house, the place I'd hoped would be his safe haven in the eye of the storm that was our lives. I would have to work hard to get him to tell me what he'd been through. But for now he was here, alive, safe, his little hand stroking my hair, mirroring the way I always stroked his, because he was a sweet, loving, beautiful soul and there wasn't a drop of malice in him. If only she could have seen that, she would have been so much happier. But she would never go near my son again.

'Come on, darling. Let's get out of here.' I pulled back and saw how heavy his eyes were again, already trying to close. 'Tommy, did Grandma give you a drink? Do you remember how you got up here?'

'Warm milk...' he said, his voice already slipping away into sleep. 'With cinnamon on top. I didn't like it, but she said I had to...' His head tipped back, and I caught him, scooping him up, cradling him like I had when he was a tiny newborn.

Careful not to bump his head against the many boxes, I carried him back through the loft to the open hatch. 'Rhodri? Are you there?'

I heard the creak of the ladder, then his face appeared below me.

'He's been drugged. I think he's okay; he was talking. He just needs to sleep it off.' I was surprised at how matter-of-fact my words sounded. 'Can I pass him to you so I can get down?'

'Give him here.' Rhodri held him against his strong chest, climbing slowly back down the ladder. I followed, seeing that Mirium and Jeff were still standing there, unusually quiet.

'Is he all right?' Jeff met my eyes, and I saw how tense he was, how scared.

I nodded. 'He's alive. He's going to be okay.'

'Oh, thank God!'

He grabbed Mirium, pulling her into a hug, and she hugged him back, surprising me with her tears. I couldn't read her; still couldn't understand her.

'So this is my nephew.' Rhodri smiled as he looked down at my son in his arms. 'He looks so familiar. I feel like I already know him.'

Mirium stepped forward, her cheek red from the slap, but I couldn't find it in me to apologise. 'You should get him home to his own bed. Jeff can drive you.'

Rhodri shook his head. 'I'll take them. Chloe, go and grab his teddy and anything else he needs. You won't be coming back here.'

'No,' I murmured. 'I suppose you're right.'

The teddy was on a shelf in Tommy's room, high out of his reach, I noted, my stomach tightening as I realised how little comfort he'd had here. I should have known, should never have trusted her so blindly.

I traipsed after the solemn group, into the kitchen. Mum was sitting at the table, a half-eaten cream slice on a plate in front of her, a mug of tea clutched between her hands. She didn't look up as we walked in. I didn't know what to say, where to even begin. Now that I had Tommy back with me, everything seemed dim in comparison. There would be things to deal with. But not yet.

'Ready?' Rhodri asked, looking pointedly at the back door.

I nodded and was about to move when a cascade of knocks sounded at the front door.

Jeff, standing in the kitchen doorway, frowned, then broke into a wry smile, shaking his head. 'Well I never,' he said. 'They pulled their finger out after all.'

FORTY-FIVE

CLARISSA

'I'll thank you not to go answering the door in my home, Jeff,' I snapped, pushing back my chair and walking across the kitchen.

He gave an irritating grin and shrugged. 'Be my guest.'

I shoved past him, my eyes meeting Miri's for a moment, delivering a silent message. And then I saw what had him so smug. Behind the stained-glass panel of the front door were the unmistakable blue flashing lights that made my heart race. 'Did you call the police?' I demanded, spinning to face the group.

Mirium grabbed my wrist. 'We didn't. None of us – I swear it,' she said, her tone pleading as she gripped tighter, her finger-nails digging into the soft skin. Her eyes were wide, afraid as she met mine, imploring. 'Honestly, Clarissa. Chloe suggested it, but I told her this was a family matter. I said we could deal with it ourselves. Isn't that right, Jeff?' she said, looking at him with a beseeching expression.

'So explain this then!' I gestured to the door as another resounding rap battered against it.

'About damn time, if you ask me,' Jeff said, folding his arms, clearly having no intention of leaving.

No, of course he wouldn't. He'd want to watch me squirm.

Love nothing better than seeing me dragged out of this house so he could finally claim victory over me. But I wouldn't go down so easily.

I looked at Chloe as she reached out to touch Tommy's forehead, lolling against her brother's chest. 'I told you he was fine,' I said quietly. 'I only did it for his own good. The world isn't the same as it once was, darling. Entitled men need to learn their place. It's the one positive that's come with this modern world.' I willed her to nod – to say that she understood, that she knew I was only trying to help – but her expression was blank as she stared back, and I felt a cold trickle of fear that perhaps this time I'd gone too far.

'Chloe... we'll get through this. It's a different parenting style, that's all. I don't want to fall out with you over it. I won't lose you again,' I added as I heard the back gate open, knowing the police had come round the side.

Chloe broke into a smile, and I felt a surge of hope deep in my heart, but then I saw the way her eyes were fixed on mine, two hard little rocks filled with a hatred I hadn't known she was capable of. Not my sweet girl, the golden child who'd made my narrow little life bearable. I'd given up everything for her. Couldn't she see that?

'Do you really think there's a way back from this, Mum?' She shook her head. 'You lost me the moment you drugged me so you could hurt my younger brother. You lost me when you let me believe I was a murderer. You lost me when you tried to make me believe I could be a danger to my child, and most of all, you lost me the moment you laid eyes on my son and failed to see him for the pure soul he is and thought he needed a lesson – the kind I wouldn't subject a dog to. The woman I loved as a little girl doesn't exist. She was a fragment of a person, a fiction I held on to. I was blind to her faults, and had I been older and wiser, I would have seen through the mask. The mother I loved wasn't real. Because any good you did, any love you gave me, was tainted by the way you treated everyone else. You killed my dad. You lost me my brother, and you've traumatised my son. My storybook mother is dead. And you...' She took a shaky breath, glancing at the window as two uniformed officers passed it, heading for the door. 'You can rot in hell,' she finished, her tone filled with malice.

Her words were like a slap in the face, the sting no less painful than if she'd attacked me with a blade. I blinked, tears filling my eyes, heedless of everyone but her. I couldn't believe she was speaking to me this way, not when we'd been so close, two peas in a pod, since the moment she was born. Beside me, I was aware of a struggle as Jeff made to open the door to the waiting police.

'Jeff,' Mirium whispered, holding his arm. 'No, wait!'

'Let go of me, woman! What the hell is the matter with you?'

I locked eyes with Mirium as she held firm to her husband, but when I broke my stare and turned back to Chloe, I saw that my daughter had gone to open the door herself. She was shaking, I realised. She didn't have the stomach for any of this. I'd failed in raising her to be strong. To see through the tricks the opposite sex liked to play. She was being manipulated by everyone around her. If only she'd come home to me earlier, I might have made a difference, led her down the right path.

The two police officers stepped through the door, and I jutted out my chin defiantly, noting that both were male, young, eager to prove themselves, like a couple of unneutered puppies. They were practically bouncing on their toes in their jubilation.

'We're looking for Clarissa Phillips,' said the first one, glancing around the group.

Mirium shrank back behind Jeff, and I knew her support would be far less vocal from this point on. Jeff, however, couldn't hold his tongue.

'You've found her. And you've picked your moment, I'll say that.'

I shot him a hateful look, and he didn't even bother to cover up his grin. Turning to the PC, I clasped my hands in front of me. 'How can I help you?' I asked, offering a tight smile.

'Are you familiar with a Mr Scott Radley?'

Chloe stepped forward. 'This is about Scott? Is he... Has he died?'

I held my breath, waiting for the answer, though I was certain that if he had died, they wouldn't be here now. No, their presence could only mean one thing. That I had failed. And in doing so, I'd let my daughter down again.

'He woke up this morning.' The officer turned back to me. 'And he claims that *you're* the reason he was in the hospital. That he woke up to find you standing at the foot of his bed with a needle already pressed beneath his toenail, and before he had time to do anything, you injected him with the heroin, causing a near-fatal overdose.'

Chloe gasped, and Rhodri gave another of his irritating laughs.

'Of course she did,' he said. 'If she knew you were having trouble with your ex, she'd do anything in her power to get him out of the picture. Anything to protect her little girl,' he added, as if it were something to be ashamed of.

'Don't, Rhodri.' Chloe was pale as she shook her head. 'It's too much. Today has been... a living nightmare. I feel numb—' She broke off, looking to the PC with a resigned expression. 'I have a statement of my own I'd like to make. I think you need to hear about the things I've learned today. But right now I want to take my son home. I'll come down to the station tomorrow. You'll watch Tommy, won't you?' she asked Rhodri.

He gave a nod, his jaw stiff.

The PC raised an eyebrow, slowly realising that he'd hit the jackpot in turning up today of all days. 'Please do. Clarissa

Phillips, I'm arresting you for the attempted murder of Scott Radley.' He stepped forward, holding a pair of handcuffs.

I backed away, shaking my head. 'Don't you fucking touch me!' I growled. 'You keep your disgusting hands away from me. I won't go! I've done nothing wrong!'

'You don't have a choice,' Jeff said, coming up behind me, his massive frame preventing me from getting into the hallway.

The second officer had removed his truncheon from his belt, his eyes sparkling as if he couldn't believe his luck.

'*You're* the one they should be taking,' I shouted at Jeff. 'If it weren't for your meddling, everything would have been fine! Rhodri would never have had your worm tongue in his ear, would never have rebelled so hard against my boundaries! Then Chloe wouldn't have had to leave and she'd never have settled for a scumbag like Scott!'

'So I should have just let you get on with abusing your son, killing your husband? Is that it?' Jeff demanded.

I stumbled back, my spine colliding hard with the door frame. 'How dare you!' I reached to rub the bruise I knew was already blooming under the surface of the skin, and in my moment of vulnerability, I heard the awful metallic click as the PC swooped in, securing the cuffs around my wrists, pinning my hands behind my back. Cowards. That's what they were.

I stared at my daughter, willing her to say something in my defence, but she looked down, unable to meet my eyes.

'Chloe! Chloe, don't you get it? It was for you! I did it all out of love for you. How can you let them treat me like this? How can you bear it?'

She gave a choked sob but didn't raise her head as the cocky man-child of a police officer forcibly shoved me in the direction of the door.

'Let's go,' he said, his body odour and cheap aftershave filling my nostrils as he pressed up against me, making me squirm to one side. 'I have a feeling you won't be coming back here for a very long time,' he added softly into my ear.

I looked behind me, seeing Mirium's pale face peeking out from behind Jeff. I stared at her, knowing she understood exactly what I was communicating. She gave a short nod, not daring to look away. She wouldn't make a statement corroborating their hateful lies. She would vouch for me. She had no choice. Because her life was in my hands. It was the one card I had left, and she knew that if she let me down now, I would play it without hesitation.

FORTY-SIX

CHLOE

'Do you know how much this kid eats?' Rhodri laughed down the phone. 'I mean, I know he's growing, but he can put away nearly as much as me. We're on round three of sandwiches already. I might have to break out the chocolate!'

I heard an excited squeal of approval in the background and smiled, pressing the phone to my ear, hoping that I'd be back with them before they knew it. I'd hated having to leave Tommy so soon after all that had happened yesterday, but within minutes of meeting his uncle this morning, the two of them had been laughing and joking, Tommy clambering all over Rhodri with seemingly no residual effects of the drugs he'd been slipped, and Rhodri grinning like it was all perfectly normal. For someone who'd claimed he wasn't interested in kids, he certainly seemed to be a natural with them.

I'd spent the night cuddled up with Tommy in our cosy bedroom, inspecting his body for bruises and finding just one or two in addition to the one on his face. And after an hour or so of holding him close, feeling his breath warm on my cheek, I had slept. I had let go of the fear that I would rise up in the depths of some dream and hurt my son, and for the first time in memory, I hadn't fought the sleepiness when it came. I'd allowed it to wash over me, carry me into a safe, rejuvenating state, and this morning I'd woken with Tommy's foot pressing into my bladder, the birds singing outside my window and a feeling of a new beginning enveloping me from the inside out.

I ended the call, telling Rhodri to ring if he needed me, that I would keep my phone on loud. He would be coming here later to make his statement, and I knew it was something he was dreading. He had said he wasn't going to hold back, but that would mean delving into the locked box of memories he'd tried so hard to move on from. But he was determined to make our mother pay for what she had done to him, Dad and every male who was unfortunate enough to have been in her life.

I glanced over at the police station from the bench I'd sat down on, dropping my phone into my bag and thinking of my mother in there now, locked in a tiny cell. Would she be frightened? Or would that vindictive anger I'd witnessed from her be keeping the fear at bay?

It had been her reaction to being caught that had been the worst part to bear. The fact that she'd cited me as her primary motivation, her behaviour supposedly fed by her love of me, her desire to rid the world of toxic masculinity in order to keep me safe.

I couldn't help but wonder if she would have gone down this awful path if it wasn't for getting pregnant. If my father had chosen another girl to marry and start a family with. If she'd lived the life she claimed she'd had planned for herself: the travel, the freedom, a single, childless woman with nobody to answer to – nobody to hurt but herself – perhaps she might have been able to keep this evil side of herself restrained. It was hard not to consider the part my birth had played in her choices. And along with that, I felt as though a mirror had been shone on my own shortcomings, her traits reflected back in my personality.

Was it because of her that I found it so easy to lie? That the words could roll off my tongue without my ever having to think of them, the deception as natural as breathing? I'd thought that my experience with Scott had hardened me, brought out this side of me that was almost a form of self-preservation, but was it *her* influence all along? I didn't want to have any part of her in me, but I wasn't sure that was my choice to make.

I stood up, wanting to get the statement over with and go home to my son. Heading towards the door of the station, I glanced up as it opened only to find myself face to face with Irene.

'Chloe!' she exclaimed, rushing forward and grabbing my wrist.

I pulled away, shocked that she would have the audacity to even speak to me having only recently threatened me with social services.

'Are you okay? I just drove Scott here to make his statement – he's finishing up in there now.' She shook her head. 'I can't believe any of this. I don't suppose you can either.'

I glared at her. 'Yes, it's been a shocking week. Your threats to try to get custody of my son didn't help,' I said, refusing to beat around the bush.

She let go of my wrist, scraping her hand through her short copper hair, the lines around her mouth deepening as she puckered her lips. 'I know. And I'm sorry about that. It appears my son hasn't been entirely truthful with me – not that I should be surprised.' She sighed. 'He told me he was fighting to see little Tommy and that you were refusing him access. I didn't know what was going on; I only asked him to get you to visit me so we could sort it all out, but in his attempt to hide the truth from me, he panicked and made up the custody stuff so you would avoid me all the more. Didn't want me to find out what had really happened.'

I folded my arms, raising an eyebrow. 'And what was that then?' I asked, wondering what bullshit story he'd fed her now.

She shook her head sadly. 'Don't think I condone any of it, Chloe. I don't. I know everything that happened, and it makes me sick. I think coming so close to nearly dying impacted him, and when he woke up from the overdose, he was a mess. He told me how he had treated you. How he'd disowned his son because he couldn't bear being tied down.'

'Really?' I asked, shocked that he'd ever admit to any fault on his part.

She nodded. 'I know he hurt you, and I understand why you left. Why you cut all ties. And,' she added with a sad little smile, 'I finally get why you and I have never been close.'

I frowned. 'What do you mean?'

'You think he got it from me, don't you? The violent nature. You think he was just a damaged child acting out his trauma on you.' She gave a wry laugh, looking down at her feet. 'I bet every time he hit you, there was a part of you that blamed me, wasn't there? That thought that if I'd been a better mum, he'd have been a good partner to you. But it wasn't like that.'

She looked at me, her eyes glistening with tears I hadn't known she was capable of. She'd always come across as hard, cold, but as she spoke now, she looked so vulnerable.

'I'm not well off. I didn't have a lot of money, and I was on my own,' she said, pulling a packet of cigarettes from her back pocket and lighting one. She was silent as she took a drag, her eyes fixed on the road. 'I thought I was doing the best for him. I wanted him to believe he was just as good as all the other kids, so every penny I had went on him. New trainers. Money to go out with his mates. I worked three jobs to buy him the video games he wanted, a TV for his room, and he never went hungry, even when I couldn't feed myself. I gave him everything he asked for, but I forgot the one thing he really needed. Boundaries.'

She took another puff of her cigarette, blowing the smoke to one side. 'I fucked it all up, Chloe. *I* made him the way he was –

a spoiled, entitled brat who was never satisfied. That was why he left home. It wasn't because I abused him, though I know that's what he led you to believe. It was because I realised how badly I'd messed up parenting him and tried to backtrack. I told him there would be no more gifts, no more money for nothing. He was given a list of chores around the house – you know, things like tidying his room and washing the dishes – and I said he needed to start going to school rather than bunking off whenever it suited him. He pushed back, but I wouldn't relent, wouldn't give him a penny. I hoped it would make him see sense, mend his ways, but he couldn't stand to be dictated to, and he just walked out. I lost him because I tried too hard to make his world what I thought he deserved, and forgot to teach him to be grateful for the life he had. It was my fault but not for the reasons he let you believe. I never laid a hand on that boy. Not once.'

Her eyes finally met mine as I stared at her, absorbing what she'd told me in a haze of shock.

She gave a shrug. 'I'm just glad he's finally told me everything so I can try to make amends. I know you won't want him involved with Tommy, and I don't blame you. But I would love a relationship with my grandson. On your terms, anywhere, any time. I just want to see him, Chloe. It will break my heart if I've lost him for good.'

I looked over her shoulder as the door opened behind her. Scott stepped out into the bright June sunshine, then paused, catching my eye before looking away. The anger I'd grown to expect from him was conspicuously absent, and I wondered if perhaps Irene was right – that his encounter with my mother and subsequent brush with death had shaken him, taken a bit of the bluster from his sails. I half expected him to start yelling at me about what she'd done, but instead, he plucked a rollie from behind his ear and lit it, then looked at Irene.

'I'll wait by the car.'

'Go on,' she said, not turning to meet his eye.

He gave me a brief nod and then loped off in the direction of a rusty blue Nissan.

As I watched him go, I reflected on Irene's words. I had disliked her from the moment we'd met, sure that she'd treated the man I loved poorly. I'd made her into a character in my mind, a cold, hate-filled woman, and her brusque tone and no-nonsense demeanour had only served to feed my opinion. But now I realised that while I'd put my own mother on a pedestal for her soft curves, home-baked puddings and gentle tone, I'd written off Irene for being the polar opposite. And yet I'd got them both so wrong.

Irene was brusque because she was busy. A single mum working every hour she could at low-paid jobs, no doubt on an empty stomach from what she was telling me now. She wasn't the picture-perfect storybook mother of my childhood, but someone real and flawed and honest. And I would rather have had that than the lie I'd been fed.

I reached forward, giving her hand a squeeze, and saw the hope bloom in her deep-set eyes. 'Sunday suit you? We could meet at the park. Take a picnic and make an afternoon of it.'

Her eyes filled with tears once more, and she gave a brief nod. 'Thank you, Chloe,' she whispered. 'And don't worry. He won't be there. It'll just be me, I promise.'

I nodded, letting go of her hand, and she walked over to Scott, unlocking the car so he could climb in.

Turning back to the door, I sucked in a breath and readied myself for what I was about to do. Once I'd told the police everything my mum had confessed yesterday, there would be no turning back. She would be as good as dead to me. It broke my heart, and for a second, all I could think of was how she used to stroke my hair when I was afraid to fall asleep. How she'd read to me for hours, never tiring. But as I pictured Tommy lying in the dark on those bare floorboards, locked in that awful cupboard in the loft, I hardened my heart and stepped forward. She only had herself to blame.

EPILOGUE

MIRIUM

Six months later

The mouth-watering scents of nutmeg and cinnamon wafted through the house as I opened the oven to check on the flapjack. I'd almost forgotten to make it, what with the endless to-do list occupying my mind, but I'd remembered just in time and now I wouldn't be guilty of breaking a Christmas tradition. The kids would never forgive me.

Closing the door to give it a few more minutes, I turned, double-checking that the table was laid, the plum wine already uncorked, the raspberry cordial waiting in the special reindeer jug I brought out each year – another tradition the grandkids loved. They would pour their own drinks and pretend they were sipping wine, giggling as they stuck out their little fingers and put on regal accents.

The colourful fairy lights twinkled on the huge tree Jeff had bought from a nearby farm, reflecting in the window, making the kitchen feel cosy and warm in contrast to the grey sky beyond. The turkey was a glistening golden brown, a mouth-watering centrepiece, the potatoes and veg waiting in covered dishes, and all I had left to do was to take the gravy off the hob and sit back with a glass of wine to enjoy the day with my family.

It was especially precious to me this year, having feared that I might be at risk of losing them entirely. Keeping my silence had nearly cost me my marriage when I'd refused to corroborate Jeff, Rhodri and Chloe's stories after Clarissa's arrest.

When Jeff had forcibly put me in the car and driven me to the station, I'd told the police that Clarissa – my best friend of nearly thirty years – had been a fantastic mother to both of her children. That Rhodri had been a wild child with a penchant for lying, who'd required a firm hand. And that Reece had been notorious for forgetting to take his blood-pressure pills, and Clarissa was always on at him to take better care of himself for fear that he would put too much strain on his heart. In short, I'd put on an Oscar-winning performance of pure lies, and the moment I'd had my chance to visit Clarissa, I'd made sure she knew that I'd gone above and beyond to protect her. She'd been refused bail, considered too dangerous, too manipulative to be allowed to await her court date from the comfort of her home, instead being placed on remand and shepherded into prison to await her trial.

I'd done my best to help her, but even so, I'd been terrified that it wouldn't be enough. It was clear that as much as my testimony might soften the sentence somewhat, she would still be going to prison, and for a good long time.

Beneath the bright lights of the visiting room, she had quietly shared with me the evidence that had been uncovered since the investigation began. There were the recent searches on her computer, which she'd thought she'd made on an incognito page. Where to buy heroin. How to prepare it. How much to use and how much would kill a grown man. Then there had been the CCTV showing her on Scott's estate the night of the crime, the order for hypodermic syringes and thick leather gloves. It was damning, especially with Scott identifying her categorically and claiming she'd already threatened him once before, though of course he hadn't taken her seriously the first time.

And the police hadn't stopped there. They'd looked at Rhodri's hospital records. A broken wrist at six years old that had begun to set by the time he was brought in. The burn on his arm that Clarissa claimed was accidental. A list of maladies spanning the course of years that really should have been picked up on at the time. His records screamed abuse, but nobody had stepped in and helped him, despite the obvious going on right before their eyes.

As for Reece's sudden heart attack, I hadn't imagined they would be able to prove anything so many years on. His body would have decomposed by now, any meddling on Clarissa's part erased, and yet, they'd investigated every avenue and discovered that she'd borrowed several books on pharmaceuticals from the library in the months leading up to his death. Textbooks on toxicity.

And then there was the box of letters under her bed – letters he had written to me in secret desperation, hoping I might help somehow, because I'd led him to believe I was his friend; that he could trust me. Letters I'd read, cried about, and then, feeling like the most wretched human on the planet, handed back to his tormentor. It might not be conclusive, but there was enough in her file now to make her realise that she wouldn't be coming home.

I feared that sitting in that cell with nothing but her bitterness and resentment for company, she might use the small scrap of power she had left to destroy me – as much for her own vindictive satisfaction as anything else. A woman with nothing left to lose is a dangerous creature. But one with everything to lose is so much worse.

And so, as the months passed and I lost weight, sleep, sanity over my fears of what she might do or say next, I began to lay my own preparations. I invited Chloe and Rhodri round, and with Jeff sulking in the corner of the room, our relationship balancing on a knife edge over my lack of willingness to help convict my friend, I told them how she'd been threatening me for years. How I was scared of her, and how she was far more unhinged than even they realised. I wove a web of lies intermingled with the absolute truth, discrediting her to the point where I knew she was no longer a threat to me and my family.

I took her obsession with Jeff and told them how she believed he was already married and that I had stolen him from his true family. I took her hatred of men and told them that our own grandson had been in danger, though I'd never left him alone with her for a second. And I told them how I'd been too afraid of her to speak up, because she'd made up lies about me being infertile, stealing my son from another woman, faking my pregnancy...

I had to make sure that if she ever decided to tell the truth, they would already have heard my side and know it was just spite, insanity, a sick fantasy she'd concocted to wreak havoc on our lives. That they wouldn't believe a word.

I pulled the tray of flapjack from the oven, leaving it on the side to cool, and remembered the day she'd come to me all those years ago, a sobbing mess, having discovered that the abortion she'd gone ahead with behind Reece's back had failed, and she'd just learned that she was carrying twin boys. She was hysterical, couldn't stand that they were growing inside her, the thought of them feeding from her body making her want to slice open her own belly and rip them out.

I'd been too shocked to speak as I realised that she would do anything to make 'the problem', as she called it, go away. And I'd had to listen to all of it after having failed to conceive over three gruelling years of trying. It had stung – no, more than that: it had made me angry, bitter, opportunistic. It had taken only minutes for me to suggest the obvious. That Jeff and I adopt the babies.

I was afraid he would say no, that he didn't like Clarissa enough to take on a child with her DNA. He wanted his own baby, birthed by his wife. We'd discussed adoption over the years and he'd always been so resistant. But even before I'd had the chance to run through the list of reasons why it couldn't work, she'd shaken her head, explaining that Reece would never agree to it either. That he desperately wanted a son, and the moment he heard the news, he would get tunnel vision and never dream of giving the babies away. He'd be horrified if he ever discovered she'd tried to abort them.

We'd gone back and forth, the idea sticking between my teeth, for what seemed like hours, and finally decided to do the only thing that felt possible. Clarissa said if she absolutely had to, she could manage one boy. It felt far less overwhelming to her, though she would still have to carry them both. And I felt that her giving me the other would be the greatest gift imaginable. She'd been told that the twins were dizygotic – non-identical, each in their own sac with their own placenta – and so the plan was formed. It spoke volumes to me how easily she agreed to hand over her baby, but I was too hopeful to focus on the red flags, pushing aside any doubts I might have had.

That night, I went to Jeff and told him that I'd been keeping a secret for fear it wouldn't stick, and that I was sixteen weeks pregnant with his son. The look on his face had made any lingering uncertainty at the lies I was going to have to tell melt away. I gave up shellfish and soft cheese, and disappeared off to imaginary appointments, and as the months passed, I bought prosthetic bellies and undressed in the bathroom and told him I was too nauseous, too nervous of harming the baby, to keep up a sex life. And he'd been so elated at the prospect of becoming a father that he'd given me all the space I needed.

Over the years, Clarissa and I regularly brought up the story of the day we had the babies, as if reinforcing our version of events. We always laughed about how the two of us were so close we went into labour on the same day.

After the event, we'd told Jeff and Reece that we'd been out for a drive in the countryside when my waters broke, and the shock of finding herself alone with a labouring first-time mum had brought on Clarissa's labour too. We'd made up an elaborate tale of her driving us to the hospital, of us being given rooms side by side as we both brought our sons into the world, how there had been no time to call the fathers as we screamed in unison.

The reality was, when she'd felt those first twinges of labour, she'd dashed across the road to bang on my door. It had all been planned. I'd driven us to the outskirts of a nearby village, to a secluded holiday cottage I'd rented using cash she'd stolen from Reece, then watched helpless and terrified as she screamed and contorted, pushing the babies from her body with a force that seemed to declare, *Get out, give me my life back!* She hadn't allowed me to touch the first twin as he lay on the floor, still tethered to her body, blood dripping onto his tiny face as she birthed his brother. He'd been soundless, *still*, but she wouldn't let me come near.

When at last they were both born, there was a moment of absolute silence, save for the heavy panting as she caught her breath, and I wondered if it had all been for nothing. If her poisonous soul had seeped into these vulnerable little beings and ended their lives before they had even begun. But as their tiny bodies nestled together, I saw their chests rise and fall, then the glorious sound of their cries filled the room. Clarissa's face dropped in disappointment as my heart exploded with a love I couldn't even begin to describe.

I'd tried again, then, to take them both, telling her I could pretend the second baby was missed at my scan, that she could tell Reece she'd had a stillbirth. But she'd refused. Said we'd never get away with it. And looking at the babies, I had to admit she was right. She chose first, the one she said looked most like Reece, and as he grew, it became apparent that he was a mirror image of his father. But my sweet Joseph, thankfully, didn't share the same features. He was more wiry, his hair a honey brown, and by some miracle, we were never questioned.

I tried, time and again to protect Rhodri. If I'd known how bad it would be for him, I might have made a different decision, but in interweaving my happiness with her lies, I couldn't speak up for him. Couldn't call social services to have him removed. I was powerless, trapped by my unwillingness to lose the son I had no right to keep. And so, as the years passed, and I realised how cold Clarissa was towards the twin she'd insisted on keeping, I had to maintain a distance between us for my sanity, because it broke my heart to know his brother was going to get all the love in my heart, and Rhodri was going to have such a hard life in comparison. I had hoped she would learn to love him, but she never did.

I think Jeff sensed a connection with him though. He took him under his wing. Loved nothing more than seeing Rhodri and Joseph sitting side by side at our table. I was forever thankful that they looked so different.

When Reece died, I thought Clarissa might relent and send Rhodri to live with us so that she could focus her energy on the daughter she doted on, but by then, we had fallen out over our parenting styles. She said I was too soft, that Joseph ran rings around me – though he never did. She threatened to take him back, told me I was irresponsible for not breaking the toxicity from his nature, and so I stopped asking for guardianship of Rhodri, my focus needing to be on my family. But we were always under her control.

She wanted me to divorce Jeff, a constant source of anxiety for me, and when I suggested we might move away, she quickly put a stop to that. I guess that slowly I learned to shut out what I knew to be happening, because I felt I had no choice. I pretended not to see the bruises on Rhodri. I didn't entertain Jeff when he ranted and raved about the madwoman who'd killed his friend. I feigned ignorance time and again and instead talked with her about recipes and knitting patterns and book club recommendations, until the other stuff faded into the background.

Until Tommy arrived on her doorstep and I saw history repeating itself. I knew the moment Chloe got that phone call from Scott that I had to try to seek out his address and warn him what Clarissa was capable of, though I hadn't been quick enough to stop her. Seeing that witch of a woman playing the perfect grandmother to Tommy brought back a thousand memories from the past, and I knew that in her heart, nothing would ever change.

And now, despite the guilt in my belly at not telling the police every scrap of what I knew, I would never make that statement. Would never admit any guilt or knowledge on my part. It would ruin me. Some secrets you take to the grave.

I heard the sound of an engine outside and rushed to the front door, smiling as Jeff pulled up, Joseph's wife Emma in the passenger seat. Joseph and the kids poured out of the back, all wearing knitted Christmas jumpers and elf hats. I rushed forward, kissing Emma first, then wrapped my son in a hug.

'Merry Christmas, darling,' I whispered into his ear. 'Lunch is ready.'

He hugged me tight, then pulled back, smiling. 'Merry Christmas, Mum. Thank you for hosting – you're a star.' He opened the boot, lifting out a bag overflowing with presents. 'I'll pop these under the tree,' he said, heading inside.

My phone pinged in my pocket and I pulled it out, smiling

as I saw Rhodri's name on the screen. I opened the text, reading quickly.

Just round the corner. Chloe's driving and it's terrifying! ;) Be with you very soon. Tommy's hyped up on chocolate – sorry! X

I felt a slow grin spread across my face, picturing my two grown-up boys at my table, the pair reunited again. Having Rhodri back in my life had been the best thing to come out of all of this. He should have always been mine. The two of them belonged together, a perfect set. And now that bitch would never know how I'd finally got what I wanted.

Her son was slowly opening up to me, growing more comfortable in my presence, more tactile when I hugged him. He might be all grown up, but he still needed a family, and we were it. It was what I had wanted all along. I would never tell him the truth, nor Joseph. They would be the best of friends without ever knowing that the same blood flowed in their veins.

I reread the message, my eyes lingering a moment too long over Tommy's name. The only complication, the only potential problem in my plan. The resemblance between him and Joseph was already so obvious to me, though nobody else seemed to have noticed it yet. But if it became too strong... I didn't know what I might be forced to do. Because there was no doubt in my mind, I would do *anything* to protect my secret.

I slid the phone back into my pocket, imagining Clarissa eating a microwave turkey dinner, surrounded by criminals. She could have had this happiness too, if she'd only forced herself to grow, to be a better mother, a kinder, more tolerant person. I shook my head, pushing her from my thoughts, ready to celebrate with the family I'd created for myself. I was a good person. In my heart, I knew that to be true. But even good people can do despicable things when the price is high enough.

I smiled to myself, listening to the excited squeals of Berty and Lola coming from inside. Enough of this reminiscing, I thought, heading back into the house. It was time for me to close the door on the past and look towards a happy future with my family.

I walked towards the kitchen, where the sound of 'Jingle Bells' was playing on the radio, and whispered to myself the mantra that had kept me going through good times and bad. 'Tomorrow is a new day after all.'

A LETTER FROM SAM

I want to say a huge thank you for choosing to read *The Child at My Door*. If you enjoyed it, and want to keep up to date with all my latest releases, just sign up at the following link. Your email address will never be shared, and you can unsubscribe at any time.

www.bookouture.com/sam-vickery

As someone who has experienced a volatile relationship with sleep since childhood, it was particularly interesting for me to delve into the topic of Chloe's sleep disorders in this story. I still have vivid memories of my childhood night terrors, and to this day am prone to lasting bouts of insomnia, so that feeling of being desperately exhausted, the shaky adrenaline that overtakes you a few nights into an episode, was all too familiar to me. I connected deeply with her struggles.

I had an image in my mind of a sickly-sweet Dolores Umbridge type when writing Clarissa, though I tried to tone her down somewhat and make her easier to relate to – that is, until her true character is revealed! Her hatred of men impacts every decision she makes, and as such, she was the worst person little Tommy could have ended up with.

But in my mind, the character who scared me the most was Mirium. She was the person who had the most to lose, the biggest secrets to hide, and that made her by far the most dangerous person in this story. I loved ending with the threat of what might come next, the feeling that this story isn't quite over, leaving us to let our imaginations run riot and fill in the gaps.

I hope you enjoyed reading *The Child at My Door* as much as I enjoyed writing it. If you did, I would be very grateful if you could leave a review. I'd love to hear what you think, and it makes such a difference in helping new readers to discover one of my books for the first time.

I always enjoy hearing from my readers – you can get in touch at www.samvickery.com, or find me on my Facebook page.

Until the next time,

Sam

www.samvickery.com

 facebook.com/SamVickeryWrites

ACKNOWLEDGEMENTS

I have been very lucky to work with some extremely talented people in bringing this book to my readers. I want to thank my wonderful editor, Jennifer Hunt, who has been such a support to me. I love working with you and have learned such a lot from you. To Lauren Finger, who managed to make the line edits for this book actually very painless, thank you so much for your input and your lovely comments, which helped propel me through the task! To Aaron Munday who came up with the perfect cover – so sinister and compelling – thank you, I love it! To Sarah Hardy, for all your hard work organising the publicity for this story, thank you so much.

To my family. You distract me when my head is spinning, feed me when I get lost in my characters and inspire me beyond anything else in my life. Thank you, my loves!

And most of all, to my readers, without whom this story would never get the chance to come alive. Thank you for choosing to read my story. I hope you'll come back for the next one.

PUBLISHING TEAM

Turning a manuscript into a book requires the efforts of many people. The publishing team at Bookouture would like to acknowledge everyone who contributed to this publication.

Audio
Alba Proko
Sinead O'Connor
Melissa Tran

Commercial
Lauren Morrissette
Jil Thielen
Imogen Allport

Data and analysis
Mark Alder
Mohamed Bussuri

Cover design
Aaron Munday

Editorial
Billi-Dee Jones
Nadia Michael

Made in the USA
Las Vegas, NV
02 April 2024

88130557R00177